Best wishes

Judith Mather

A TWIST OF FATE

Also by Judith Mather:

Vengeance Visits Cornwall
   – A Sanders & Wade Trilogy

A TWIST
OF FATE

Judith Mather

UNITED WRITERS
Cornwall

UNITED WRITERS PUBLICATIONS LTD
Ailsa, Castle Gate, Penzance, Cornwall.
www.unitedwriters.co.uk

British Library Cataloguing in Publication Data:
A catalogue record for this book is
available from the British Library.

ISBN 9781852002084

Printed and bound in Great Britain by
United Writers Publications Ltd.,
Cornwall.

For my remarkable
daughter Amy.

"Blame it on a simple twist of fate."
Bob Dylan, 1974

Chapter One

DI Cassandra Wade sat alone at the breakfast table, listlessly stirring her scrambled egg and smoked salmon. This was the first time she had spent an Easter weekend alone since before the kids were born. Had Micky and Tanya been here, there would have been chatter and delight at the Easter treats Cassie would have provided. Not so much now that they were teenagers: Micky nearly sixteen and studying hard for his GCSEs, Tanya just eighteen months younger but, as is often the way with girls, far more sophisticated than her older brother.

Deciding that her eggs had gone too cold to eat, Cassie scraped them into the pedal bin and, taking her coffee with her, went out into the small, uninteresting garden that came with the house she rented. Her only additions to the space were a garden swing and a fire pit, which the kids had pestered her to get after they had experienced a beach barbecue. When they found that the ambience in the tiny fenced garden wasn't of the same quality, the pit became unused and waterlogged.

Maybe I'll get my old clothes on and tackle the garden, she mused, not feeling enthusiastic about the task. Rocking backwards and forwards on the swing, Cassie thought that perhaps it was time to set down roots. She had been in Cornwall for almost two years now and she should really make a decision whether to stay or go back to her native Liverpool. Never wanting the posting here in the first place, Cassie had slowly been seduced by the county's rugged beauty. Not just that, though. She had been surprised that the work

7

here in the Serious Incident Squad led by DCI Peter Sanders had been more challenging than she could have imagined. Peter couldn't be more different to her. She was a five-foot-six black woman, he a six-foot-three muscular, rugby-player of a man, his impressive frame belying a calm temperament. Whereas she was impulsive and a natural rule-breaker, he was methodical and evidence-driven. These differences had led to clashes on more than one occasion. However, after initially feeling she had to assert her authority, she had learned to respect not only Peter, but also his team.

The kids had settled, too. Micky had taken up surfing and was getting quite good at the sport. Robbie, her DC, was an instructor at the surf school and he thought that Micky could be competition-standard in a couple of years. Tanya had made a group of really nice friends. She had been bullied in her school in Liverpool, seemingly for being too bright; a swat they called her, which Cassie translated into, *you're very pretty and clever so we hate you.* Nevertheless, the taunts were having an effect on her daughter, whose work had begun to suffer. No such problem here. Tanya was a star student and admired for it. She was blossoming and turning into a very lovely young woman.

Cassie was returning briefly to Liverpool the next day and not looking forward to it. She was to give evidence in the case which had led to her unwelcome posting to Cornwall. She and her family had been threatened by a prominent drugs gang, most of whom were now incarcerated. The gang leader had now been apprehended and awaited trial. Cassie's evidence should put him away for a long time.

Shaking off her worrying thoughts, Cassie decided to phone the kids and wish them a happy Easter. They were in London with their dad and his wife, enjoying the attractions of the capital. She'd always got on with her ex-husband. The divorce, when it came, had seemed like an inevitability, so no shock or recriminations, just an acknowledgement that they shouldn't have got married in the first place, except, of course, that Cassie was pregnant, and Jack was too much of a traditionalist to suggest otherwise. The pregnancy almost prevented her taking up her place at police training college but, fortunately, her parents were there to lend a hand, as they were through the tough days following her divorce.

'They've been asking to come to stay,' she thought out loud. 'I really must arrange that.'

As Cassie reached for her phone it started to ring. 'DI Wade,' she said automatically.

'Sorry to bother you on a Sunday, ma'am,' said Maggie, the squad's DS and research whizz, 'but the Chief has asked me to contact you. There's been an incident in Penzance.'

Setting her SATNAV to the address DS Maggie Williams had given to her, Cassie sped off, her mind still reeling from the realisation that the address where a body had been found was familiar to her. Cursing the Sunday morning traffic, Cassie decided to activate the blues and twos. 'Get out of the way!' she shouted at a driver who was crawling along at twenty miles per hour. As she passed the car, she saw a white-haired old lady gripping the steering wheel, her nose almost resting on the dashboard. 'Deaf *and* blind are we?' she yelled, glancing over at the woman, who seemed oblivious. 'Shouldn't be allowed on the road,' Cassie murmured, before turning her concentration to the directions from the SATNAV. Cassie knew her way to Penzance, but was still new enough to Cornwall to appreciate the calm voice giving instructions. Right now, it allowed her space to think what she might be heading towards.

DCI Peter Sanders stood in the corner of the small room, allowing space for his longtime colleague, pathologist Ben Samuels, to complete his examination of the body lying half hidden behind the sofa. Peter took in the room, committing details to memory. There was a table and two chairs in one corner, and a small desk and bookshelf in the opposite one. The table had been set for breakfast with mugs and plates and a full cafetière of coffee. The sofa was old but clean and a blanket and pillow had been folded neatly at one end. The smell of coffee and toast mingled with the all too familiar iron tang of fresh blood. 'What's the verdict, Ben?' Peter looked over at the squatting figure.

'Knife wound to the chest, most probably piercing the heart. And look here,' Ben lifted the woman's arms to allow Peter to see cuts and bruises to her forearms.

'Defensive wounds?'

'Almost certainly, Peter, but I'll know more when I've examined her.'

'Murder weapon?'

'A large-bladed knife by the looks of it. Could be a kitchen knife.'

Peter edged his way over to the tiny kitchen. A knife block on the worktop had spaces for five knives. Two were missing. A small paring knife lay on a chopping board next to two tomatoes and a piece of cheese, which left one unaccounted for. By the looks of the gaps in the block, the missing knife could have been large. A spur of the moment crime maybe, Peter thought.

'Any sign of the knife, Ben?' Peter called from the kitchen.

'Not in the immediate vicinity,' Ben called back, pushing himself to his feet with a groan. 'Doesn't get any easier. My knees are not as supple as they once were.' He picked his bag from off the arm of the sofa, being careful to avoid the wet patch on the seat cushion. 'This looks and smells like urine,' he observed, turning to Peter, who was standing in the kitchen doorway, his phone in his hand. Peter nodded, 'SOCO will collect a sample for analysis, but our victim was either very frightened or the murderer peed on the sofa for some reason. DNA analysis should tell us.'

Ben smiled at his old friend. 'I'll leave that to you then. Shall we say eleven tomorrow? I've got a sudden infant death first thing. I wouldn't want that to wait.'

Pausing before he made for the stairs, Ben turned. 'How's that lovely wife of yours, by the way? Managing the new baby alright?'

Peter lifted his head. 'Actually, not as well as I'd have thought, Ben. Rachel is the most calm and capable person I know, but little Charlotte has completely deskilled her.' He smiled ruefully. 'She loves her and wants more than anything to be a good mum but. . .'

'Give it time, my friend, I'm sure she'll get the hang of it.'

'Yes, sure. SuLin is coming tomorrow for a few days, so that should help.'

'Mother-in-law as well as new baby. You'll have your hands full.'

Peter smiled and nodded. 'Eleven tomorrow, then,' said Peter, giving a farewell wave to Ben as he completed his call to SOCO.

As Ben descended the stairs, he almost collided with Cassie, who was pulling on gloves and trying to slip plastic covers over her shoes whilst still hurrying upwards.

'Steady on there, DI Wade,' laughed Ben. 'Don't want to be treating any broken bones this morning.'

'Sorry, doc.' Cassie stepped aside to let Ben through. 'Is she dead?'

Ben looked surprised. 'Well you're right, it is a woman, and she is dead. Knife wound. Do you know the victim?'

Cassie's face fell and she steadied herself against the wall. 'Oh no,' she whispered, before pushing past Ben and continuing upstairs.

Ben shrugged thoughtfully. 'Now what was that all about?' he said to himself before turning and making his way out of the building.

Peter looked up as Cassie entered the room. 'SOCO are on their way.'

Cassie only had eyes for the pair of legs sticking out from behind the sofa. Her hand flew to her mouth as a small sob escaped. Cassie rocked on her heels and might have fallen if Peter hadn't jumped over to steady her.

'You okay, Cassie? Only you've gone very pale. Come on, let's get some fresh air.'

'No! I have to see her.' Cassie shrugged Peter off and strode over to the sofa. Hardly daring to look, she peeped over to see a woman lying on her back, her one good eye staring sightless at the ceiling. It took her a few seconds to take it in, but she eventually looked over at Peter and said, 'It's not her.'

Peter and Cassie stood at the door to the flats looking out over the road to the railway line and the sea beyond. A uniformed constable stood a little way away on the pavement, moving would-be onlookers along.

'Want to tell me what that was about?' Peter asked a still stricken looking Cassie.

'This address, it's where my old school friend Suzi lives. She's been in Cornwall for a couple of years, only I didn't find out until recently.'

'But that's not her?'

Cassie shook her head emphatically. 'No. Suzi is small and blonde, similar to the woman up there, but it's definitely not her. I don't know who she might be.'

'You noticed the table set for breakfast?'

Cassie nodded, feeling irritated by the obvious conclusion being drawn. 'I know what it looks like, Peter. A cosy domestic scene. Possibly an argument and a fight. Suzi picks up a knife and stabs her... what? Flat-mate? Partner?'

'You have to admit, Cassie, there's room for conjecture.' Peter chose his words carefully. 'We need to locate your friend Suzi as soon as possible, and eliminate her if we can.'

'I don't know what to tell you, Peter. I know nothing about her life now, except what she told me a couple of weeks ago when she phoned out of the blue. She got my number from my mum. She wanted to meet up but I was busy. You know how it is, thought I'd contact her soon and arrange something.' Cassie shrugged then carried on. 'She met a man, online she said, and came to stay with him in Cornwall, somewhere near St Austell. She'd been working as a children and families social work manager in Merseyside, St Helens I think, but became disillusioned with it all and wanted a change.'

'Big change, to come all the way to Cornwall to a man she'd met online,' said Peter.

'That's Suzi all over. Impulsive. She told me he was okay though, and they got on really well. "An online success story" she called it. Not the love of her life, but comfortable. Oh, that sounds a bit pipe and slippers, and I don't think it was like that exactly. From the little time I spoke to her I got the impression that he was a nice guy. However, she found she couldn't live with him despite that. She said she had developed such a poor opinion of men that she couldn't help but find fault, even when there was none. So she left.'

'And came to live in Penzance?'

Cassie nodded. 'She sent me a note with her address and a recent photo. She was with a small group of people from Women's Aid; she'd been volunteering there.'

'That's helpful. We'll need the photo. Was she working?'

'I don't think so. She said she'd taken a counselling course in Camborne and wanted to set herself up doing that, but as I said, we didn't find time to chat.'

'Okay, Cassie, you go back to the station. You're going to Liverpool tomorrow, aren't you? Giving evidence?'

'Mmm, supposed to be.'

'You're definitely going, Cassie. I don't want you anywhere near this case so it's best all round that you're out of the way.'

Cassie opened her mouth to protest but Peter cut her off. 'The Liverpool case is important, as is your evidence, so there's no question. Your kids being looked after?'

Cassie was still thinking of objecting but knew there was no point, and anyway, Peter was right. 'They're with their dad in London for another week yet.'

'Right. Leave me that photo of Suzi. What's her other name?' Peter said as he took out a notebook.

'Delaney, Susan Mary Delaney. Unless she'd been married.'

'Write up what else you know about her and leave it on my desk. Good luck in Liverpool, keep away from the nasty men.' Peter was referring to the threats of harm that Cassie and her family had had from local gang members.

'Thanks, sir, I'm staying with an old university friend. They offered me a safe house for a couple of nights, but I don't think I could stand that.' Especially now, she thought.

Chapter Two

Cassie had chosen to travel to Liverpool by train with the intention of re-familiarising herself with the drugs case and going through her evidence. In the event, all she could think about was the body in Suzi's flat and her missing friend. She had tried Suzi's phone but it was either switched off or out of power. She itched to get involved in the investigation. Deep down she knew that Suzi was incapable of killing someone, but she also knew how it must look to Peter.

They'd been best friends at school, inseparable. Even though to most people's eyes they were an unlikely pairing. Cassie a black girl, dumpy and plain-looking with a studious nature. Susan (call me Suzi, it's more grown up) was slim and pretty. Long silvery blonde hair and wide blue eyes. But, although she looked as if butter wouldn't melt, she was tough for her size and defended Cassie when she was bullied by the school in-crowd. Suzi was anything but studious and blatantly copied Cassie's homework, making Cassie suspect that Suzi's interest in her was based on this fact alone.

But the friendship lasted, and Cassie loved being with Suzi, falling into fits of laughter at her outrageous suggestions. 'Let's get dolled up and go down the park – there's a footy match on and we can show the boys our legs and put them off.' When the pair were fourteen, Suzi made a plan to go to a club in the city centre. 'It'll be great, Cassie, The Human League are playing. We can get changed in the toilets at Lime Street station.'

Suzi's parents were strongly religious and not very welcoming, so the pair always met at Cassie's house. Cassie suspected that Mr and Mrs Delaney were racists, and it was for this reason that Suzi didn't introduce Cassie to them.

Cassie resisted the plan, but Suzi could be very persuasive, and, anyway, The Human League were Cassie's favourite band. 'Tell your parents that you are staying at mine and I'll do the same. It'll be great, Cass, Come on, I'll have to go by myself if you say no.'

The train was pulling into a station and Cassie was surprised to find it was Bristol Temple Meads, where she had to change. Gathering her belongings hurriedly, she made her way off the train and onto the platform. Having missed her breakfast, Cassie was hungry and headed to the station buffet for a coffee and bacon roll.

After settling herself back on a train, Cassie took out her phone to call Peter. She was desperate to find out what progress had been made in the case. Had they found Suzi? What did she have to say about events? Cassie felt sick at the thought of her friend going through the procedures in the police station. She might be scared and upset, and Cassie wouldn't be there to help her. Just then, Peter answered the phone.

In reply to Cassie's question, Peter said that they had not yet located Suzi. 'I can't tell you any more than that, Cassie. Her car is still here so we can assume she's on foot or public transport. It doesn't look good for your friend though, Cassie.'

'I know how it must seem, sir, but I can't believe Suzi is capable of murder, even if it looks that way. There must be another explanation. Perhaps the murderer abducted her.'

'Well that's a possibility, Cassie. Look, I can't let you be involved in this case, you know that.'

Cassie was silent, and Peter carried on. 'But, while you are in Liverpool you can do one thing to help. I want you to go to Suzi's parents, if they are still around, and find out if she has had contact with them. Can you do that?'

'I know where they used to live, but I don't know if they are still there, or even if they're still alive, but I'll be glad to go. I honestly don't think she'd go to them, though. As far as I know, they have completely lost touch.'

'When people are desperate, they do desperate things, Cassie.' Peter ended the call.

Thoughts of Suzi's parents took Cassie back to being fourteen.

The club turned out to be a back-street dive and The Human League wouldn't be seen dead there. Cassie held back at the entrance, looking nervously at the two large bouncers at the door. 'I'm not going in there, Suzi.'

'Don't be wet. It'll be great, come on.' Suzi tugged at Cassie's arm.

'They won't let us in, anyway,' protested Cassie. 'Just look at those two.'

Suzi laughed. 'Pussy cats. Come on.'

Cassie allowed herself to be led over to the doorway, feeling sure they would be turned away and could go home. She couldn't have been more wrong. The biggest of the bouncers simply leered suggestively at Suzi, taking in her short skirt and long legs. ' 'Ave a nice time, girls,' he said as he waved them through.

Inside it was dark, with red lights illuminating booths to either side of a small dance-floor. The bar was on the left and that's where Suzi headed, still dragging Cassie along. Suzi ordered Vodka. 'Tonic with mine,' shouted Cassie, trying to make herself heard over the deafening music.

Cassie felt sick and worried. The dance-floor was packed with writhing bodies dancing to a loud techno beat, arms waving in the air. She had never felt so out of place, but Suzi was smiling broadly and swaying to the music. 'Come on, Cass, let's dance,' she shouted. Cassie still had her coat on and a drink in one hand, so was surprised to find that Suzi had left hers somewhere and had on just a skimpy silver top with her short black skirt. Nevertheless, Cassie joined her on the fringes of the dance-floor, taking off her coat and placing it on the floor between them. Suzi was clearly enjoying herself, dancing wildly and attracting glances from men standing around the edge.

After a few minutes, the music stopped and the DJ introduced the band. Cassie's ears were ringing from the noise and she didn't hear their name, but it wasn't The Human League. Suzi grabbed Cassie and pulled her to the front of the stage just as the band were starting up.

They turned out to be not too bad, even played some Human League numbers, and Cassie found herself enjoying the music. The lead singer was good-looking, and Suzi was blatantly making eyes at him. When they got to their last number, which was *Don't You*

Want Me?, Suzi climbed up onto the stage and started to dance and sing like The Human League's backing singers. The band made no objections as Suzi was sexy and sang in tune. When the song was finished the lead singer took Suzi's hand and they bowed to the audience. Suzi looked entranced. Perhaps we can go home now, thought Cassie. But, instead of getting down from the stage, Suzi followed the band backstage.

It had been at least half an hour since Suzi had disappeared with the band, and Cassie was becoming increasingly concerned. She looked around to see if she could find someone in management or a waiter, but it was impossible. The DJ had started up again and the dance-floor was packed. Just as she thought of trying to find her way backstage, Suzi reappeared, looking flushed and wobbly. She approached Cassie, peering at her blearily. 'Can we go now?' she said, slurring her words slightly.

Cassie managed to tear herself away from the disturbing thoughts from the past and concentrate on the task at hand, her upcoming appearance at Liverpool Crown Court. She had been instrumental in putting away several members of the drugs gang, but one, calling himself Jasper, had evaded the police and escaped to Spain. He had been arrested at Manchester airport on a tip-off when he had tried to return to Liverpool. It was at his trial that Cassie was giving evidence tomorrow.

Cassie was pleased that she had retained a grasp of the drugs case and the part Jasper played in the death by overdose of a young woman who had been drawn into their circle. She hoped that he would be put away for a long time, but knew that his brief would argue for manslaughter, and that could mean a short sentence if Jasper played well in front of the jury. Still, she could only do her bit as well as she could. Cassie prided herself on performing competently in court, keeping a cool head when cross-examined by a hostile defence council. When she looked up from her notes, the train was arriving at Liverpool Lime Street Station, and this brought with it a tang of nostalgia.

Cassie had arranged to meet Steve at the Adelphi Hotel, so she made her way to the rear of the station and the busy taxi rank. Steve was waiting in the hotel's main bar as Cassie arrived, overnight-bag and briefcase in hand. He stood and waved her over. 'Long time, Cassie,' he said as he hugged her. 'Let me look at you.'

'Give over, you daft fool,' she replied laughing. 'You sound like me auntie.'

Steve returned her laugh. 'It is you then, I thought someone had kidnapped my friend and replaced her with this slim, sexy model.'

'You're gonna get a thump,' she quipped playfully, but was pleased with the compliment nevertheless. She had indeed lost weight since going to Cornwall. Being a detective in Liverpool had meant drinks in the pub almost every night, and fast food snatched on the way home. With her parents only too pleased to look after Micky and Tanya, Cassie had been drawn into what was a self-destructive lifestyle. Cornwall had introduced her to coastal walks and fresh food, and she felt the benefit of it on her waistline.

Driving out of the city, Steve turned to Cassie. 'What's all this about your mad friend then?'

'Mmm. She's not mad exactly, not these days at any rate, but she may be in trouble.' Cassie paused. 'I was wondering if you could do me a favour later.'

'Name it.'

'Can you take me to Childwall? I have to check out Suzi's parents' place. My boss thinks she may be with them, or at least have contacted them. Even though I know it's a non-starter, I have to rule it out, just to be thorough.'

'No problem, love. Shall we drop your bag and freshen up or do you want to go now?'

'Let's get it over with, Steve, then we can relax.'

'Your wish is my command.'

Driving down the familiar streets of her home city, Cassie felt a pang of regret that she couldn't visit her parents. Her old team had advised her that it wouldn't be safe as the drugs gang knew where they lived, and might be watching the house. Turning into a side street, Cassie indicated to Steve to pull over beside a neat semi. She sat in the car remembering the last time she had called at this house.

Suzi had not been her usual lively self after their experience at the club. She was absent from school regularly, and eventually word got round that she was being home-schooled. Of course, the grapevine soon reported that Suzi was pregnant. Cassie was furious that her best friend had not confided this in person, and went round to the Delaneys' to confront her. Mrs Delaney answered the door and told Cassie that Susan didn't want to speak to her, looking her up and down as if she had a bad taste in her mouth. As Cassie turned away, she noticed Suzi at a bedroom window, her hand pressed against the glass.

Walking up the path this time, Cassie felt nervous, as if she was fourteen again. 'Stop being so daft, Cassie,' she said to herself, 'You're a grown woman and a detective inspector.' This made her laugh inside, so that when the door opened, she had a smile on her face.

The grey-haired woman who stood there couldn't have been more different from the sour-faced blonde who had confronted Cassie all those years ago. This woman's face spoke of regret and sadness, her shoulders slumped and her hands shaking. 'Can I help you, love?' she said, half smiling.

'Mrs Delaney, it's Cassie Wade, Cassandra Spencer as was.'

Mrs Delaney studied the woman before her. 'Cassandra? Of course, I'm sorry, love, I didn't recognise you. Come on in.'

Cassie was taken by surprise by this welcome, but followed Mrs Delaney through the hall and into a comfortable sitting room, noting that this was the first time she had set foot in this house.

'Sit down, love. Can I get you a cup of tea?'

'No thanks, Mrs Delaney, I'm here on official business actually. I'm a detective inspector with Devon and Cornwall Police.' She took out her warrant card and Mrs Delaney studied it, not quite comprehending what was happening.

'The police? I don't understand, love, what's wrong?'

'It's about Suzi. . . er, Susan, Mrs Delaney. I wonder if you'd heard from her lately?'

The older woman stiffened. 'Susan? No, we don't speak.'

'It's just that we need to find her, she may be a witness to a crime.'

'Cassandra, you know as well as anyone what happened with Susan. I try not to think about those days now, it's too painful. Susan left home when she was sixteen, and I have never heard from her since. It broke Mr Delaney's heart. He died not a year after she left, and I couldn't even let her know. I've been on my own since.' The bitterness in her voice spoke of years dwelling in the past, despite her protests that the past was too painful to think about.

'I'm so sorry, Mrs Delaney, but I had to check.'

'Have you seen her? I mean recently?'

'Not for a while.'

'How did she look, when you did see her? Was she alright?' A look of longing was evident on the mother's face.

'Susan has made a success of her life; you'd be proud of her. She looked well and happy the last time I saw her. I'm sorry she hasn't found the time to see you.'

'Found the time? No love, she hated me and still hates me by the look of things. Is she in trouble? She must be, you wouldn't be here otherwise would you?'

'At the moment we are trying to find her in connection with a crime. She may be able to help us, that's all.'

'Wait a minute. Did you say Devon and Cornwall Police?' Cassie nodded. 'I don't understand.'

'Susan was living in Cornwall when she... well, when she disappeared.' Mrs Delaney's face registered dismay. 'But I'm sure it's nothing to worry about, really,' reassured Cassie. 'When we locate her, shall I say you've been asking about her?'

'Don't bother, love. She knows where I live if she wants me.'

Cassie stood, took a card out of her pocket and handed it to Mrs Delaney. 'Please contact me if you hear from Susan, or if you can think of anything that could help us locate her.'

The older woman nodded and stared at the card. 'I will, love, but don't hold your breath.'

Steve drove the silent Cassie back through the city centre. Travelling up Mount Pleasant, they passed part of the university they used to frequent. An old red-brick building with wide steps leading up to ornate double doors. Steve looked over at his passenger. 'Remember this place?'

'Of course I do. Child Development, Criminology and Deviance.'

'What was the name of that old duffer who used to do T groups with us?'

'Therapy groups? Yes, George something. Watkins, Watkinson? Something like that.'

'Yes, George Watkinson. D'you remember how he used to fall asleep during our discussions?'

Cassie laughed. 'It all seems so long ago, Steve.' Cassie was reminded of the time she bumped into Suzi outside Lewis's when she was dashing to the shops between lectures.

They were both entering the swing doors at the same time, and literally bumped shoulders. After a double take, Suzi shrieked, 'Cassie!'

They hugged and laughed at the random nature of life. 'This was our old meeting place, under *Nobbie Lewis*, remember?' The reference was to the Jacob Epstein statue of a naked man on top of the store's impressive portico on the Lewis's store corner, named thus by the Liverpool wits. Standing five and a half metres tall, it was quite a landmark for the local residents. Cassie recalled the place had been immortalised in song by Pete McGovern, and made popular by The Spinners in their song *In My Liverpool Home*: '*meet under a statue exceedingly bare.*'

On that occasion, the pair had talked non-stop over coffee, updating each other on what had happened in their lives since they were fifteen. Suzi wasn't at all surprised that Cassie had done well in GCSEs and A levels and congratulated her on being in her final year at John Moore's. 'Then it's police training college, eh? You'll make a great copper, Cassie, always had a strong sense of right and wrong, unlike me.'

'What happened, Suzi? I tried to see you but …'

'I know, Cass, my lovely caring mother shooed you away. I had my baby, a boy, but they whisked him away before I saw him.'

'Oh, I'm so sorry, Suzi. It must have been an awful time.'

'You don't know the half of it.'

Cassie had been so lost in thought that she had hardly registered the drive to Steve's flat. 'Earth to Cassie,' he said gently.

'Sorry, Steve. I was somewhere else.'

'Come on, love, let's get inside and you can tell me where exactly "somewhere else" is.'

After a welcome shower, and dressed in comfortable jeans and sweater, Cassie relaxed and she and Steve talked as they sipped their G&Ts.

'Your friend had it rough then?' said Steve.

'Her parents were strong Catholics, you know the sort, the priest practically lived with them. Suzi told me that, when they found out she was pregnant, they called in the old priest. He told her that she had sinned and that her sin would leave a stain on her soul forever. She was forced to go to confession every day because the priest didn't think she was sufficiently remorseful. She said he liked to hear the details of her sexual encounter with the boy, Johnnie, so much so that Suzi was sure he got a vicarious thrill out of it.

Her parents wouldn't let her out of the house, apart from going to church, and they arranged for an adoption through a Catholic adoption society. The baby was taken away at birth.'

'She went back to school though?'

'Yes, but she was different. She kept away from me and, I'm ashamed to say, I was glad. I wanted to concentrate on my studies, and I knew she'd be a bad influence. Some friend I turned out to be.'

'You mustn't blame yourself, Cassie. She made her choices, bad ones as it turned out.'

'She was raped, Steve. She was fourteen and he plied her with Vodka and raped her.'

Steve nodded thoughtfully. 'What was she doing when you met up with her again?'

'Surprisingly, she'd got her life together, eventually. She left home when she was sixteen and moved into a squat with a boy who knocked her about. Ultimately, he beat her so much she finished up in hospital. She'd been pregnant at the time and he accused her of going with another bloke. He broke her jaw and kicked her in the guts so badly that she needed a hysterectomy.'

'Cassie, that's awful.'

'Yeah, tell me about it. A nurse got someone from Women's Aid to visit her and Suzi was taken to a refuge. And that was the beginning of her salvation, she says.' Cassie remembered the excited look on Suzi's face as she described her vocation to help women and children who were victims of domestic abuse. 'Because of her volunteer work with Women's Aid, and her excellent results from an access course, she had just been accepted at Manchester University to do a social work degree. She was so happy when I saw her.'

'And since then?'

'A couple of years ago she was all over social media as a spokeswoman for Women's Aid. She'd had a bit of a meteoric rise in social work and managed a children's division as well as working with women. A workaholic by all accounts.'

'What about now?'

Cassie remembered a phone conversation with Suzi just before she came to Cornwall. She was clearly looking for something new.

'I'm sick of social work, Cassie. I really thought I could make a difference, you know? But nothing changes. Children are still abused and too many die as a result. As a manager I tried to drum into my social workers that they must always concentrate on the child. You know what the first words in The Children Act are?' Cassie said no. *The welfare of the child is paramount.* Paramount. Doesn't leave much room for interpretation does it? Time after time when a child is killed, the serious case review, that includes all agencies, always concludes that, *lessons must be learned*, and this should never happen again. Has a hollow ring, doesn't it?'

'So you're disillusioned, Suzi. Surely though, you're better in the fight than out of it? I sometimes don't think the police are effective enough.'

Suzi shook her head on the end of the phone. 'The very last straw, Cassie, was when a child that all the agencies were working with, died of nappy rash.'

'Nappy rash?'

'Officially sepsis, but it was brought on because the poor mite was lying in urine-soaked nappies for days on end. His mattress was sodden, Cassie. Worse case of neglect I've seen. We were just as responsible as anyone.'

'Didn't anyone notice?' Cassie was clearly shocked.

'The trouble is, Cass, the workers focus on the parents, feel sorry for them, lone mothers more often than not, in the hopes that they'll get their act together. It's normally the unholy trinity of domestic abuse, drug or alcohol misuse and mental health issues. All very sad, tragic even, but the problem, Cassie, is that kids can't wait for mum to get her act together, they need parenting now.'

Suzi sighed and gave a hollow laugh. 'Anyway, that's enough of me on my soapbox. I've handed in my notice and I'm going to have a change.'

'What about your other stuff? Women's Aid? You're quite the national figure for them.'

'I'll carry on with that for now, but who knows, I might join the police.' Suzi laughed as Cassie gasped. 'Only joking, love. Out of the frying pan and all that.'

Cassie was suddenly very tired. 'I'm off to bed, Steve, if that's alright. Big day tomorrow. In reality, Cassie was sick with worry about Suzi and needed sleep to calm her troubled thoughts.

The next day started with a rushed breakfast, Cassie not able to eat much because of suddenly feeling nervous about her court appearance.

'I'm never like this, Steve,' she said, brushing down her black jacket. 'I can't count the number of times I've given evidence and I'm always calm. Now look at me, shaking like a leaf.'

'I bet you've never given evidence with a death-threat hanging over you, though.'

Cassie smiled ruefully. 'I suppose. But my old team are on the ball. They're picking me up from here and I'll go into court the back way. Afterwards, they'll take me straight to the airport. The gang will be expecting me to take a train so the railway station will be well covered by them.'

'Sounds like a good plan. I'm only sorry that you can't stay longer.'

Cassie hugged her friend. 'Me too, chuck, you'll have to come to Cornwall for a visit. I'll show you the sights.'

'I'll hold you to that,' Steve said. 'And I think that's your lift.' He looked out of the window to see a grey car pull up.

After a quick check in the mirror, Cassie picked up her bag, feeling less nervous now that she was on the move.

John Lennon Airport came into view. Cassie's court appearance had gone according to plan. Her nerves had disappeared as she was sworn in, and even the very expensive defence barrister couldn't shake her. The whole thing was over in less than an hour and her ex-colleague Martin whisked Cassie away from the court's rear entrance. Conversation in the car had been about Cassie's new posting, with Martin giving his condolences about the Cornwall job. 'Talk about woolly-backs, Cassie. They're probably sheep-shaggers as well.'

'Ha! I've missed you and your razor-sharp wit, Martin. As a matter of fact, it's not too bad. We're starting our fourth murder investigation since I joined the team. A good team, too.'

Martin glanced over sharply.

'Oh, not as good as our team,' Cassie said quickly, 'but not too shabby all the same.'

Martin pulled the car into the drop-off point. Cassie grabbed her bag. 'Give my best to everyone and remember me when you have a drink to your success tonight. I'm sure it'll be a guilty verdict. One more moron off the streets.'

Martin watched his ex-boss walk away. She's looking good, he thought. Cornwall must suit her after all.

The flight was on time and Cassie barely had time to order a coffee and glance at the in-flight magazine, before the pilot announced their descent into Newquay airport. This is the way to travel, she thought. Now I can find out what's happening with Suzi's case.

Chapter Three

Cassie had asked to be taken straight to the team room. 'I know I've only been away a day, Robbie, but I need to know what's happening with the murder investigation.'

Robbie looked uncomfortable. 'I'm not supposed to say anything to you about that, ma'am, seeing as you know the suspect.'

'I can't see that she's a suspect yet, Robbie,' said Cassie sharply. 'We've got a dead body and a missing person. It's good to keep an open mind about these things.'

'Yes, ma'am.' Nevertheless, Robbie concentrated on his driving and managed to avoid filling Cassie in on progress with the case despite her curiosity. Not that there was much, he mused, there had been no sightings of Susan Delaney. Her car was still parked in a side road by the flats, so they were checking bus and train stations and CCTV on the streets nearby. The chief was giving a press conference today hoping that a strong media focus would bring results.

Cassie understood that Robbie was under orders not to involve her in the case, and she didn't press him. It would be a different story when she met with DCI Sanders though. Cassie was determined not to be idle whilst the team chased after her old friend, believing her to be the prime suspect in a murder. She didn't have long to wait when they arrived at the station. Cassie jumped out of the car as Robbie pulled into the parking bay. 'Grab my bag, Robbie. I'll be with the Chief.'

DCI Sanders was briefing the team as Cassie burst into the

squad room. He stopped talking and held his hand up to call a halt to the general chatter. 'DI Wade. My office please, I'll be with you shortly.'

Cassie glanced around the room and tried to quickly take in the information on the white board before nodding towards Peter and heading for his office.

As soon as Peter had closed the door, Cassie made her move. 'You can't leave me out of this one, sir. I know Suzi Delaney and she just isn't capable of murder.'

'Good to see you're keeping an open mind, Cassie,' said Peter, not hiding the sarcasm. 'That's precisely why you can't be anywhere near this investigation.'

Cassie realised her mistake. 'Of course I'll keep an open mind, but at the moment Suzi is a missing person, that's all.'

'That is not all, Cassie. There was a body found in her flat, a flat which she more than likely shared with the victim, and she is missing under extremely suspicious circumstances. Get your head out of your arse, Cassie!' She was taken aback by the unfamiliar phrase from her usually calm boss. 'What would you be thinking if this was anyone else but your friend?'

Peter invited Cassie to sit down. 'Now, understand this. I will not have you involved in this case, except where your knowledge of the suspect would be helpful. Do you get that?' Cassie nodded glumly. 'On that subject, how did you get on with the parents?'

Cassie filled Peter in on her meeting with Mrs Delaney. 'I really don't think she knows anything. I bet Suzi doesn't even know her dad's dead, unless she still reads the obits in the *Liverpool Echo*.'

Peter smiled at the weak joke. 'Okay, Cassie. I have got something that I want you to lead on though.' He pulled a thin file out from his desk drawer. 'It's a rape case. Only reported last night and it needs immediate attention. The victim is fourteen...' This made Cassie jump considering where her thoughts had been for the last couple of days.

Cassie took the file from Peter. He continued. 'The Trevellian family live on a farm near Stithians. I'll give you the post code for the SATNAV. The accusation is that a man jumped Erica, that's the victim, on her way home from her grandma's last night. She's refusing a medical examination and is back home with her parents. That's all we have. You can have Robbie to help you.'

Cassie was intrigued, despite her desire to be involved in Suzi's case. 'Yes, sir. I'll get on it straight away.'

'Good. And Cassie? It's best this way. If your friend is innocent, we'll find out. No witch hunts here, you know that.'

'Yes, sir. I know.'

Peter took in Cassie's smart black suit and cream shirt. Glancing at her footwear, he said, 'You may want to go home and pick up some wellingtons. If I know anything about the farms around here it's that they are invariably muddy.'

Cassie smiled. 'You have to remember, sir, I came straight from court.'

'Of course. How did you get on?'

'We had a watertight case, sir. Evidence from an undercover op plus an eye witness to the overdose the suspect administered to the dead woman. One of the gang members also testified in return for a lighter sentence. And it's a good job we had his testimony on tape because he had a nasty accident whilst on remand. He's still in a coma.'

'These cases are a nightmare, Cassie. But you and your family are safe?'

'My mum and dad are staying with my aunt in Southport. As soon as I gave my evidence they were safe, at least that's what we hope. They'll stay away for a bit. I think they're enjoying the seaside.'

'Okay, off you go. I'll tell Robbie to expect your call. In the meantime, he may be able to find out a bit more about your rape case.'

'Right, sir. I believe you're giving a press conference today.'

'On your way, Cassie,' Peter said, determined not to respond to any fishing expedition from his DI.

Cassie smiled. 'I'll catch you on TV then, sir.'

'Out, DI Wade.' Peter smiled. He had some sympathy with Cassie. He would probably be just the same in her shoes.

'I'm gone, sir.'

After Cassie had left the station, Peter resumed his briefing to the team. 'I attended the PM this morning.' He took out a sheet of paper from his pocket. 'Ben Samuels found multiple injuries of

varying ages on our victim, who I'll call Jane for the time being.'
He pointed towards the crime scene photos on the white board.
'Jane was found on her back with a knife wound to her chest. She
also had a number of fresh bruises and cuts to her forearms which
suggest defensive wounds.

'As I said, Jane also had old injuries. She was missing an eye,
with a fracture to the eye socket consistent with that event. She had
sustained several broken bones, most extensively to her ribs, where
there were signs of different degrees of healing. Jane also had a
broken foot, four metatarsals, semi-healed, crushed by something
heavy, or having been stamped on violently. There were old and
healed twist fractures to one arm.' Peter looked around the room at
the shocked and saddened faces of his team. 'All that and
numerous bruises over her body, inflicted over a period of time.'
Peter dropped the report on the desk in front of him. 'Jane had
clearly been systematically abused over a long period. Ben felt
sure that the injuries could only have been inflicted by a strong
person, most likely a male, so not likely to have been Susan
Delaney who we know to be a slight person. That's not to say she
didn't kill Jane, for reasons we've yet to establish, but it may put
another suspect in the frame.'

Peter paused to let this sink in. 'What do we know about
domestic abuse?'

DS Saroj Kapoor was the first to answer. 'Statistically most
often perpetrated by men against women, though more cases of
women abusing men and violence in same sex couples are being
reported.'

'So,' said Peter, '*Statistically*, who is most likely to have killed
Jane?'

DS Kevin Sharp spoke up. 'The most likely is a male partner.
The one who was responsible for the old injuries probably.'

Peter nodded. 'That gives us another line of enquiry. Kevin,
contact Women's Aid in Penzance and show them Jane's photo. If
they know her, they could give us a lead to her long-time abuser.
They may also know something about why she was where she was
when she was killed.'

'What about time of death, sir?' asked Kevin.

'We can be fairly accurate on that. A neighbour in the flats heard
loud screaming from flat eight at ten o'clock that morning. She is

sure about the time because a programme she watches on TV was just about to start. The neighbour, a Miss Connolly, says that they all look out for each other in the flats, so she paid particular attention to the event. The screaming and shouting went on for a few minutes, and then all was quiet. Then Miss Connolly heard someone coming up the stairs, followed by a muted argument, she thinks between a man and a woman. She heard footsteps going down the stairs, then nothing more. Miss Connolly was aware that Suzi had a friend staying but had heard no arguments or anything like that since the friend moved in. Anyway, she was concerned and called the police.'

'Sounds like she'd make an excellent witness, sir,' said Saroj.

'Thank goodness for busy bodies,' said Kevin.

'Indeed, Kevin. We may not have found the body for days if she hadn't been so vigilant. Thanks to Miss Connolly we've got a jump start on the case. Susan Delaney didn't go up in a puff of smoke, did she? So someone will have seen her when she left the flat. Remember, from what Miss Connolly said, there may have been a man present also.

'I'm going back to the scene after I've finished with the press. There must be some clue in the flat as to where Susan Delaney is hiding out. SOCO found a number of fingerprints, as we expected. If Jane's ex was a violent man, he may be known to us, so if his prints are there, we can place him at the scene, and that would make him our prime suspect. Maggie, let me know as soon as their report comes in.'

'Yes, sir.'

'Robbie, you'll be working with Cassie on the Stithians rape case. The rest of you, I want you searching CCTV and doing house-to-house around the murder scene. Let's get some more information. It feels like we're working in the dark.'

Peter dismissed the team and went into his office to prepare for his press conference. He was sorry not to have Cassie to bounce ideas off in this case. He had promised Rachel that he would delegate more responsibility to his DI now that they had a baby to consider. However, Cassie had shown him that she would find it hard to remain objective when it came to her old friend. He felt sure that Cassie had more information about Susan Delaney that might give them a clue as to her whereabouts. He would need to tread carefully but resolved to speak to her again soon.

Chapter Four

Cassie had taken a taxi home and decided to change into something more suited to visiting a farm. Dressed in dark trousers and a smart but serviceable jacket, she waited for Robbie to collect her. Forcing herself to concentrate on the case in hand, Cassie wondered why the victim had refused medical attention. According to the file, Erica had been found around eleven-thirty at night by a waitress cycling home from the pub where she worked. The girl was lying on the grass verge and was conscious but very shaken. The waitress, Marcia, had offered to call for an ambulance, but Erica became hysterical and insisted on going home. Marcia walked home with Erica where her dad took control and seemed disinclined to take the matter further. However, Marcia was alarmed to think of a rapist in the vicinity and reported the matter to the police.

Well done, Marcia, thought Cassie. But why would any parents not want the rape of their daughter investigated? Cassie's thoughts went back to her conversation with Suzi about her parents' reaction to her pregnancy: how they were ashamed of their daughter and wanted to keep the whole event private. Could Mr and Mrs Trevellian feel the same? Cassie felt that she would need her wits about her on this case. Family dynamics were tricky subjects. There would be a lot to take in on this visit.

Robbie pulled into the short drive to Cassie's house. He hoped that she wouldn't be angling for information about the Susan Delaney case. He found it difficult to stonewall a senior officer, but he would have to. DCI Sanders had warned everyone what would happen if they shared anything with the DI.

'Afternoon, ma'am,' he said, as he opened the car door for his boss.

'Pop these in the boot, Robbie,' said Cassie, as she handed him a clean pair of wellingtons.

Robbie glanced at the boots. 'Not seen much wear, these, ma'am,' he remarked, smiling.

'Just put them in the boot and wipe that silly grin off your face,' said Cassie, not really minding the cheeky young constable's attempt at a joke. 'I hope you've come fully equipped yourself?'

The smile disappeared from Robbie's face as he realised that he hadn't thought to bring boots. 'Shouldn't be a problem ma'am.'

Cassie chuckled to herself. Let's hope not, she thought.

The dark clouds scudded overhead, the spring sun blinking in and out between them. 'Looks like rain,' said Cassie.

Robbie nodded. 'Could be a downpour if those clouds are anything to go by.'

Cassie thought she would quiz her colleague to see if he had his thinking cap on. 'Why would parents not report the rape of their daughter, Robbie?'

He thought for a moment. 'If they blamed her? Or if they knew the attacker and wanted to protect him? Locals can be very defensive, ma'am, don't take kindly to interference. They might try to cover something up.'

'Very good, Robbie. Now when we get to the Trevellians' I want you to keep your eyes and ears open. Watch everyone closely, see how they are with each other. Remember all your body-language training – using your third eye and all that.'

'Aye, I remember it well, ma'am. At the time I thought it was a bit of hippy mumbo jumbo, you know, but people do give themselves away unconsciously, don't they?'

'They do indeed, Robbie. So let's see what the Trevellians are hiding.'

Robbie turned off the narrow country road and pulled into a rutted driveway suited to tractors and four-wheel drives, but not so good for the average police car. Rounding a bend, the farmhouse came into view. A large muddy courtyard fronted the house which was built of granite with small window openings. Outside the front door were various pieces of farm equipment haphazardly placed. There was no attempt at making the entrance attractive. That was not the way with farmers, Robbie acknowledged to himself, it was, after all, a workplace first and a home second.

Cassie made few observations at this point, other than being pleased she had heeded Peter's advice about the wellingtons, the rain had begun to fall in earnest now and the conditions could only get worse. She waited until Robbie had opened the boot and handed her the much-needed footwear before emerging from the car. She noticed that Robbie's smart boots were already splashed with mud and she smiled to herself. A dog barked loudly and came running towards them. Robbie bent to pet the animal which snapped and snarled at him. A man's voice called from the doorway. 'Heel, Margo!' At which command, the dog turned and ran to its master. 'Can I 'elp thee?' he said.

Cassie held out her warrant card. 'Mr Trevellian? DI Wade, Devon and Cornwall Police, and this is DC Green. I'd like to have a word with you about the incident concerning your daughter Erica.'

'Nuthen' to be said, Miss. It wer all a misunderstandin'.'

'Nevertheless, the police have been called and we have a duty to check it out. Could we speak to your daughter, sir?'

Mr Trevellian stood stony-faced for a few seconds, his large frame filling the doorway. Then he turned to enter the house, leaving the door open. 'A man of few words,' whispered Cassie, as she and Robbie followed him into the house.

The entrance led directly into a sizeable kitchen which doubled as a living space. A large, old black Aga took up the most of one wall. A clothes-dryer was hoisted above with items of clothing dangling from it. The centre of the room was taken up by a huge pine table with several chairs surrounding it. The table was littered with mugs and dishes, with the remnants of a meal evident in the loaf of bread and large cooking pot in the centre.

Mr Trevellian stood behind the table, hands on hips. Cassie spotted an old lady sitting by the Aga in a tattered armchair, staring at her as if she had just descended from outer space. Looking up at Mr Trevellian, the old lady shouted, 'Who's that maid? What's a coloured doin' 'ere?'

33

'She's a policewoman, ma.'

'Don't talk daft, boy. She's black.'

Cassie shook her head, amazed that such attitudes could still exist. 'Mr Trevellian, can we get on with the matter at hand. Is Mrs Trevellian around, perhaps?'

The old lady chirped in again. 'What's her saying, Saul?'

' 'Tes alright, ma. It's nuthen.' Looking steadily at Cassie he said, 'Wife left two years back.'

'I'm sorry to hear that. It must be hard for you bringing up a daughter.'

Saul glared at her. 'We manage,' he said.

Cassie nodded, knowing she wouldn't get any more out of the belligerent farmer. 'I'd like to speak to your daughter.'

The farmer scowled at Cassie and, without moving, shouted, 'Erica! Get down 'ere.'

Just then the front door crashed open and two large young men burst in, arguing about something. They stopped in their tracks when they saw Cassie. 'Who's this, pa?' said one. Cassie noticed that the young men were very similar in size and appearance, like two bookends.

'Nuthen fer you to concern yerself wi'. Is they fence posts fixed?'

The same young man spoke again. 'Need fresh wood, pa. Yon's rotten.'

Cassie spoke up again. 'Mr Trevellian, as fascinating as this is…'

At that moment a girl entered the room. She was small and timid-looking, scruffily dressed in leggings and a stained T shirt.

Mr Trevellian turned to her. 'Police 'ere want to know about tuther night. Nuthen 'appened, right?' His demeanour was imposing and Cassie could see that the girl was afraid.

'I'd prefer to speak to Erica myself, Mr Trevellian, if you don't mind.' Cassie turned to the girl. 'Shall we sit here, Erica? There's nothing to be afraid of; I just want to ask you a couple of questions. Okay?'

Erica nodded slightly and sat down at the table. Cassie pulled a chair out and sat next to her. Mr Trevellian seated himself opposite, never taking his eyes off Erica. 'Before we start, Mr Trevellian, would you introduce me to the others in the room?'

The man looked startled, and looked around. 'That's me ma, and these is me sons, Paul an Andy.'

'Thank you. I'll leave my sergeant here while I speak to Erica alone, if that's okay.' Cassie knew she was on thin ice as PACE requirements dictated that an appropriate adult be present in interviews, but she decided that an informal conversation wasn't strictly an interview. She looked at Mr Trevellian hopefully. 'Perhaps she could take me up to her room?'

Erica looked wild-eyed, like a startled deer. 'Would that be alright, Erica?' Cassie said.

Mr Trevellian gave the slightest of nods and Erica stood.

As Cassie followed the girl to the stairs, Robbie took over, to distract the farmer. 'You been farming long, Mr Trevellian?'

He looked Robbie up and down. ' 'T'was me father's afore me.'

'I saw sheep on the way in. D'you have any other livestock?'

The conversation limped along as Robbie tried to engage the farmer and his sons, ignoring the old lady who seemed to be falling asleep.

Cassie could hear the murmur of voices from below as she and Erica reached the landing. *Good work, Robbie*, she thought. Erica opened a small door and preceded Cassie into a largish room with sloping ceilings. The smell of urine was evident, and Cassie wrinkled her nose.

Erica noticed the inspector's reaction. 'It's me nanny, she wets the bed. I 'aven't 'ad time to wash this week.'

'You share a room with your nanny?' Erica nodded. And a bed too, thought Cassie. There was nothing in this room to tell you that a teenaged girl owned it. No posters on the walls, no dressing table with jewellery and make up, no laptop or TV. A single chest of drawers and wardrobe in dark wood stood against the only non-sloping wall in the room, and a chair by the bed held a lamp.

Cassie was reluctant to sit on the bed, but the window ledge was deep, and she perched on it. 'Now, Erica, I just want you to tell me what happened when you were on your way home from your gran's the other night. We had a call from a young woman who found you at the roadside. Do you remember her?'

Erica started crying quietly, her shoulders hunched. Cassie thought she had never seen such a pathetic little creature in her life.

Being more used to stroppy teenagers, this poor girl seemed alien in comparison.

'I can see it's upsetting, Erica. Look at me, love.'

Erica raised her head and focused her eyes on Cassie, sniffing away tears. Cassie handed her a tissue from her pocket.

Taking in the girl's face, Cassie could see that she was quite pretty really, with amazingly bright green eyes. A wash and some nice clothes and she would be a different girl, she thought.

'Now, take your time. What time did you leave your gran's?'

Mr Trevellian stood in the doorway of the farmhouse, scowling as the police car disappeared down the driveway. He hoped that was the last he would see of the bolshie black woman. Why they let women into the police was beyond him anyway, let alone a black one. Of course, he knew about the various movements to promote the role of women and ethnic minorities, but that didn't mean he had to agree with them. Women's place was definitely in the home as far as he was concerned. Leave the decision making and politics to the men. He turned and shouted for his sons to follow him over to the bottom field. He was proud that his two boys were keen to carry on the farm. Big lads, too, and twins at that, two for the price of one he had often said to his mates in the pub, and no one could argue with the benefit of that.

The boys ran ahead of their father as the three made their way to check out the rotten fence posts. Boys are good, Saul thought, not like Erica bringing trouble to the house. Since his wife left two years ago, claiming rough treatment, he had to rely on the girl to do the woman's work. His ma was too old and not all there at times. He had no conscience about keeping Erica off school. Why do women need an education beyond that which would help them run a household? Erica could cook well enough and, if the cleaning was a bit haphazard he didn't mind, couldn't stand too much tidiness anyway. She could do better helping out with the farm though. Chickens were always the woman's job, as well as feeding the pigs. She'd have to put more effort in there, perhaps she'd grow into it. Better still, marry somebody who would provide an extra hand.

The boys had reached the fence and were patiently waiting for their father. Now all we have to hope is that Erica will forget this silly nonsense about rape. Saul could hardly think of the word, let alone say it out aloud. She'll have to stay at home and not visit that old busybody of a grandma. Soon all be forgotten, he thought. But he couldn't be more wrong.

Cassie had turned to watch Mr Trevellian as Robbie drove away from the farm. 'Got any observations, Robbie?'

'Mr Trevellian is tight-lipped but the boys know something. They hinted at dealing with trouble themselves, but before they could say more, their dad silenced them with a look.'

Cassie thought for a moment. 'If they're under eighteen, which it seems they are – just, PACE rules say we can't interview them without an adult present. But, if we think another crime may be prevented through that interview, we can call on the services of an appropriate adult instead of a parent.'

'Do you think that's the case here, ma'am?'

'We could stretch the point, Robbie. From what you say, we definitely wouldn't get anything out of them with their dad present.'

'What about Erica, ma'am? Did you get anything from her?'

'What do you know about The Children Act, Robbie?'

'Not much, I have to admit.'

'Well, Erica has been kept from attending school. She's also taken the place of her mother in the household, and that makes her a *young carer* and a *child in need* under the provisions of the Act. And that means that social services have a duty to offer support, especially as Erica also qualifies as a child "who's health and development is being impaired", that's another provision in The Children Act.'

Robbie was impressed with the wide knowledge his DI had and made a mental note to look out a copy of The Children Act. 'So does that mean we can hand the case over to social services?'

'Well said, Robbie. Probably. Almost certainly, in fact. Erica is determined not to make a complaint of rape, and with no other evidence apart from that of the woman who found her, we've nothing to investigate.'

Robbie detected a note of triumph in Cassie's voice. He knew that the chief thought that this case would keep Cassie from interfering in the murder investigation. I wonder what he'll do now? thought Robbie. He glanced over at his DI who was absorbed in scrolling through her phone.

Suddenly she said, 'Found it! There's a multi-agency group set up to deal with issues of children in need. There's usually one in each local authority. I want you to contact them, Robbie, and call a meeting about Erica Trevellian. It won't need me to attend, you can deal with it.'

'Yes, ma'am, if you think it's appropriate.'

'I do, Robbie. I'll give you a few pointers if you've never attended this type of meeting before, but, basically, the outcome I want is for social services and education to take responsibility. No need for us to remain involved.'

'Ma'am. I'll get on to it right away,' said Robbie, his mind still on the clash which was bound to take place between his DI and the Chief. He couldn't see Cassie twiddling her thumbs whilst her friend was still a major suspect. The next couple of days should be very interesting indeed.

Chapter Five

Peter stood in the centre of the living room in Susan Delaney's flat. A small desk in one corner had obviously held a laptop, as the leads were still visible. He knew that SOCO would have removed it for analysis. Above the desk was a bookshelf. Peter wandered over to inspect it. There were mainly feminist books, counselling and psychology reference books, and several volumes concerning childcare, including legal texts like *The Children Act* and *Every Child Matters*. A stack of papers filled an in-tray and, as he flicked through them, he could see that they consisted of copies of newspaper articles going back a few years, and other research documents, all concerning domestic abuse. It looked to Peter as if Susan was writing a book. The contents of her laptop should confirm that.

Peter moved to the kitchen. This was a small but tidy and cheerful space decorated in bright colours. The fridge door contained photographs and a shopping list attached by magnets. The photos showed groups of women at what looked like a barbecue, mugging for the camera. He recognised Susan and thought that one of the other women could be the victim. Taking an evidence bag out of his pocket, he collected the photos and placed them inside. The bedroom was neat, but the bed remained unmade. Peter could see the evidence of fingerprint powder everywhere, but despite that, he felt that Susan liked her place to be clean and tidy. The bathroom had a shower cubicle with an electric shower, a washbasin and toilet, all clean. Opening the bathroom cabinet, Peter examined pill bottles, noting the date of prescription. He collected all but a pack of Paracetamol, and bagged them for further analysis.

As he was leaving, Peter paused and looked back into the flat. The overall feeling he had was of a comfortable and settled home. What happened here to disturb that peaceful existence? he thought. Was it Jane? Was she the disruptive influence? The impression of Susan that he gained through examining her flat suggested a studious and well-ordered person. Did Jane upset the rhythm of Susan's life? And could Susan have struck out at her lodger when it all got too much? Surely it would be easier to simply ask Jane to leave. But if it wasn't Susan, why had she disappeared? All Peter's instincts said that Susan wasn't a killer. Cassie certainly refused to believe that she was. Perhaps all would become clearer with the SOCO report. He certainly hoped so.

Back in the squad room, Kevin was making notes on the whiteboard. He stopped when he heard Peter come in. 'Sir,' he said, 'some good information from my contact at Women's Aid.' 'Right, let's have it then, I could do with some good news.' Peter took off his coat and pulled up a chair.

Kevin carried on. 'Okay. Our victim was identified as Carol Lightfoot from the photo we have; she's twenty-four. According to Christine Taylor, that's the Women's Aid contact, Carol was in an abusive relationship with this man...' Kevin wrote a name on the board. 'Matthew Penworth. According to Christine, he practically kept Carol prisoner for years. She said that the rescue of Carol was harrowing. Women's Aid came to see her in hospital, but she was refusing to go with them. While they were there, Matthew Penworth came in and, when he twigged what was going on, he attacked the workers and tried to drag Carol out by her hair. The staff called for security and Matthew was brought under control. Apparently, he ran off at this point and they were able to persuade Carol to come with them. Penworth had made sure she had no friends and was estranged from her family, so a refuge was the best solution.'

'She could have met Susan Delaney there, I suppose. What did your Women's Aid contact have to say about her?'

'Christine knew her well. Susan had been a spokesperson for

the Women's Aid movement for a number of years and was a bit of a hero to the Penzance group. Since moving to Cornwall, Susan had been active within the group, delivering training and liaising with other agencies, especially Housing, where Susan had great success in finding accommodation for the women in their care. It's entirely possible that she could have come into contact with Carol when she was in the refuge.'

Peter nodded and turned to the rest of the team. 'Do we have any information about family?'

DC Maggie Williams spoke up. 'I've done a search and come up with a couple in Birmingham called Lightfoot who seem to be a fit. They reported their daughter Carol missing seven years ago. Haven't heard anything from her since then. I've printed off the missing person's photo.' She handed it to Peter. He looked at the pretty teenager depicted in the photograph and glanced over at the crime scene picture of their victim. It could be her, but the murdered woman's face was so altered by her previous injuries, it was hard to tell.

'Good work, Maggie. Let's get them down for an ID. Go on, Kevin.'

'Right, sir. Matthew Penworth is known to us for a number of minor affrays. Pub brawls, that sort of thing, and we have an address.'

'What would really make my day is if we can place him at the scene. SOCO report, Saroj?'

'We have it, sir, but no match for Penworth's fingerprints at the flat I'm afraid. Of course, he could have been wearing gloves.'

'Anything else to indicate he might have been there?'

'SOCO found some black hairs on the body. Both of the women were blonde, so that suggests at least one other visitor to the flat. I've fast tracked DNA analysis so we should get results in a couple of days.'

'Well, I suppose that's something. We'll have Penworth's DNA on file for comparison.'

The room became quiet for a moment as everyone absorbed the new information. Then Saroj broke the silence. 'Shall we pick him up, sir?'

'Definitely, Saroj. You and I will do that. Maggie, you contact the Birmingham couple. Gently though, if this is their daughter, it's going to be very emotional.'

'Yes, sir.'

'Right. Give me a few minutes, Saroj, I just have to make a phone call.' Peter was not looking forward to telling Rachel that he would be late. At least SuLin was with her, but in a way that made it worse for Peter. He knew his mother-in-law would judge him more harshly than his wife. At least Rachel knew how demanding and unpredictable the job could be.

Chapter Six

Cassie burst into the squad room, eager to find out where the murder investigation was up to. Looking around, she saw Maggie and Kevin busily typing. They looked up and smiled but carried on with their work. Cassie looked over towards Peter's office. 'Is the Chief in?'

Kevin answered. 'No, ma'am. He and Saroj are out.'

'Out? Out where?'

Kevin looked uncomfortable, exchanging a glance with Maggie. 'We're not supposed to discuss the case with you, ma'am.'

'Hmmph, bloody stupid if you ask me.' Cassie walked over to the white board. The team had been busy, she thought, as she noted the name of the victim and a possible perpetrator. 'No sign of Suzi yet?' She looked at the embarrassed faces. 'Oh, never mind.' And with that she left the office.

Maggie let out a long sigh. 'How long can we keep this up, Kevin? She can see progress from the white board anyway. It might be better if the boss gave her a few days' leave then we wouldn't be put in this awkward position.'

It was six o'clock and Cassie was hungry. She thought she might as well pick up a takeaway and head home. The kids were due back in a couple of days, and she wanted to make the most of her time alone. As she walked across the car park a voice called. 'DI Wade? Is that you?'

Looking up, Cassie saw DI Mark Andrews, the contact she had made in Plymouth during a previous investigation. She had liked him very much and he had been extremely helpful to her enquiry. 'Mark Andrews! What are you doing in these parts?'

He wandered over and shook Cassie's hand warmly. 'Training, would you believe, delivering, not receiving.' Cassie took in his tanned face, handsome despite his lack of hair. It seemed that Mark had gone down the route of shaving his head when his hair became sparse, and it suited him well. He wore smart dark-rimmed glasses and was dressed casually in grey chinos and a black leather jacket.

He looked towards the station entrance. 'Just popping in to see my old mate Peter.'

'You'll be out of luck then,' said Cassie. 'He's out, and I imagine he won't be back any time soon.'

'Damn, I was hoping he'd keep me company tonight. I hate eating alone.' Mark tilted his head enquiringly. 'I don't suppose you're free?'

'As a matter of fact I've got a date with a takeaway and bad TV, but I could be persuaded.'

'That's settled then,' Mark said delightedly. 'Now, this is your patch, so you choose; only please not curry, it seems to be the copper's meal of choice, but I can't stand it.'

Cassie chose an Italian restaurant in the centre of Truro. Before that, though, they called at a quaint old pub for a drink. They found a corner table easily and Mark brought their drinks over. 'G&T for you and a pint of the local for me.' He set the glasses on the table and sat opposite Cassie. 'Cheers!'

'Cheers,' chimed Cassie. 'This is a nice surprise. How's life treating you in Plymouth?'

'Well, I could tell you about our ongoing battle with drug gangs, or the latest knife crime figures, and then you could tell me about your latest investigations, but, frankly, I'd rather talk about anything other than work.'

Cassie took a sip of her drink and smiled broadly. She raised her glass towards Mark, 'I'll drink to that,' she said, relieved that she wouldn't be drawn into revealing the awkward situation in the office.

Over the next hour, their conversation ranged from music to books to films, and Cassie found that she shared many of Mark's tastes. He made her laugh, recounting stories about playing rugby with Peter, no doubt revealing too much about what went on in

44

changing rooms and the scrapes they got into on tour. It was, however, very entertaining, and Mark was a great storyteller. By the time they decided to go to the restaurant, the pair were chatting like old friends.

Cassie chose a seafood linguini and Mark plumped for the carbonara. Before the mains, they shared a cheese fondue, dipping the warm bread into the delicious gooey, cheesy mixture and sipping a robust Italian red wine. Cassie couldn't remember the last time she had enjoyed herself so much. She completely forgot about the disappearance of Suzi Delaney, and relaxed in Mark's wonderful company.

At the end of the evening, Mark called a taxi for Cassie. While they were waiting, he caught hold of her hand and pulled her towards him. Placing a kiss on her cheek he said, 'I've really enjoyed myself tonight, Cassie. I'm here for another night and would love to repeat this if you could stand it.'

'I thought you wanted to see Peter.'

'I could see Peter, no doubt, but I'd much rather spend time with you.'

Cassie felt a flutter of excitement. It had been a long time since she had had a date, and with someone so attractive too. 'I'd really like that. How about if I cook for you?'

Mark tentatively said, 'That would be great. I could get to meet your kids.'

Cassie laughed at his diplomatic answer. 'Don't worry, my kids are with their dad at the moment. You don't think I'd subject you to that, do you?'

'In that case, I'll look forward to it even more. Text me your address.' As the taxi drove up, Mark kissed Cassie again, this time a proper kiss. 'Goodnight, Cassie,' he said as she slid into the taxi.

He watched as the tail lights disappeared. Well, well, Mark old boy, I think you're a bit smitten, he said to himself, a beaming smile on his face.

Whilst his DI and long-time friend were enjoying a pleasant evening out, Peter and Saroj had been sitting opposite one of the most objectionable men either of them had ever met, and they'd met a few in their time. Matthew Penworth was a big man, at least six foot and broad across his shoulders. Peter guessed that Matthew worked out in a gym, muscle building, perhaps enhancing his physique with steroids. But it wasn't just the man's size that was offensive, Matthew Penworth oozed arrogance as he sat back in the plastic chair, his legs spread wide and a leer on his face. Saroj tried not to show how uncomfortable she felt as he looked her up and down, licking his lips suggestively.

Peter knew that he would have to hold back his distaste for the man if he was to avoid Penworth clamming up and stating 'no comment' to his questions.

'Thank you for agreeing to speak to us, Mr Penworth,' Peter said. 'I will be recording this interview. It helps us if we don't have to take notes.'

'That's okay, mate, I've got nothing to hide.' He flashed his eyes at Saroj. 'And the scenery's good.'

Saroj was sure that Penworth would see the contempt on her face so looked down at the case file in front of her. 'Could you tell us where you were at ten am yesterday?' she said, raising her eyes.

'Always have a lie in on Sundays, sweet'art, especially if I've got company, if you see what I mean.'

'And did you have company yesterday?'

'Unfortunately no, all on me lonesome, darlin'.' Matthew leered suggestively.

Peter took over the questioning. 'Do you have anyone who could confirm that?'

'I just told you, mate, I was on me own.' Matthew feigned disbelief, spreading his hands wide, as if to an audience.

'Did you leave your home at all that day?' Peter kept his voice low and calm.

'Yeah, I went the pub at dinner time, lunch you might call it. Met some mates and had a few drinks.'

'We'll need the names of your friends and the pub.'

'What! You don't believe me? What d'you think I've done anyway? You haven't said yet.'

'I told you we were questioning you in connection with a serious crime.'

'Yeah, but what exactly? And why me?'

Saroj took over. 'Do you know a woman called Carol Lightfoot?'

46

Matthew's eyes darted around the room and he shifted uncomfortably in his seat. 'What's that cow been sayin' about me now?'

'When was the last time you saw Miss Lightfoot?'

'Ages ago. Her left me, just walked out, after all I'd done for her.'

Saroj resisted the temptation to respond with the catalogue of injuries Matthew had 'done' to Carol. 'Can you remember when that was, exactly?'

'Couple of months ago. Can't say exactly.'

'And you haven't seen her since?'

'I told yer. Never seen the maid. I gave all her stuff away to one of them charity shops. Good riddance to her.'

Peter fixed Matthew with a hard stare. 'Would it surprise you to learn that Carol is dead?'

Matthew's eyes widened and he shook his head, appearing shocked. 'Dead! Blimey. Overdose was it?'

'Why would you think that?'

'Her loved the stuff. It was me who stopped her taking too much. Her never knew when to stop.'

Peter checked the medical report in the file. There had been no drugs in her system when she died, but needle marks were present in a few areas. 'No, it wasn't drugs, Mr Penworth, Carol was murdered.'

Matthew held his hands up defensively. 'Woah, hold on a minute. You think I did it?'

'We're just trying to eliminate anyone who knew Miss Lightfoot, and you did know her.'

'I told you, I ain't seen her in ages.' Matthew shook his head nervously. 'Yer not gonna pin this on me. I know how you lot work. I'm sayin' nuthen else without a solicitor.'

'Of course,' said Peter. 'We can arrange one for you or you can contact your own. But we will be keeping you here while we check out your alibi. So, Matthew Penworth, I'm arresting you in connection with the murder of Carol Lightfoot. You do not have to say anything. But it may harm your defence if you do not mention when questioned something which you later rely on in court. Anything you do say may be given in evidence. Do you understand?'

'This is a fuckin' set up.'

Peter felt weary as he and Saroj walked out onto the car park. 'Did you believe any of that, Saroj?'

'What? the *shocked and outraged* act? Not at all, sir. I'll see you tomorrow.'

Peter waved goodbye to Saroj. He would like nothing more than to cuddle up on the sofa with Rachel, sharing a drink and offloading his problems with the case like they used to. But he knew that would be impossible, and he felt terrible that he was wishing away his beautiful new daughter and the joy of the family life he had always dreamed of. If only Cassie was available to take charge of this damn case. There was no one else he could hand the responsibility to. Peter sighed as he started his journey home. Would it be impossible for Cassie to be involved in some way? Just take some of the burden off him for a while? He knew he would have to give it some serious thought. Perhaps Rachel would be up to discussing it with him. She had a cool head, or she used to. Since Charlotte came along Rachel had become a bit muddle-headed, all the pressure of a newborn, he knew that. But, the truth was, he longed for her to get back to the Rachel he had learned to depend upon. And those thoughts made him feel guilty as hell.

Chapter Seven

Cassie woke the next morning feeling happier than she had in a long time. Her evening with Mark had been as lovely as it was unexpected, and all the more thrilling for that. She stretched out in her bed, luxuriating in the unfamiliar feeling and, as she ran her hands over the sheets, she realised that they had not been changed for a week. It wasn't as though she expected Mark to stay the night, but who knew how things would turn out, better to be prepared. Cassie jumped up and stripped the bed, bundling the bedding up and taking the pile through to the kitchen. As she loaded the washing machine, she thought about the evening ahead. What to wear? And what to cook? Looking around, she became aware that the place needed a bit of a spruce-up too. Coming to a decision, Cassie picked up her phone and called the squad room.

Maggie answered and took the message that Cassie would be going to St Piran's school regarding Erica Trevellian, and then to Erica's grandma. After that she would be taking some time off as she wasn't needed in the office anyway. Maggie was a little surprised at the change of tone in the DI's voice, and that she was clearly backing off from the murder investigation. Maggie was sure that the Chief would appreciate this turn of events and couldn't wait to share the news with him.

'She's what?' said Peter when Maggie gave him the message from Cassie. 'Not coming in at all?'

'No sir, she was very clear about that. Sounded happy.' Maggie couldn't understand her boss's reaction, wasn't this what he

49

wanted? She walked back to her desk, a puzzled expression on her face. Peter shouted after her.

'Maggie! We got the DNA on that hair in Susan Delaney's flat?'

'Not yet, sir.'

'Then chase it up.'

'Sir.' Maggie sighed and shook her head. Saroj was coming in and noticed Maggie's expression.

'Something wrong?'

'The Chief's in a stinking mood. Best keep your head down.'

'We're re-interviewing Matthew Penworth this morning. I hope Peter calms down before then. Penworth could wind up a saint.' Saroj sat down just as the phone rang on her desk. 'DS Kapoor. Right, have him wait would you.' She stood and went over to Peter's office. The door was closed but she could see that he was having an animated conversation over the phone. She knocked gently and he waved her in.

'Yes okay, I know it's important. One o'clock you say? Right, I'll do my very best to be there. Okay, love, have to go now so see you later.'

Turning to Saroj he sighed and shook his head. 'Charlotte has got a sniffle and Rachel's got us an appointment with the paediatrician.'

'Yes, sir. Babies are certainly a worry.'

'Anyway, what did you want to see me about?'

'Mathew Penworth's solicitor is here, sir.'

'Bloody hell, he's keen.'

'She, sir, it's Sylvia Moorcroft.'

'Well, it'll be interesting to see how this plays out; she's a bit of a stunner by all accounts. Penworth will be chomping at the bit.' This seemed to cheer the Chief up somewhat.

'Shall we say half an hour, sir?'

Peter smiled up at Saroj. 'Sorry I'm a bit grumpy this morning. Charlotte had us both up most of the night. Half an hour is fine.'

Matthew Penworth was looking nervous. Peter thought he would have lapped up being represented by a lovely young woman, but his body language said otherwise. He had pulled his seat away from Sylvia Moorcroft and had turned sideways with his back towards her. She must have had a few sharp words with him, he thought. Good for her.

After Sylvia had introduced herself, followed by the others in the room, she launched into a strident defence of Penworth. 'You have no reason to keep my client here. He has given you an explanation of his whereabouts when the attack on Carol Lightfoot took place and, as far as I can see, you have not a shred of evidence to place him at the scene.' She looked steadily at the two detectives. 'So, unless you have anything new to share with me...'

Peter held up his hand to stop the flow of words. 'Ms Moorcroft, as you know this is a murder investigation and we have every right to interview and hold anyone we believe has a motive for the killing. Your client has previously committed serious attacks on Ms Lightfoot, the last one leading to hospitalisation.' Peter produced a photograph. 'These injuries,' pointing to the facial deformities, 'were not caused by the knife attack, but were perpetrated by your client.'

Sylvia looked suitably shocked, but held her ground. 'As you are aware, Detective Chief Inspector, my client has been cleared of any involvement in these injuries to Ms Lightfoot. And, in any event, his previous behaviour cannot be used as an indicator of current actions. I say again, Mr Penworth told you where he was on the morning in question, and I suggest you look into that before you detain my client any longer.'

Peter knew that, until he could establish a match between Penworth and the hair found at the scene, he had nothing to justify holding the man any longer. 'Okay, Mr Penworth, you're free to go for now, but we will want to speak to you again, so don't leave the area.'

Ms Moorcroft patted Matthew on his arm. Only then did he acknowledge her presence. He had said nothing all through the interview. 'Is that it then?' he asked.

Sylvia gave a self-satisfied smile. 'You're free to go, Mr Penworth. I'm sure we won't have to meet again.'

Cassie glanced around the bedroom, all clean and fresh, she thought as she smoothed the newly-made bed. I wonder if we'll finish up here tonight or is that rushing things a bit? She made a quick swizz over the en-suite bathroom and put fresh towels in place. At least that part of the house was fit for visitors, she mused. I'll see to the kitchen and living room when I get back.

Driving up in front of St Piran's brought back the feeling that Cassie associated with school. These were never to do with her work, she was a good student and diligent about homework. Her anxiety was more related to the group of girls who hung about by the entrance door giving grief to anyone who didn't fit their standards. You only had to have a spot or a bad haircut and the ridicule started. Given that Cassie was fat, black and with the most unruly frizzy hair, she came in for the most hurtful comments. Funny how those things stay with you, she thought, as she locked her car and headed for the entrance. Gathering all her confidence, Cassie stepped over the threshold. Two young girls were inside waiting by the secretary's office. 'Morning, miss,' they said in unison. 'Can we help you?'

Cassie was a little taken aback by the polite welcome. 'I've come to see Mr Simmonds,' She had noted the name of the headteacher on the sign outside the school.

'I'll just see if he's available,' one girl said, as she knocked on the secretary's door, then opened it. 'A lady to see the head, miss.'

A well-dressed woman of about fifty came out smiling. 'Well done, Tabatha.' Then looking over to Cassie, she said, 'Citizenship lessons. Thank you, girls. Can I help you, madam?'

When Cassie was ensconced with Mr Simmonds, cup of tea in hand, she came straight to the point. 'Tell me what you know about Erica Trevellian.'

'Not as much as I probably should, inspector. My member of staff in charge of special needs will probably be more able to answer your questions better than I.' He stood and peered through his office door. 'Mrs Jackson, will you get Mrs Smythe for me, tell her it's urgent.'

Turning back to Cassie he said, 'I knew the boys better, Paul and Andrew. They played rugby for the school and I was their coach for a while, when I was Deputy.'

'Cassie was interested to know more about the family as a whole. 'What was your impression of them?'

'Boisterous lads, not the brightest but not the worst either. They definitely saw their future at the farm and didn't see the point in continuing their education beyond GCSEs.'

'What do you know about their parents?'

'Not much. Dad was rarely seen at school, and I think mum left them, maybe a divorce? Not sure of the details. Ah, here's Mrs Smythe.'

Driving to Erica's grandmother's, Cassie thought about what Mrs Smythe had told her. Erica had begun missing school in year eight when she was just thirteen, one of the oldest in her year as her birthday was in September. 'She seemed mature too,' Mrs Smythe had said. 'Not giddy like some of them can be at that age, and a bright girl. Could have done well if she'd not missed so much school.'

Mrs Smythe had visited the family home when Erica had been away from school for two weeks, with Mr Trevellian claiming that his daughter was unwell. She found Erica fit and well and hanging out washing. 'I had a few sharp words with Mr Trevellian who told me that his wife was away, and Erica was just helping out. After that, Erica came back, but she'd just come in the morning and then skip off in the afternoon, or sometimes the other way round.'

Cassie realised that Mr Trevellian was trying to keep the 'authorities' off his back by allowing Erica to go to school just enough to stop the interference. Well, she was determined to put a spoke in his wheel.

The grandmother's house was one of a row of cottages on the lane leading to the Trevellian's farm. It was a fair walk to there though, about two miles by Cassie's reckoning. There was a pub, The Plough, at the halfway point, and it was from here that the waitress who found Erica was cycling home.

Cassie parked on the grass verge; the door was opened before she had got out of her car. A bent old lady stood in the doorway. 'Come about James?' she shouted.

Cassie took out her warrant card as she walked up the short path. 'Devon and Cornwall police, madam, I'm Detective Inspector Wade.'

'Not from round 'ere is yer, me lovely?'

'Could I come in, please? I want to ask about your granddaughter Erica.'

'Not James then?'

The sitting room was crowded with old dark furniture, the size and design of which was not meant for a small cottage, but the overall effect was comfortable. There was a fresh smell of lavender and soap. A fire was made up in the hearth, ready to be lit later, Cassie thought. Mrs Trevose sat down heavily in a worn armchair. 'What's this about Erica? She's a good maid that one, alers comes to see her old gran.'

'We believe Erica was attacked two nights ago. Do you know about that?'

'Attacked, yer say? No, sweet'art, not round 'ere anyhow. Safe as 'ouses this place.'

'She was found on the roadside in some distress.'

The old lady tapped her head. 'Two nights ago, yer say? She was 'ere then. Couldn't 'ave been attacked. James walked her 'ome when it went dark.'

'Can I ask who James is?'

'My lodger, sweet'art, James Tandy. 'E's not getting' on too well wi' 'is folks so I said 'e could stop 'ere for a bit. 'He's some good lad, 'elps me out.'

Cassie felt a tingle of interest. Erica had not mentioned James. In fact, she had said she walked home alone. 'Could I speak to James, Mrs Trevose?'

'He's not 'ere, is 'e? 'He's in 'orspital. That's what I thought you'd come about. 'Was beaten up, sweet'art, right bad by all accounts. Anyway, I'm forgettin' me manners. Like some tea would you, me dear?'

While the old lady made the tea, Cassie took out her phone and called Robbie. 'Get over to Trevan hospital and find out about a James Tandy. He would have been brought in with injuries after a beating. He walked Erica Trevellian home, her grandma says, the night she was attacked, so he's definitely a person of interest. Call me when you've spoken to him.'

'Yes, ma'am. Will you be coming into the office?'

'No, Robbie, I'm taking the rest of the day off, but you can call me anytime. I've been to the school, so I'll let you have my report on that and my visit to Erica's grandmother later today. Have you fixed up that multi-agency meeting yet?'

'Social services are getting back to me, ma'am. They chair the meetings so they're making the arrangements. I told them it was urgent.'

'Good. This case is getting interesting, Robbie. When you've spoken to James Tandy and the medics, get over to Trevellian's farm and find out where those two lads were when he was being beaten up. I'd put my not insubstantial police pension on them being involved.'

'Yes, ma'am, I'm on it.'

Chapter Eight

Cassie preferred the shops in Truro to those in Liverpool, or Manchester for that matter. These large city shopping centres looked glamorous, but the shops were all the same chains, John Lewis, Debenhams, Harvey Nichols. But here in Truro you could find small independent boutiques tucked away down alleyways. And they sold the sort of clothes that suited the area. Soft flowing fabrics that filled the gap between casual and formal. Cassie was looking forward to treating herself to something new and sexy. First, undies, she decided. Since losing weight, her bras sagged on her once ample breasts and her briefs were in danger of sliding down over her slimmer hips. Something lacy and feminine, she thought. Then a dress and maybe some new sandals. She sat in a window seat in Costa and made a plan of action. There was food to think of as well. She had decided on a few appetisers served in the garden, then back inside for mussels in a wine and cream sauce with some crusty bread, and a rich chocolate mousse to follow, plus some interesting artisan cheese to nibble if they still had room after the meal. It was market day in Truro so Cassie planned to buy most of her ingredients from local suppliers.

It would also be an opportunity to use the fire-pit once she'd cleaned it up. This was the perfect occasion for a late evening drink around the fire. I'll call for some logs on the way home, she thought, and watched the shoppers as she sipped her latte, anticipating a lovely evening ahead.

Mark was due to arrive at seven o'clock, but Cassie was already showered and dressed by six. Her new lacy undies in ivory silk made her feel ultra-feminine and the dress she had plumped for was soft cream linen which skimmed her still curvy body beautifully. Sandals with a touch of gold completed her outfit and, as she twirled in front of the mirror, she felt the excitement rise. As she was finishing fixing her hair and donning some jewellery the doorbell rang. He's early, she thought, just as well I am too. A smile played on her lips as she opened the door to find Peter standing there.

'Sorry, Cassie... you look amazing by the way. You're expecting company. I should go.'

'Not at all, Peter, and thanks for the compliment. Come in.' Cassie opened the door wide.

Peter felt awkward, but now he was here, he thought he might as well say what he came to say. 'Look, Cassie...'

'Would you like a drink, Peter? I'm having wine but there's beer if you prefer.'

'I could do with a glass of wine actually, goes well with humble pie.'

Cassie looked at him quizzically as she passed him the glass. 'What's this about, Peter?'

'I know I've made a big fuss about you not being involved in the Susan Delaney case, but, to be quite honest, I need you on the team.' He paused waiting for a smug reply, but none came, so he carried on. 'I am beginning to think that Susan is not the killer and, if this is so, she may be in danger. I need your help to find her. I don't want to go into much detail now, especially as you're expecting guests, so could you come to see me tomorrow morning?'

'Of course, Peter. I'll be glad to help, you know that.'

'Good, that's settled. I'll get out of your hair now.'

'Finish your drink first. Actually, it's one guest and you know him.'

'Really?' Peter was intrigued.

Just then the doorbell rang again. Cassie shrugged, 'Now you'll get to meet him.'

Mark stood in the doorway with a bunch of roses and a bottle of wine. 'You look fantastic,' he said and came forward to kiss her.

Looking past her into the kitchen he spotted a familiar face. 'You didn't tell me it was a threesome,' he joked. 'Peter, me old mate, how's tricks?'

'Don't worry, Mark, I'm just leaving. Spot of business, that's all.'

'Look, I'm sorry I didn't find time to see you this trip…'

'Completely understand. I probably wouldn't have been able to find time anyway, what with the baby and all.'

'Yes, of course.' Mark smacked his head. 'I've not got used to Peter the dad yet. Promise I'll come and see her and Rachel very soon.'

The dinner had been a great success, the candlelight adding to the ambience as Cassie and Mark chatted and flirted over each delicious course. Later, on the small terrace, Mark lit the fire-pit as Cassie brought out a plate of cheese and a full-bodied red wine. Cassie had placed candles out here too and they flickered in the gentle evening breeze. Along with her purchase of the fire-pit, Cassie had treated herself to a garden swing and it was here that the couple sat, swinging gently and sipping their wine.

Cassie couldn't remember a more perfect evening. In her experience, the phone would usually ring when she was settling down to have a quiet night in, with an urgent call to be somewhere else. She had been a little alarmed when Peter had called earlier, fearing that he was there to take her to a crime scene. However, she had been surprised and pleased that he had changed his mind about her involvement in the murder investigation. Secretly, she suspected that Rachel and the new baby had something to do with that. Peter had told her before Charlotte was born, that he would be giving her more responsibility to allow him time to be at home helping out. Ah well, it's an ill wind…' Cassie mused.

'Penny for them,' said Mark, snuggling closer to Cassie.

'Just thinking that I haven't enjoyed myself so much for a long time.' She leaned over and kissed Mark lightly on the lips.

Taking her glass from her and placing it on the table with his, he leant over. 'Oh, I think we can do better than that.' He kissed her deeply, his hands caressing her body. 'Shall we get even more comfortable?' He felt Cassie stiffen slightly. 'Only if you want to,' he said quickly, sensing a change of mood.

Cassie looked into Mark's eyes and placed her hand on his cheek. 'Are we going too fast, Mark? I've not felt like this about anyone for a very long time and I could easily lose my head over you.'

Mark took her hand and kissed the palm. 'I can assure you I don't proposition women at the drop of a hat, Cassie. I felt it the day we met last year, a connection between us, if that doesn't sound too melodramatic. And last night I sensed something special too, didn't you?'

'I did, Mark. Cassie stood and tugged at Mark's arm. Let's see if we can make it even more special, shall we? Or am I being too forward?'

Mark stood and swung Cassie around. 'Not forward at all; it's been the only thing on my mind since I saw you tonight.'

Cassie leaned on her elbow and watched Mark's sleeping face. Without his glasses he looked younger despite his shaved head. He had been a considerate lover, though the first time had been fast and furious, with both of them eager to satisfy their lustful feelings. After that, they took their time, exploring each other's bodies, finding unexpected scars as well as a tattoo on Mark's leg; a souvenir of a rugby trip.

'Why an anchor, though? You've not been in the navy, have you?'

'It's a long story, Cass, has to do with me being the 'anchor' of the team. Rubbish really. The things you do when you're drunk.'

Breakfast turned out to be a hasty affair after Mark had joined Cassie in the shower, delaying them both in a most delicious way. Cassie dressed quickly and gulped her coffee, snatching a banana before telling Mark to let himself out. They had arranged to meet for lunch before his train back to Plymouth and they could say a better goodbye then.

Before Cassie could meet with Peter, Robbie stopped her with the latest on the Erica Trevellian case. 'I'm in a bit of a hurry, Robbie,' she said, noticing Peter standing by his office door waiting for her.

'Just the highlights then, ma'am.' Robbie took out his notebook.

'James Tandy is in an induced coma, may not wake up. He received an injury to his head. A vicious blow administered with some force, the doctor said, and he was kicked so hard in his genitals that the doctor thought he might need surgery. The Trevellian brothers say they were in the pub all evening when James was being attacked. Apparently, James has had only one visitor – Erica Trevellian.'

'Very interesting, Robbie. Check the brothers' alibi and get Erica Trevellian in for questioning. Get a social services representative to be the appropriate adult.'

'The multi-agency meeting has been set up for Friday, ma'am, so I could get whoever is attending that if he or she is available.'

'I'll leave that to you, Robbie. Now I really have to go. Keep me informed, though; you can reach me anytime.'

'Righto, ma'am.'

Cassie hurried over to Peter's office. 'Sorry to be late, sir. D'you mind if I grab a coffee.'

'That's okay, Cassie. Get one for me, too.'

When they were settled in Peter's office, he began. 'I'll not beat about the bush, Cassie, I could do with your help. We had a man in custody in the Lightfoot murder investigation. His name is Matthew Penworth, he's the ex-partner of Carol Lightfoot, the victim. He had been extremely violent towards her in the past, but we've not enough to hold him and we had to let him go for now. I'll give you the details of that later. We suspect that he discovered where she was staying and attacked her.'

'Do you have evidence that he was at the scene?'

'Nothing confirmed yet, but a neighbour heard a man's voice in the flat just after the attack took place; she's certain of that.'

'So, what are you thinking about Suzi?'

'I just can't see her as the murderer, Cassie. Everything about the flat tells me that she's a stable and studious woman, and she has long-term ties with Women's Aid who speak very highly of her. Does that chime with what you know about her?'

'Absolutely, sir. I've known Suzi since we were best friends at school. There were gaps in our contact, but I still feel I know her. She has championed women for most of her life and is, in my opinion, incapable of any sort of abuse against anyone, especially another woman.'

60

'Well, if we're right, Cassie, she may be in trouble. We have no trace of her. Her car is still at the scene, she hasn't used her bank cards and there's no CCTV of her on the roads around the flat. We have some information from a local shopkeeper who says that Susan called in at around nine-forty for bread and milk, and another neighbour saw someone who might have been her walking down the road with a man at around ten-twenty.'

'What's your feeling, sir?'

'Matthew Penworth arrived at the flat whilst Susan was out at the shop. He killed Carol then was disturbed by Susan returning. The raised voices the neighbour heard were his and Susan's. He abducted her, making a getaway in his car, and he's either killed her too, or is holding her somewhere.'

'No evidence at all for any of that, though?'

Peter gave a rueful smile. 'None. There has been some black hair found on Carol Lightfoot's body and we're waiting DNA analysis on that.'

'Fingerprints?' Peter shook his head. 'The witness who saw the man and woman in the street, could she describe the man?'

'Very sketchy. Said he was medium height and looked young. Wearing dark clothing. Possibly jeans and T shirt.'

Cassie sighed. 'I've tried Suzi's mobile several times but it's not responding.'

'We can only trace where the phone was when it was powered down, and that was...' Peter consulted the file, 'on the A30 near the Long Rock roundabout.'

'Not far out then, a mile at most from her flat.'

'Penworth could have switched it off then; maybe threw it out of the car.'

Cassie didn't feel confident. 'All this is too speculative, Peter. We need some hard evidence. Has his car been picked up on CCTV around that time?'

'No, not found anything as yet.'

'Okay, so we're assuming that Suzi is being kept against her will somewhere, or Penworth has killed her too and disposed of the body.' Cassie forced herself to treat this case as any other. If she allowed herself to think of Suzi dead and buried in a shallow grave, she wouldn't be able to function as a detective. 'Can we put a trace on Penworth's phone over the last couple of days? And does he have access to a place where he could be holding Suzi – a lockup maybe?'

'I'll get Maggie on to that,' said Peter, feeling much more confident with his DI on board.

Cassie nodded. 'I'll chase up the DNA and check out the pub where Penworth said he had lunch that Sunday. If he killed Carol at ten o'clock and was in the pub by lunchtime, he can't have gone far. Perhaps the bar staff will have some information – the time he arrived and left, his general state, agitated or not? If he'd just killed someone and abducted another, he would be a very cool customer indeed if he managed to appear calm after that. He must have had blood on him, too, so that's a factor. Did he go home to change?'

'It's a pity we didn't have enough on him to get a search warrant. He's got time now to dispose of his bloody clothing,' Peter said.

'He may have dumped his clothes somewhere. Let's check out the bins and hedgerows. It's a long shot, but even long shots come off sometimes.' Cassie felt energised. 'I'll check out the pub, sir. I'm meeting Mark for lunch, and the Royal Oak is as good a place as any.'

'Yes, Cassie,' said Peter smiling mischievously. 'You kept that one quiet.'

'As much a surprise to me as you, sir, I can assure you. I'll tell you about it sometime, if you promise to tell me why Mark has a tattoo of an anchor on his leg.'

Peter laughed out loud, causing heads to turn in the squad room. 'It's a deal, Cassie.'

The Royal Oak in Threemilestone was quiet on this Wednesday lunchtime. Nevertheless, Mark and Cassie found a table in a secluded corner and held hands, gazing lovingly at each other. 'I feel like a schoolboy,' said Mark, 'sneaking off to see his first girlfriend.'

Cassie laughed warmly. 'You didn't seem much like a schoolboy last night. At least, none that I remember.'

The reminder of the previous night brought a wide grin to Mark's face. 'We wouldn't have time to nip back to your place, would we?'

'I wish,' replied Cassie. 'Unfortunately, I've got a bit of business to attend to here. I need to ask the landlord a few questions about a suspect.'

Mark threw his head back and laughed. 'It's a good job I'm a copper or I'd be very offended. This is exactly why I've never managed to find a woman to stick with me. Married to the job, they always said, and couldn't understand why some things took priority over them.' He patted Cassie on the arm. 'Off you go then, and you can order for us while you're there. I'll have the steak pie and chips and a pint of Doombar.'

Cassie placed the order, opting for a chicken salad and a sparkling water for herself. She was pleased to know that the landlord was behind the bar on the previous Sunday and that he remembered Matthew Penworth being in for the Sunday roast. 'Matt? He never misses. My lady does a mean roast beef and all the trimmings; you should try it yourself sometime.'

'What time did Matthew arrive, Mr Smithfield?'

'Oh, let me see. Around twelve-thirty, I'd say. We hadn't been serving long and we start at twelve.'

'And did you see him leave?'

'Chucking out time. Him and his mates usually have a skinful and then go home to sleep it off. So that'd be four-ish, or just after.'

'That's very helpful, Mr Smithfield. How did he seem to you?'

'What d'you mean?'

'Was he his usual self?'

'Oh aye, sweet'art. Always quick with a joke, and he's chatting up my best barmaid at the moment, so he flirted with her a bit too.'

'Is she around?'

'Not right now, she's on tonight, though. Name's Sally, Sally Nixon.'

Coming back over to the table with the drinks, Cassie looked at Mark as he perused a newspaper which had been left on the adjacent seat. He was dressed smartly-casual as usual, this time in a black polo neck over jeans, with a tan suede jacket. He wasn't really her type, she thought. Back in Liverpool the men she dated were taller and more muscular, and very often black, but Mark definitely had something about him. Confidence and an intelligent wit. He was never short of conversation which was focused on her, and she found that refreshing after being with men who were full

63

of themselves. Mark could never be accused of that, self-deprecating if anything, which she found most attractive.

He looked up as Cassie approached. 'Got what you wanted?' He put the paper down and stood to take his pint and hold the chair for her.

'Yeah, very helpful, but I do need to come back tonight to speak to someone else.' Cassie liked Mark's old-fashioned manners, something her feminist friends would scold her about. Thinking of that brought Suzi to mind, and she frowned slightly.

'You okay, Cass?' Mark enquired.

'Oh, just a bit distracted for a moment. I'm all yours now. At least for the next hour or so.'

'I'll have to settle for that then.' And he kissed her lightly on her lips. 'Until next time.'

After dropping Mark at the railway station, Cassie returned to Threemilestone to find Penworth's house. Stopping on the roadside outside a neat, detached house, Cassie checked her notes and was slightly surprised to confirm that this was where Matthew Penworth lived. Can't always judge a man by his actions, she thought. She noticed that the vertical blinds at the front window twitched and was aware that she was being watched. She got out of her car and approached the neat driveway leading to number seven. The door opened before she had chance to knock. 'What d'you want with me now?' Penworth scowled.

Cassie was taken aback as she had never met Matthew Penworth. 'Mr Penworth? I don't believe we've met.'

'I can spot a copper a mile off. I'll say again, what d'you want?'

Cassie took out her warrant card, undeterred by the man's hostile attitude. 'DI Wade. Can I come in? I've just got a few things to clear up with you.'

Penworth didn't move.

'Or we could do this on your doorstep if you prefer.'

He sullenly stepped back and opened the door wide, making a sweeping gesture with his hand. 'As you wish, detective.'

Cassie stepped into a wide hallway, neatly furnished with modern light-oak furniture. Framed photographs adorned the walls, mostly black and white and, from the dress of the subjects she could see that they were old images.

Matthew led the way into a stunning modern kitchen. The units were white with chrome handles and the black granite worktops gleamed and sparkled. Penworth was dressed casually in a track suit, but it was obviously an expensive brand, and he was clean-shaven and smelling of a subtly fragrant aftershave. If Cassie hadn't known better, she would never have suspected him of the kind of violence she knew he had committed. 'Nice place,' she said. 'Have you lived here long?'

'We don't need small talk. Ask your questions and leave.'

Cassie nodded slowly. 'Tell me about your movements last Sunday morning. Particularly around ten o'clock.'

'I told your colleague, I was in bed reading the Sunday papers. It's my one lie-in of the week.'

'Can anyone corroborate that?'

Penworth gave an exasperated sigh. 'Like I've already said. No. I live alone.'

Cassie struggled to find anything new to ask. She was aware that Peter would have covered this ground, and while it was always good to repeat questions, she doubted she'd learn anything new. Desperate for something original to ask, she said, 'Do you get your paper delivered, Mr Penworth?'

For the first time he seemed uneasy, and Cassie thought she had hit upon something that could be important. She could see Penworth's mind racing before he answered.

Cassie took advantage of Penworth's disquiet. 'We will check, of course.'

'No, I don't like people coming to the 'ouse.'

'So where did you get your Sunday paper? As you said, you were in bed reading it.'

Penworth's eyes shot around the room as he considered his answer. Finally, he said, 'I forgot, I had to go out for milk, and I picked up a paper while I was out.'

Cassie took out her notebook. 'And could you tell me where you went?'

'To the Sainsbury's down the road.'

'I noticed a corner shop at the end of your road, why didn't you go there? The Sainsbury's is a couple of miles away.'

Penworth fiddled with a mug which was on the worktop. 'It's rude of me not to offer you a coffee, detective, there's some made.'

'No thanks. The corner shop?'

'I don't like that shop. Their stuff is often out of date. I prefer the supermarket.'

'Do you still have the receipt from the supermarket?'

'No, it was just a couple of things, so I didn't get one.'

'And how did you pay?'

'Cash; it wasn't much.'

Cassie felt that she had enough to go on for the time being. 'I may want to talk to you again, Mr Penworth. I hope you don't have any plans to go away.' He shook his head. 'By the way, what is it that you do?'

'I'm a market trader; I've got a stall in the Pannier market. Ladies clothes, you should come and see, I've got some nice stuff.'

'It's been interesting talking to you, Mr Penworth,' Cassie said as she headed for the door. 'I'm sure we'll meet again soon.'

Cassie deliberately left her car parked outside Penworth's house. She noted that he had an attached garage. I'd like to get a warrant to search his place, she thought. Now that I've broken his alibi that might be possible.

The corner shop was bright and well stocked. Out of interest, Cassie checked some of the use by labels on the produce. Everything she picked up was well inside the date stated, and looked good quality. After the sole customer had left, Cassie approached the man behind the counter, who she noticed was of Indian origin. Could this be the reason Penworth didn't shop here? Simple racism? She showed her warrant card and introduced herself. 'I wonder if you can help me out,' she said.

'Of course, DI Wade. How can I assist you?'

'The man in number seven, Mr Penworth, do you know him?'

The shop owner gave a hollow laugh. 'Indeed I do, detective.'

Driving home Cassie relived the pleasure she got from seeing Penworth watching her as she knocked on his neighbours' doors. Good to rattle his cage a bit, she had thought, he's clearly worried about something. One neighbour reported seeing Penworth get his car out of his garage and drive off at around 9 o'clock on Sunday morning. She described the tracksuit he was wearing and Cassie recognised it as similar to the one he had on today. The neighbour told Cassie that Matthew seemed to be in a bit of a hurry when he left, but hadn't seen him return.

When asked about other people at the house, the two adjacent neighbours said they knew that a woman was living there at one time because they had seen her in the garden once or twice. The descriptions they gave were a possible match to Carol Lightfoot and Cassie made a mental note to return with a photograph of the dead young woman. Of course, Penworth had never denied being in a relationship with Carol, but any excuse to keep the pressure on was worthwhile in Cassie's view.

What the shopkeeper had told Cassie was interesting too. Mr Kamal, that was the man's name, had been instrumental in saving Carol from Penworth. One morning, about six months previously, a woman he didn't know then, but now knew was Carol Lightfoot, stumbled into his shop covered in blood and clearly terrified. Mr Kamal had taken her into the back room and called the police and an ambulance. Carol wouldn't say what had happened to her, but Mr Kamal saw Penworth running towards the shop only to stop and run the other way when he realised where Carol had gone.

'They took her to the hospital and a policeman went to interview Mr Penworth,' Mr Kamal said. 'I thought they might have taken him away to question him, but they didn't. He hung around until the ambulance left and seemed very concerned about the lady. Wanted to go with her to the hospital, I think.'

Mr Kamal didn't know anything else about the incident, but had seen Penworth in the street the next day. When he approached the man to ask about Carol, Matthew Penworth dismissed him with a few words, saying she was nothing to do with him. Mr Kamal told Cassie that, before this incident, Mr Penworth was a good customer, but that he hadn't been in the shop since.

Cassie determined to check out the incident report from the time Carol Lightfoot was attacked, to find out exactly what had been done. In the meantime, she had enough suspicion to re-arrest Penworth based on the fact that he had lied about his whereabouts on Sunday morning. He could easily have had the time to drive from home to Penzance and back in an hour, carry out the murder and abduct Suzi before appearing at The Royal Oak at twelve-thirty. They only had his word that he went to the supermarket and straight back home. This time we should be able to get a warrant, she thought, and was eager to get back to the station to talk to Peter about it.

First, though, she returned to the pub to talk to the barmaid that Penworth had been chatting up. Sally was petite and pretty, and told Cassie that Matthew Penworth had suddenly taken a keen interest in her, even though she had been working behind the bar for a couple of years. 'I hadn't really noticed him before, but he came on to me quite strong. I thought he was a bit creepy to be honest.'

Cassie was careful not to give too much away, but suggested to Sally that she trust her instincts in the case of Matthew Penworth. Cassie perceived that the young woman had got the message, and was content with that

Matthew Penworth was back in a cell and mad as hell. The arrest had been made at Pannier market and it was this that seemed to upset Penworth the most. The other stall-holders were obviously shocked, with one man protesting that Matthew was an upstanding citizen and that there must be a mistake. This man took a set of keys from Penworth and promised to lock his stall up. 'Don't worry, mate,' Penworth had said. 'It's just a big mix up. I'll see you here tomorrow morning.' He had now been told that there was a warrant to search his house and any other premises he owned or had access to. It turned out that he had a self-storage unit where he kept his goods for the stall and that gave Cassie a jolt, thinking that it was a possible place to hide someone, dead or alive. For that reason, the team decided to search this place first.

The unit was on a small industrial estate just off the A30 by the Chiverton Cross roundabout. It was called Truro Lock and Leave, and Cassie had the keys to unit 641. She and Saroj parked their car and hurried over to the site office. They were given directions to 641 and wasted no time in getting there and opening it up. Cassie shouted, 'Suzi!' as they entered the container and switched on the light. But there was no sound at all from inside. The walls were stacked with boxes marked China and Romania, and, opening a couple, Saroj found that they contained clothing. Cassie pushed boxes aside and looked into the corners of the unit, but there was no sign of her friend or discarded clothing that could belong to

Penworth. Saroj was examining a table on the far wall on which was a laptop and a printer, as well as box files of invoices and paperwork concerning the shipping of goods into the UK.

Cassie slumped down onto the desk chair and looked forlornly at Saroj. 'I was so sure she'd be here,' she said. Saroj patted Cassie's shoulder affectionately. 'There was a good chance, ma'am, but there's no sign now. I'll get SOCO over to carry out forensics. If she was held here, there'll be traces.'

Cassie nodded. Okay, you wait here for SOCO and I'll join the search of his house. Can you get a lift back?'

'No problem, ma'am. The Chief and Kevin are at Threemilestone; maybe they've found something.'

However, the search of Penworth's house proved just as fruitless. They, and now Cassie as well, took the place apart. The one thing that spooked them all was a bedroom set out like a shrine, with glossy photographs of Carol Lightfoot on the walls and tables. The bed was like a fairytale bed, with pink satin covers and heart-shaped cushions. Remembering that Penworth had said he'd got rid of Carol's possessions, she checked out the wardrobes. They held rows of dresses, mostly pink or floral. 'Blimey,' said Kevin, opening a drawer to find neatly folded pink underwear, 'talk about obsessed.'

Cassie just stood and stared at the room. He was obviously lying about ditching her stuff. 'This looks like motive to me,' she said. 'He's obviously never got over Carol. There's no sign of any other woman having been in the house, either. If he knew where she was staying, I wouldn't put it past him to go and get her. We know he attempted it when she was in hospital, so he's definitely got the nerve to try it. Maybe killing her wasn't part of the plan, but she fought back, and he picked up the kitchen knife and stabbed her.'

Peter nodded his agreement. 'But then Susan Delaney came home and found him there. He would have been desperate to make his escape and get her away as well. What we haven't discovered yet is where he took her. From ten o'clock, he would have had two hours at most before he needed to get back here, change and get down to the pub for his lunch. So let's think where he could have gone from Penzance that was secluded enough to dispose of a body, and, after doing that, not be more than an hour from home.'

Peter was aware that Cassie would be hurting at the thought of her friend being disposed of in this way, and was impressed that she was able to keep a cool professional head.

'Let's let SOCO go through this place with a fine-tooth comb. If we find any trace of Suzi, we've got him.' Cassie was impatient to get back to the office and start to put together a search area.

Peter agreed. 'Yes there's nothing obvious here. We'll get back and put our heads together. He seems like the sort of bloke who keeps himself to himself, but there must be someone who knows him well enough to suggest possible sites of interest.'

'The landlord of The Royal Oak said that Penworth met with mates each Sunday, so maybe they can tell us something. And what do we know about his family? Either way, he may have had assistance.'

'It's certainly something to think about, Cassie. Okay, no time to waste, let's get back.'

Chapter Nine

Robbie walked down the hospital corridor early on Thursday morning. James Tandy's doctor had told him that they were still very concerned about the young man's condition. He had fitted several times during the night and there were no signs of the swelling in his brain diminishing. Robbie wanted to see James for himself before he reported back to the DI. This was fast beginning to look like it might become a murder investigation and Cassie would want to act quickly before any suspects had a chance to establish an alibi. Robbie knew that Cassie favoured the Trevellian boys for the attack, so they would need to be brought in for questioning. She also wanted to speak to Erica without her dad present, and Robbie had arranged for her to come into the station this afternoon with the social worker from the children and families team to act as an appropriate adult during the interview.

As Robbie approached the private room where James was being cared for, he saw that the young man had a visitor. Erica Trevellian sat weeping by the bedside, stroking James's hand. Entering the room, Robbie spoke quietly to the girl. 'You care a lot about him,' he said. A statement, not a question.

'He's a good person, he didn't deserve this,' she sobbed.

Robbie nodded. 'No one deserves this sort of treatment, Erica. The doctor told me that he was hit with some force on the head with an implement, that's why he's got major swelling in his brain.'

Erica looked frightened. 'D'you know who did it?' she asked.

'Not yet, but we will soon enough.' Robbie checked his watch.

71

'Come on, it's getting on for two o'clock. I'll give you a lift to the station for your interview.'

'You don't think I did this, do you!' Erica said, obviously alarmed.

'No, we don't, but we do think you might have information that will help us catch whoever did.'

Erica looked worried but stood to join Robbie at the door. 'Does my dad have to be there?'

'No. We've asked a social worker to be with you. There's nothing to worry about. Just tell the truth, that's all we ask.'

Cassie was in the squad room when Robbie returned. There was a large map of the Penzance area on the wall and Peter was using the team's knowledge of the surrounding lanes and villages to identify any possible dump sites for a body.

He managed to catch Cassie's eye. 'Erica Trevellian and the social worker are in interview one, ma'am.'

Cassie looked over at Peter who nodded. 'That's fine, Cassie, we can manage here for an hour or so. I'll catch up with you later.'

Interview room one had been set up to be comfortable and non-threatening. It was often used for rape victims and younger children, where the object was to avoid confrontation and encourage the person to give their evidence without fear. Erica sat on a comfortable armchair with the social worker, Barbara Penwithen, on a similar chair next to her. The two were having a discussion as Cassie and Robbie entered.

Having completed introductions, Cassie began by telling Erica that she wasn't in any trouble, but she may have remembered something now that she forgot to mention when they saw her at home. This was a diplomatic way of saying that Cassie didn't think that Erica had been completely truthful earlier, and this was her chance to set the record straight.

Erica looked over at the social worker. Barbara smiled. 'Just tell them what you were telling me. Don't leave anything out.'

Erica hesitated, clearly struggling with the situation.

Cassie gently nudged the girl along. 'Things have changed since we last talked, haven't they, Erica?' The girl nodded, dabbing her eyes with a tissue. Cassie continued. 'We know now that James

72

Tandy walked you home on the night you were attacked.' Erica didn't protest this time that she hadn't been attacked, so Cassie carried on. 'Your grandma says that the two of you were friends. Is that right?'

Erica nodded. 'Yeah, he's a nice lad, we get on.'

'Tell me again what happened after you left your grandma's. Don't leave anything out this time, eh?'

Erica took a sip of water and sighed. 'We'd been having a good time at gran's, playing cards, the three of us. Gran brought out the port bottle and mixed me a port and lemon. I'm not used to drink, and I gulped it down like lemonade. We were laughing and enjoying ourselves. I had another port and lemon, and James was on his third glass of port, I think. We were probably tipsy.' Erica blushed and looked embarrassed.

'Don't worry about that, Erica,' said Cassie. 'Believe me, we've all been there.'

Erica smiled weakly. 'Anyway, gran said it was getting late and I should go home. I wanted to stay over. I did sometimes, but gran reminded me that dad wanted me back so that I could be there when the vet came early next morning. James said he'd walk me home, probably because he could see that I was a bit unsteady and giggling. We do like each other, and James held my hand as we walked, it was the first time he'd done that, and it felt nice. I leant against him and we were both giggling at nothing really, being a bit silly.' Erica took another sip of water.

'You're doing great, Erica,' said Cassie. 'You were laughing and walking…?'

'Yeah. Then James stopped and pulled me over to a farm gate. He pressed me against the gate and kissed me. Just gently. It was nice so I didn't try to stop him. But then he kissed me harder and pushed me to the ground. I really thought I'd fallen, but I remember now that he pushed me. What happened then is a bit hazy though. He pulled up my skirt and put his hand between my legs.' Erica looked at Robbie and blushed. 'After that, I just felt this sharp pain, and James was shouting out, then he got up quickly and ran away. I touched myself where the pain was and there was blood, and my knickers were down by my ankles. I think I passed out then, 'cause the next I knew that woman from the pub was there asking if I was alright.' Erica stopped and started crying. 'I

73

don't know how he could hurt me like that,' she said through her sobs.

'You're doing very well, Erica. Just a couple more things,' Cassie said gently. 'What happened when you got home?'

'My dad sent the woman who found me away. He said he'd deal with it. She didn't look too happy though, and kept asking if he'd call the police, but he wouldn't answer. When she'd gone, he grabbed me and said, 'nuthen' 'appened, you hear me?' And I just started crying and ran upstairs for a bath. He didn't even complain about me using the hot water. Then I just went to bed and cried. I really missed my mum.' Erica started sobbing loudly.

Barbara Penwithen put her arm around Erica. 'I think that's enough for now, detectives. Erica has been very brave but you can see she's upset.'

Cassie agreed. 'Of course. You've been extremely helpful, Erica, and very grown up about everything. I'll get someone to bring you some tea and then I've just got a few more things you may be able to help us with if that's okay? Or we could do it another time if you don't feel up to it.'

Erica shook her head. 'No, I'll be okay in a bit. I'd rather just get it over with. I'd like some tea, though.'

When Cassie and Robbie left the interview room, the duty sergeant approached them. 'DI Wade? There's a Mr Trevellian in reception wanting to speak to you. He looks quite agitated.'

'Ask him to wait, will you sergeant. Tell him I'm tied up at the moment and I'll get to him as soon as I'm free.' Turning to Robbie, she said, 'I don't want to get into an argument with him right now, just as Erica is being co-operative. She could clam up if she knows he's here.'

'Well, you know what they say, ma'am. It's often better to apologise after than ask permission before.'

Cassie laughed. 'Too right, Robbie. Let's organise that tea.'

Cassie asked Robbie to lead the next part of the interview as he was the one who had first hand knowledge of the attack on James Tandy. Erica had calmed down considerably and seemed relieved to have got things off her chest. Robbie used a more business-like tone, which Erica seemed to respond to. 'You know that James

Tandy is badly hurt, Erica?' She nodded. 'I just want to ask you a couple of questions that may help us find out who did it. You'd like to know that too, wouldn't you?' Erica nodded again.

'Now, I want you to think very carefully. Do you have any ideas about who might have wanted to hurt James?'

Erica stared at her tea, then seemed to come to a decision. 'It could have been Paul and Andy.'

'Why do you say that, Erica?'

'I heard them talking. Andy said, "He's not getting away with that. She's our sister." And Paul swore, the F word, and said, "He'll f...in' not know what's hit him". Then they said something I couldn't quite catch but I did hear, "tomorrow night", and then they walked off.'

'And when did you hear this conversation, Erica?'

'It was Tuesday afternoon. They were in the barn and I was by the door after collecting some eggs.'

'So, they would have been talking about doing something on Wednesday night? Is that what you think?'

'Yeah, I suppose so.'

'That's really helpful, Erica.'

'There's somethin' else,' Erica said.

'Go on,' said Robbie.

'It was Wednesday night, late. I was in my bedroom when I heard Paul's motorbike. Paul was driving and Andy was on the pillion. They were laughing and foolin' around. Paul waved something in the air, it looked like an iron bar of some sort, I think it was a crowbar. Then he went to the barn with it in his hand and Andy came into the house.'

'You're sure it was a crowbar? That's pretty specialist knowledge for a fourteen-year-old girl.'

Erica laughed. 'You weren't brought up on a farm then, were you? I use all the tools now and again. Dad's taught me what they are and how to use them. Everybody has to pull their weight on a farm, is what he says.'

'I apologise, Erica,' said Robbie, noticing that Cassie was trying her best to hide a giggle at his discomfort. 'Can you remember what time it was when you saw your brothers arrive home?'

'Must have been about eleven. I'd gone to bed at quarter to. Nan was fast asleep by then, which is better for me 'cause otherwise she starts asking for drinks of water or to help her to the loo.'

Robbie looked over at Cassie. 'Do you have any questions, ma'am?'

'No thank you, Robbie. You've been incredibly helpful, Erica. I know this can't have been easy for you.' Cassie hesitated. 'Your dad's in reception. I think he's here to take you home, but I'd like a word with him first if you don't mind waiting? Or I could get someone to take you back if you prefer?'

Erica's eyes widened. 'Could someone take me?'

Barbara spoke up. 'I'm going that way. I could give you a lift if you like?' Erica nodded.

'Okay. If you'll just wait here for a few minutes first, then Robbie will come and show you out.'

Cassie made sure that Mr Trevellian was safely out of the way in an interview room before telling Robbie to escort Erica and Barbara Penwithen out of the building. 'I'll see what he wants, Robbie. I want you to bring those two lads in. Let's hear what they've got to say for themselves.'

'Yes, ma'am. Erica's testimony was damning, wasn't it?'

'Yes, she seemed very clear about what she saw and heard, but it's best not to rely on the uncorroborated testimony of a minor. They're often seen as unreliable witnesses. If we can get something else on the boys, we may be able to obtain a warrant. I'd love to have a look in that barn for a crowbar. Anyway, off you go. I don't want the boys to have a chance to hide anything.'

When Robbie had left, Cassie went to see Mr Trevellian. She was itching to know what was happening with Suzi's case but couldn't keep this man waiting any longer. As she entered the room, Mr Trevellian stood, his hands placed firmly on the table. He was leaning forward in a threatening manner. 'Where's my girl?' he shouted.

'Sit down, Mr Trevellian,' said Cassie, calmly. 'Or I'll leave and get the duty sergeant to escort you out.'

He reluctantly sat, but his fists were balled and the look on his face was every bit as angry.

Cassie sat opposite him. 'We've been talking to your daughter and she's given a statement that suggests very strongly that she was raped on Monday night.'

'Never!' Trevellian shouted. 'Maid's makin' it up. Always fanciful that one.'

'Can you tell me why you didn't call the police when she was brought back home in a dishevelled state?'

'Bleddy nosey parkers, some folks. Her fell over, that's all. It was dark and her lost her footing. Why should I bother police with that?'

Changing tack, Cassie said, 'Can you tell me where Paul and Andy were on Wednesday night?'

'My boys? I don't recall. Oh aye, they was down The Plough. Saw 'em there meself.'

'At what time did you see them?'

'Why you askin' about Paul and Andy?'

'Just answer the question, Mr Trevellian.'

He looked suspiciously at Cassie, but answered just the same. 'They was there before me. I went for a last pint at ten o'clock and they was there then. Ask the landlord, he'll tell you they was there all night.'

'Oh, we will, Mr Trevellian.'

'What's they supposed to have done, then?'

'You know that James Tandy was badly beaten on Wednesday evening. We believe that your sons may have had something to do with that.'

'My boys! Never. They's some good boys. But maybe that fool Tandy got what he deserved.'

'Oh, why would that be? What do you think he did to deserve a beating?'

Mr Trevellian looked flustered and sheepish. 'He's just a bad lot. His folks don't even want him. The old lady do take him in but she should be careful.'

'The old lady being Erica's maternal grandmother?'

'Aye. She's got a bit of a screw loose, too, if you ask me.'

'You don't think he deserved a beating because he might have been the one who raped Erica then?'

'There was no rape! Her fell, I told you. Anyone could have had it in for Tandy.'

Cassie thought that she wouldn't get anything useful out of Mr Trevellian. 'Okay, sir. Your daughter has been given a ride home. So unless you have any more questions for me, you can go.'

'Aye, I'm goin' alright. Give that maid a piece of my mind; botherin' the police with her stories.'

'I'd strongly advise you, sir, not to harm or upset your daughter in any way. I'll be keeping an eye on you.'

Mr Trevellian stood suddenly and strode quickly towards the door. He turned to Cassie. 'An you'd be wise not to cross me, young woman. We country folks have our own way of doin' things, and it doesn't include talking to the police.'

'Yes, but sometimes you have no choice, Mr Trevellian,' Cassie replied, not looking at him.

Chapter Ten

While Cassie had been busy with Erica Trevellian and her father, Maggie had made some progress in locating Matthew Penworth's family. He was an only child, and, of his parents, there was just his mother alive. She had married again and was living in the Plymouth area. Maggie had spoken to her on the phone and got a strong impression that she had no time for her only child. 'She said that they hadn't spoken in years, sir. It seems that Matthew fought constantly with his dad since he was a teenager, and Mrs Penworth holds her son responsible for her husband's heart attack ten years ago. Matthew left home then, and she hasn't seen him since. She said that she pitied any woman who got tied up with him.'

Peter rubbed his hands over his face. 'So, no family to help him then. What about his mates?'

Kevin spoke up. 'I've spoken to the landlord at the Royal Oak. It seems that, even though Matthew Penworth is a frequent customer, especially for Sunday lunch, he still comes across as a bit of a loner. He drinks with a few of the regulars but always looks like he's on the fringes of the group.' Kevin consulted his notes. 'I did speak to one regular, a Mr Davies, who thought Penworth was, and I quote, 'a funny old stick'. He observed that Penworth didn't ever like losing when he occasionally played darts or pool, saying things were unfair or rigged, you know the sort?'

'No best mate, then? It's looking like, if he did abduct Susan Delaney, it was a solo effort.' Peter turned to the map on the wall. 'So where could he have taken her? Did he have any other lock-ups, Maggie?'

'Not that I can find, sir.'

'And what about SOCO? Anything from them?'

'Too early for the search of Penworth's house, sir, but we have a result on the black hair found on Carol Lightfoot's body.'

Peter's ears pricked up. 'And?'

'Not a match for Penworth, sir.'

'Damn!' said Peter, sitting down heavily.

'But it's a bit strange, sir,' Maggie went on, 'there's a familial match between the hair and Susan Delaney.'

Peter stood up again. 'What!? How do we come to have her DNA?'

'SOCO obtained it from a hairbrush in her bedroom. Just in case we needed to identify a body, sir.'

'And there's a match between a black hair and her?' Peter exclaimed.

'A familial match, sir. Did she have a brother?'

Peter took out his phone. 'I need to speak to Cassie. See if she can throw any light on this development.'

'No, sir, no brothers. She was an only child.' Cassie and Peter were in his office puzzling over this new information. 'She could have had cousins, though. I can check that with her mother.'

'That would be useful, Cassie. If we can't tie this black hair to a family member, I'm struggling to understand what's going on.'

Cassie looked steadily at Peter. 'What?' he said.

'Suzi had a son when she was fifteen. He would be twenty or twenty-one now, sir.'

Peter looked incredulous. 'A son?'

'She was raped when she was fourteen and her parents forced her to have the child. It was a boy, and he was adopted as soon as he was born.'

'Did Susan have contact with her son?'

'I don't think so, sir. Not that she told me about anyway, and it would have been a big deal for her. If she'd made contact with him, I'm sure she'd have told me.'

'Do we know anything about the adoption?'

'It was a Catholic adoption society, but Mrs Delaney will know the details. It will have been local to where they lived though, I'm sure. The family were devout, so much so that the priest practically moved in with them. He would have had a hand in the adoption, I'm convinced of it.'

'You know what I'm going to ask you, don't you?'

'How soon can I go to Liverpool? My kids are due back on Saturday so, if I get off now, I should have plenty of time.'

'Isn't Liverpool a dangerous place for you, Cassie?'

'I'll be in and out before anyone knows. Besides that scrote is behind bars now so the heat is off. I'll contact my mate Steve, see if he can pick me up from the airport.' Cassie checked flight information on her phone. 'There's a flight to Manchester at five-forty. I should just make that. Not as convenient as Liverpool airport but not bad.'

'Thanks, Cassie. Is there anything I can do with the Erica Trevellian case while you're away?'

'Thanks, Peter, but I don't think so. Robbie is bringing the Trevellian brothers in, and he can interview them about their whereabouts when Tandy was attacked. I'll ask him to report to you if anything significant crops up.'

Steve collected Cassie from arrivals at Manchester airport. 'I didn't think I'd get to see you again so soon,' he said, as he gave his good friend a warm hug. 'Just the one night, is it, madam?'

'I'm really grateful, Steve. I could have stayed with the folks on this trip, but I don't really have the time.'

'Chez Steve it is then. And you're very welcome. You tell such interesting stories and, if memory serves, you have one to finish from last time.'

As on the previous visit to Mrs Delaney, the woman was peeping from behind the curtains as Cassie parked the car she had borrowed from Steve. The front door opened and Mrs Delaney smiled a welcoming smile. 'Oh, it's you, Cassandra. How lovely to see you again so soon.'

Cassie couldn't get used to this new friendly version of Suzi's mother after the way she used to be treated in the past. 'Not welcome here,' was what she said when Cassie had tried to visit

Suzi when she was pregnant. Well, perhaps Cassie could forgive her that one time, but not for all the previous snubs and scathing remarks.

'Mrs Delaney. I wonder if I might come in and ask you a few questions?'

'Of course, dear. I'll put the kettle on.'

The mood became less warm when Cassie raised the issue of the adoption of Suzi's baby. Mrs Delaney feigned memory loss at first. *It was so long ago, my dear.* But when Cassie said she may have to go to see the priest, the older woman's memory became crystal clear.

'It was called The Catholic Children's Adoption Society. They had a very good reputation for finding parents of good character, if you know what I mean, and it was important to Mr Delaney that they were Catholic, of course.'

'Were they based around here?'

'No, dear, in Southport. The child was first taken to foster parents in Crosby by the nuns who attended Susan, and then I believe he was given over to the adoptive parents a few weeks later.'

'Have you heard anything about him since?'

Mrs Delaney gave Cassie a hard stare. 'No, and we didn't want to. He was the product of sin and we wanted nothing to do with him. Naturally, I hoped he was being well looked after, but I didn't feel that he had anything to do with me.'

'He was your grandson.'

'He was a bastard.'

That word hung in the air for a few seconds then Mrs Delaney cleared away the tea things.

'Aren't you going to ask about Suzi?' Cassie asked.

'Have you found her?' said Mrs Delaney, pausing by the door with the tea tray in her hands.

'No, she's still missing, I'm afraid.'

'Hmmph. Don't worry, she'll turn up. Like the bad penny.'

Cassie left the old woman to her sour memories and harsh comments and prepared to head for Southport. Sitting outside in her car she Googled The Catholic Children's Adoption Society, and was pleased to find out that they were still operating. Putting the post code into Steve's SATNAV she allowed the soothing voice to direct her along once familiar roads.

The building was an old Georgian mansion with the adoption society's logo subtly placed on a small brass plaque at the side of the entrance door. Cassie pressed a buzzer and a disembodied voice asked politely what her business was. After the confusing identification of herself as a DI with the Devon and Cornwall police, Cassie was allowed in.

The reception area was bright and elegant. A small half-moon desk took up one corner and there were a number of comfortable looking armchairs dotted around with coffee tables festooned with magazines. A similarly elegant receptionist rose to greet Cassie. 'You're a long way from home, detective. Or did I detect a whiff of Liverpool in your accent?'

'Yes, you're absolutely spot on. Cornwall by way of Childwall.'

'Similar really, aren't they? Cornwall – Childwall, d'you see?' Cassie smiled politely.

'Here's me prattling on when you're obviously busy. How can I help you?'

Cassie had extracted the baby boy's birthdate from Mrs Delaney and so was able to give the receptionist a fairly full set of details, which she wrote down.

'If you'd like to take a seat detective, I'll get one of our senior staff to see you. Would you like tea or coffee? A cold drink, perhaps?'

Cassie settled for water and plumped herself onto one of the armchairs, which was as comfortable as it looked. There's money in the adoption business, she thought, looking at the quality of the furnishings. One adoption society leaflet went some way to explain the salubrity, asking for people to remember them in their wills as well as making regular donations to the charity. Book your place in heaven, Cassie thought with a smile.

A door opened and a tall distinguished looking man came out and walked briskly over to Cassie, his hand extended to shake hers. 'Good morning, I'm Michael St John, I'm the deputy manager. Would you like to come through?' He indicated towards the doorway with his hand.

Following Mr St John into a well appointed office, Cassie noticed again how sumptuous everything felt. Not like most police stations, she mused.

When they were settled, Mr St John asked, 'Now, detective inspector, how can I be of service?'

'I would like some information about an adoption that I believe you handled.'

'That could be problematic, detective,' Mr St John said shaking his head. 'All our client details are confidential, as I'm sure you understand.'

Cassie carried on regardless, after making a slight nod to acknowledge Mr St John's statement. 'In most circumstances I would fully support that, sir. However, the information I need would form part of a murder investigation, and I think that changes things.'

'Mmm. I would need to know a little more. Would you like some coffee or tea whilst we discuss it?'

'That would be lovely, thanks,' Cassie said, feeling a little more hopeful at not receiving the blanket refusal she had experienced from some organisations.

After the receptionist had brought a tray with a cafetière of coffee and some delicious looking biscuits, Mr St John took out a note pad and pen. 'Shall we give that time to brew while you give me some details of the adoption you're interested in.'

Cassie also took out her note pad. 'It is a boy born tenth of February 1995. His birth mother is Susan Mary Delaney, her date of birth is the fourth of July 1980.' Cassie suddenly had a flashback to Suzi saying on her thirteenth birthday, *independence day, Cass,* and laughing out loud in the park. Cassie had saved up and bought her friend some dangly earrings which sparkled in the sun. Suzi had said, *I won't be able to wear these at home, you know that, but I love them, and I'll treasure them forever*. And she had hugged her best friend tightly.

Suddenly realising that Mr St John was holding a cup out to her, Cassie smiled. 'Sorry,' she said, taking the cup.

'That's okay, detective, you must have a lot on your mind with a murder enquiry that brings you from Cornwall all the way to Merseyside.'

Cassie acknowledged his perceptive words with a nod. 'You're right there, sir, and time is of the essence. I do hope you can help me today, a woman's life may be in the balance as well as a murderer on the loose.'

'What a murky world you police officers live in. I don't know if I could handle it myself.' He sighed and turned to face his computer screen. 'The Data Protection Act does give us some discretion, especially when sharing information with other statutory bodies. Without consulting the Act right now, I am confident that you having this information is necessary in the circumstances.'

Cassie beamed, grateful to be speaking to a professional who wasn't a jobsworth, as many could be.

'Now, let me see. Yes, the child you speak of was placed for adoption by us. The couple were on our books and approved as adopters already, so it was a fairly quick process, especially as consent was obtained from the birth mother immediately the child was born.'

Cassie asked, 'Would it make a difference if the birth mother was a minor? I know she was fifteen at the time.'

'In that case consent can be given over to the parents of the birth mother, but normally the child in question would have some say in the matter. There is a period when the baby is placed with foster carers when the birth mother can receive counselling to make sure she has not changed her mind about the decision. I imagine that didn't happen in this case as there don't seem to have been any hold ups.'

Fat chance of an offer of counselling for Suzi, Cassie thought.

Mr St John continued. 'The adoptive couple were a Mr and Mrs Makinson, Gerald and Avril. They called the boy Simon. I'll jot down their address for you but, if you'd allow, I'd like to speak to them first. Adoptive couples live in fear of having their child taken away from them for one reason or another. Even after all this time, it would be unsettling for them.'

'I have no problem with that, as long as you can do it quickly. As I said, time is pressing and I would want to visit the couple today.'

'There's one other thing, detective,' said Mr St John, consulting the screen. 'It looks like the birth mother deposited a letter with us to give to her son if he ever decided to seek her out. Some adopted people do, especially if their parents have shared the fact of their adoption and are amenable to it.'

'Can the birth mother not seek out her child?'

'No, it doesn't work that way round. You see, some children never know they have been adopted, although that is very much frowned upon by all agencies, and some are happy and settled and feel no need to find a mother that didn't want them anyway.'

'And did he, Simon, want to find his birth mother?'

St John gave a slight nod. 'Oh yes, detective, I believe he did.'

Gerald and Avril Makinson lived in Cheshire, Alderley Edge, to be precise, and Cassie felt her spirits drop a little. Checking her watch, she realised that it was already one-thirty. A trip to the Makinson's and back, even if Steve was okay about her keeping his car, would, combined with her discussions with them, take at least four hours. There was no way she was going to fly home tonight.

Just as she was about to reach for her phone to call Micky, her elder child, the phone rang out. It was Mark, and this fact brought a smile to her face. 'Hello you,' she said. 'This is a nice surprise.'

'I hope to make it even nicer,' Mark said back. 'If you're free this weekend, I can be with you tonight around eight.'

Mark's voice sounded eager and loving and Cassie's heart sank at the thought of having to turn him down.'

'Mark, I'm in Southport.'

'Tell me where that is, and I'll be there.'

Cassie laughed out loud. 'You're silly and wonderful, d'you know that?'

'I'm serious. Never heard of it but it sounds lovely.'

'Southport, Merseyside.'

'Oh, that Southport. What on earth are you doing there? And how soon can you get back? I'm a man on a mission, Cass, and determined to see you, hell or high water.'

Cassie laughed. 'I'm here as part of a murder investigation and may not be back until tomorrow sometime.' Mark started to speak but she cut him off. 'And even then I won't have any time.'

It was Mark's turn to cut Cassie off. 'Not taking no for an answer, Cass. You have to eat, even during a murder enquiry. I'll book into that hotel…'

It was Cassie's turn to butt in. 'You're not listening, Mark. As well as the murder enquiry, I've got a serious rape and assault case on the go, and my kids come home today, so, as much as I'd love to see you, it will have to be a no for this weekend.' There was silence on the other end. 'I'm really sorry.'

Mark spoke up. 'No, it's me who should be sorry, Cassie. I shouldn't pressurise you this way. If anyone should understand what you're going through it should be me. So, another time, eh?'

'Definitely. And we'll make it soon, I promise. Look, I have to get off, Mark. I'll call you tonight from Steve's when I get back, if it's not too late.'

'Steve? Should I be jealous?'

'Not when I tell you he's between boyfriends at the moment.'

Mark laughed. 'Okay, Cassie, I'll hear from you later, and you take care up in the big bad north.'

Still smiling at how keen Mark was, and enjoying the feeling of being pursued, Cassie rang Micky's number.

Leaving Southport, Cassie headed through Ormskirk and onto the M8 at the Rainford bypass, feeling pleased with herself for remembering the old familiar routes. She knew that the M8 would connect her with the M6 which was exactly where she wanted to be, heading south towards Birmingham. Cassie was disconcerted by the amount of traffic in comparison to the major roads in Cornwall. To think this was an everyday occurrence for me once upon a time, she thought, jammed between two articulated lorries. Her conversation with Micky and Tanya earlier had set her mind at rest. It was no trouble, it seemed, to stay with their dad and his wife a day longer. They had enjoyed their company, even the noisy toddler, but were looking forward to coming home. Cassie mused on the word home. That would have been Liverpool not too long ago, but it seemed they had all fallen in love with Cornwall. Cassie thought that if anyone had said that to her a couple of years ago when she joined the Serious Incident Squad in Truro, she'd have said they were mad. But now, especially with all this nose to tail traffic, she couldn't wait to get back.

Linking to the M6, Cassie set her SATNAV to the Makinson's address in Alderley Edge, and allowed her mind to wonder. Had Suzi's son made contact? Her conversation with her friend recently contained no such information, and Cassie was sure that Suzi couldn't keep such news to herself. Was there any other explanation for the hair to be found on Carol Lightfoot's body? Mrs Delaney had ruled out cousins, as the only one Suzi had now lived in Canada. Under other circumstances, Cassie would be thinking that the hair must belong to the killer, but how could that be? How could Suzi's son know Carol, and what could be his motive for killing her? Of course, Suzi could have met with her son outside her flat, and the hair could be transfer. Perhaps the information she got from the Makinsons would shed some light. She certainly hoped so. She felt very much in the dark at the moment.

The Makinson's home was a large, detached property in a mock Tudor style. Cassie pulled in by a set of wrought iron gates and pressed the intercom. She thought she detected a slight tremor to the female voice that answered the call, but it was welcoming all the same. 'We're expecting you, Detective Inspector Wade, but if you could just hold your identification up to the screen that would be lovely.'

Cassie complied and the gates swung back onto a gravel driveway bordered by decorative shrubs. To either side, neatly trimmed lawns surrounded the house which was even more impressive close-up. Stone steps led up to a tall double door which was standing open with a well-dressed woman on the threshold. The woman stepped forward to meet Cassie holding out her hand. 'Hello, detective, I'm Avril Makinson. Did you have a good journey?'

Cassie took the outstretched hand. 'Thank you for agreeing to meet me, Mrs Makinson.'

Cassie was ushered into a large hallway with a central round table on which stood an impressive display of flowers. The floor was polished stone which resounded beneath Mrs Makinson's high heels. There were four mismatched, but obviously antique, hall chairs along one wall, and a side table with another display of flowers on the opposite one. Doors led off to the left and right, but it was through the door at the far side of the hall that Cassie's host led her. Shallow steps took them down into an enormous living room with a wall of glass overlooking an immaculate garden. I could fit my whole house in here, Cassie thought, this is serious wealth. A man in his late fifties or early sixties greeted Cassie warmly. 'Come and sit down, my dear. It's an awful trek from

Southport, especially on a Friday afternoon. POETS day you know.' Cassie had heard the expression before, *piss off early tomorrow's Saturday*, so she smiled an acknowledgement.

'It's certainly different to what I'm used to, Mr Makinson,' Cassie said, choosing a comfortable looking armchair, which immediately swallowed her up into its depths. 'Cornwall's roads are never so busy.'

'But don't I detect a Liverpool accent?'

Cassie thought it could be time for elocution lessons. '*Do I detect a Liverpool accent?*' was becoming a bit tiresome. 'Absolutely correct,' she said smiling. 'And yours? Manchester I'd say.'

'Touché, detective. Now what can we get you to drink? I've just bought myself a new coffee making machine and I love to try it out on visitors.'

'I'll have a latte then, if it's not too much trouble.' Cassie felt like she'd stepped into an episode of Inspector Morse, where he visited an old wealthy family he used to know, the one where he used to be engaged to the daughter perhaps.

Casting her eye around the room, Cassie saw dozens of photographs of a boy and a girl at different stages of growing up. Standing windblown together on a yacht, laughing at the camera. A small boy in a football strip holding a trophy, a girl on a pony proudly displaying a rosette. An idyllic childhood, thought Cassie, Suzi missed out on all of that with her son. Before she could become maudlin, Mr Makinson came back into the room with a tray of coffee, his wife followed carrying some sandwiches and cakes. 'We thought you may not have had time for lunch, so please help yourself.'

While Cassie ate the tasty sandwiches, realising suddenly that she was hungry, the three chatted about general things; the weather, the garden, Cornwall sailing holidays the couple remembered. All very relaxing, but Cassie became aware of the time, and brought her hosts back to the reason for her visit.

'When was the last time you had contact with Simon?'

Mr Makinson looked at his wife. 'It would be about a week ago. Is that right, Avril?'

'Yes, about that, he phoned. But I texted him a couple of days ago and got no answer.' She looked at Cassie. 'That's not unusual is it? Young people have such busy lives. Simon is studying for his Masters. He's at LSE.'

Mr Makinson looked troubled. 'Mr St John said that you were making enquiries about a murder. How do you think Simon can help with that? He's not in any danger, is he?'

'There's not a lot I can say about the investigation, Mr Makinson, but we would like to speak to your son as soon as possible and eliminate him from our enquiries if we can.'

Mrs Makinson looked towards her husband with a worried frown on her face. 'Do you think he has contacted his birth mother, Gerald?'

He shook his head wearily. 'I don't know, Avril. It's always been a possibility, we've never tried to hide anything from him.'

Avril turned to Cassie. 'Has that woman got him into some kind of trouble? It's really not like him to have any dealings with the police.'

Cassie felt herself bridle at the description of her friend as *that woman*, but remained calm, at least on the outside. 'We don't know anything at the moment, Mrs Makinson, which is why we need to contact Simon urgently.'

Mr Makinson stood suddenly and started pacing the room. 'You're not telling us anything, detective, which leaves a lot of room for speculation and worry. Can't you at least say how Simon's name has come up in your enquiries?'

Cassie thought for a moment. She understood that she had raised the couple's anxiety levels, but maybe they would worry more if she told them about the DNA link to the murder scene. Perhaps she could give them a little more, though, she did want their co-operation after all. 'All I can tell you is that we have some evidence that Simon made contact with his birth mother recently, and that we need to speak to both of them urgently.'

'So he did get in touch with her,' Avril exclaimed, clearly alarmed.

'Does that mean that you haven't found her either? Said Mr Makinson, sounding exasperated. 'This is all very mysterious detective. Do you think that they have gone away somewhere together, is that it?'

Realising that the more they spoke, the closer Mr Makinson was to speculating accurately about the situation, Cassie thought she'd better draw the meeting to a close. 'I really can't say any more, I'm sorry. I will let you know if there are any developments concerning your son.'

The Makinsons looked at each other forlornly. 'Well, I suppose that will have to do,' said Mr Makinson, sadly.

'There's just one more thing you can do to help,' said Cassie. 'Do you have a recent photograph of Simon you could let us have?'

'Of course,' said Mrs Makinson. 'I'll get one for you.'

When Avril had left the room, Mr Makinson turned to Cassie. 'If there's something upsetting that you didn't want to say in front of my wife, you can tell me. We'll support Simon whatever trouble he might have got himself into.'

'It's really not like that, sir. And I can't tell you anything about the details of our enquiries. I'm sorry.' Cassie took the photograph off Mrs Makinson as she returned. A handsome smiling young man who held a strong resemblance to the singer in a certain band from years ago. 'This will do nicely, thank you. I will let you have it back. By the way, did Simon own a car?'

'Yes, he did,' said Mr Makinson. 'It is a white Ford Fiesta. Do you want the registration number?'

'That would be very helpful.' He jotted it down and handed the paper to Cassie.

'Thank you, and if you do hear from Simon please let me know.' Cassie passed her card to Mrs Makinson, who simply stared at it.

'We will, of course,' said Gerald, placing his arm around his wife's shoulder.

Cassie had a sudden thought. 'Do you think Simon would have said anything to his sister about his intentions? Often siblings share things their parents don't know about.'

Mrs Makinson looked up. 'Claire? It's possible, I suppose.'

'Could you give me her contact details?'

'I'll speak to her today. But there's no reason you can't have her phone number if it would help clear this matter up.' Mr Makinson jotted down the number on a note pad and tore the page out for Cassie.

'You've both been very helpful, thank you. I'll be in touch.' Cassie turned to walk into the spacious hall with the couple at her heels. As she took off in her car, she could see them in the rear-view mirror, arms around each other, grim looks on their faces.

Chapter Eleven

Robbie drove along the rutted lane that led to the Trevellians' farm. Looking to his left, he could see the two brothers at the far side of the field working on a fence. Not wishing to stop at that point, where there was no chance of turning, he carried on up to the farmhouse. He was sure that the boys had heard him arrive as they had looked up from their work. He had remembered his wellingtons this time so, pulling them on, he stood and surveyed the land. There were about fifty sheep grazing contentedly on the sloping field. They looked up simultaneously as he opened the gate, then went back to grazing. Robbie was glad of his wellingtons as the field was muddy after the previous night's rainfall. Today was bright and sunny, though, and Robbie enjoyed stretching his legs across the grass.

Paul and Andy straightened up when they saw Robbie approach, laying down their tools and shielding their eyes against the low morning sun.

'Alright?' one of them shouted. 'Dad's out.'

Robbie held up his warrant card. 'It's DC Green.'

'Right, I know who you are,' the same brother said.

Robbie had reached them and was struck again by the resemblance between the two brothers. 'I want you both to come with me to the station to answer some questions.'

'What about? Can't leave the farm anyhow 'til dad gets back.'

'And your name is?' said Robbie to the spokesperson.

'I'm Paul. He's Andy.'

'Well, Paul and Andy, if you refuse to accompany me, I will have to arrest you.'

This time Andy spoke. 'Arrest us? What for? We haven't done anything.'

'You can come with me quietly or I can call for assistance.'

Paul took out his phone. Robbie quickly stepped forward and took it from him.

'Hey, what did you do that for?'

'Let's go,' said Robbie, turning towards the house.

Paul shrugged. 'You can at least tell us what it's about.'

'James Tandy was attacked two nights ago, and we'd like you to help us with our enquiries into that incident.'

'Nothging to do with us, was it, Andy?'

Robbie stood his ground. 'Are you coming, or do I need to arrest you?'

The two brothers made eye contact and nodded, then followed Robbie to his car.

Peter took Cassie's phone call in his office. 'I'll scan in the photograph from here along with my reports of my meetings with the Makinsons and the adoption agency.' Cassie was exhausted after her long day driving around the north west and was now sipping a welcome glass of wine while Steve prepared something appetising with pasta and salmon. *He'd make someone a wonderful wife,* she thought, chuckling to herself.

'Alright in there with your drink?' Steve shouted from the kitchen. 'Dinner will be five minutes.'

Peter overheard. 'Having a nice time, then?' he said, laughing down the phone.

'You just wouldn't believe my day,' she replied, testily. 'Practically grid-locked traffic, ruining the day for a lovely couple and missing out on a date with a great guy. I think I've earned a bit of pampering.'

'You've done good work, Cassie. From what you've told me so far, we'll be able put a trace on Simon Makinson's car. That and the photo should mean we'll be able to track him down. I've got a press conference tomorrow morning, so I'll get the photo out there. Well done again, I'll see you tomorrow.'

The creamy pasta and the chilled wine put Cassie in a mellow mood. 'This is great, Steve,' she said. 'You really are a pal. There's a bed for you at mine anytime you feel like a holiday in Cornwall.'

'I'll take you up on that,' he laughed. 'Now how about finishing the story about your friend.'

Cassie didn't really feel like talking about her friend after meeting the Makinsons and seeing the photos of Suzi's baby growing up, knowing how much she had missed out on. Cassie thought of her own children and how devastated she would feel if she couldn't be a mother to them. Steve would expect a no holds barred expose of the life and times of Susan Delaney, and Cassie just didn't feel up to it. Instead, she tempted Steve with the latest developments in her love life, and he was more than happy to settle for that.

Landing at Newquay airport after an uneventful early flight from Manchester, Cassie scanned the small crowd waiting in arrivals. This area was tiny compared to Manchester domestic arrivals where she landed just two days ago, and she soon spotted Maggie waving to her. 'The car's just outside, ma'am. Did you have a good trip?'

'Yes, Maggie, very useful, but I'm glad to be back. Can you drop me home first?' Cassie was keen to get things ready for Micky and Tanya's return. She was really looking forward to giving them both a big hug.

'No problem, ma'am. The Chief wants to see you as soon as you can. He's doing a press conference at eleven and wants you to be there.' Maggie opened the car door for Cassie and put her bag on the back seat.

Cassie's heart sank. She'd hoped to be around when her kids arrived but that wasn't going to be possible now. 'Thanks, Maggie. Tell him I'll be there. Just need to change and get in a few things for tonight.' Seeing Maggie's puzzled expression, she added, 'My kids are back today so I want to do something special. It's being away from them that makes me appreciate them more.' Cassie gazed out of the car window.

Maggie thought what a great mum Cassie must be. Thinking of her children despite juggling two major investigations.

As they pulled onto the A30, Cassie asked Maggie about the Erica Trevellian case. 'Robbie had the two lads in yesterday. Apparently, they've given an alibi for the night when James Tandy was attacked. They said they were in the pub all night with several witnesses to back it up.'

'Mmm. Did Robbie go to the multi-agency meeting?'

'Yes, ma'am. The report is on your desk, but I believe social services and education are dealing with it.'

Well done, Robbie, Cassie thought. Pleased that her DC had been able to stand his ground in the meeting. She knew they could be a minefield when actions were being handed out. Feeling more engaged with this investigation suddenly, Cassie felt motivated to move it along. But first there was the press conference.

Cassie sat beside Peter as the reporters gathered in the body of the hall. She could see amongst the crowd several nationals represented. It wasn't surprising. This was fast becoming a story of profound public interest. A photograph of Suzi had been in the media for a few days now and yet there had been no sightings. The police had received several dozen phone calls, some cranks, some not credible and a few that needed to be investigated. None of these had come to anything. The press was rightly concerned on behalf of its readership, and Cassie expected some probing questions from the assembled reporters. However, she knew that Peter would be in the spotlight for these, her role was to introduce the new line of enquiry. That being the interest in speaking to Simon Makinson as a matter of urgency. His photograph had been copied and ready for circulation, but Cassie was very conscious of not linking him in any way to the murder. At this stage the message was that the police would like to speak to him as he could be a witness to a crime.

Peter drew the conference to order and introduced himself and Cassie. He read a prepared statement with the bare bones concerning the progress of the enquiry so far. The police were still interested in contacting Susan Delaney; there was nothing to suggest that she was in any danger at the moment; there was no further information on who the killer might be.

A question from the floor asked, 'Is Susan Delaney officially a missing person?'

Peter said, 'Not at this stage'.

'Has Susan Delaney been kidnapped?'

'No reason to believe that at the moment.'

'Did Susan Delaney kill her flatmate?'

'There is no evidence to support that. Now I'll hand you over to DI Wade.'

Cassie touched her keyboard and the image of Simon Makinson appeared on the screen to the right of the podium. 'We are interested in speaking to this man. His name is Simon Makinson and he is twenty-one years old. We believe he has been in the Penzance area recently, driving a white Ford Fiesta, registration LP15 PLS. If anyone has seen this man, or knows of his whereabouts, they should contact any police station or call our hotline, the number of which is on your fact sheet along with the photograph of Simon Makinson.'

'Do you think he's the killer?'

'We have no reason to believe that at the moment.' Cassie held up her hand to stop any further questions. 'I want to make an appeal to Susan Delaney.' She looked directly into the news camera. 'Susan, if you are watching this, I want you to make contact with me. You can ring the number at the bottom of the screen and ask for DI Cassie Wade, and you will be put straight through to me.' Cassie paused. 'I also would like to say to Simon Makinson, if he is listening, that your parents and sister are very concerned about you and want you to get in touch right away.'

After Cassie had finished her address, a voice called out. 'You had a man in custody for this murder, DI Wade, why did you let him go? Is he still a suspect?'

'I've nothing more to say at the moment. Thank you, ladies and gentlemen.' And with that, Peter and Cassie left the podium.

Back in the squad room, Maggie told Cassie that there had been a phone call for her from Mr Makinson. 'It seems they are on their way to Cornwall, ma'am. He also said that they had some information for you after speaking to their daughter.'

Cassie thanked Maggie and went to her desk to make the call. She was connected to Mr Makinson and could hear road noise in the background. 'Hello, DI Wade,' he said. 'I'm driving at the moment, hands free of course, just approaching Exeter on the M5.'

'Hello, Mr Makinson, I believe you have some information for me?'

'I do, but I'd rather not speak and drive. Even hands free, I find it distracting. Can we meet when we arrive?'

'Of course. I agree with you, conversations whist driving can be dangerous. I'll text you the address of the station and look forward to seeing you. Let me know when you are approaching Truro.'

'I will, detective. We'll see you soon.'

Cassie walked over to Peter's office and knocked. Hearing a muffled '*Come in,*' she opened the door to find him on the phone.

'Sorry, sir, I'll come back later.'

Peter shook his head and waved to beckon her in, then continued his conversation. 'That's great, sweetheart, it could make all the difference, by the sounds of it.' He listened for a few seconds. 'Give SuLin my best and I'll be home by six, I promise. Bye bye.'

'Everything okay, sir?' Cassie asked.

'Rachel has been struggling with low moods since Charlotte was born. Feeling helpless and tired all the time. SuLin and I persuaded her to see the doctor even though she was adamant she wasn't having anti-depressants. Anyhow, the doctor has prescribed vitamin B6, Pyridoxine. Apparently new mothers can experience a deficiency which leads to tiredness and mood changes along with a weakened immune system. Most mammals eat their placenta, apparently, which is rich in B6, and get a boost that way, but, of course, we don't. Who knew, eh?'

'I really hope it works for Rachel. Being a new mum is hard enough without your body letting you down.'

Peter smiled and nodded. 'Now, what can I do for you, Cassie?'

'I just wanted a catch up, really. The two cases we have on the go are both at critical points and I need to run a few things by you.'

'Fire away.'

'The James Tandy case. Robbie has had to let the Trevellian brothers go until he can check out their alibi. What Erica Trevellian overheard and witnessed strongly suggests their involvement in the attack on Tandy, as well as what Robbie overheard in their house. Them saying they sorted their own troubles rings alarm bells for me. My concern is that they might try to dispose of evidence, specifically the crowbar which could well be the weapon used in the attack.'

'There's not enough there to apply for a search warrant, Cassie. Where's Robbie up to with the alibi?'

'I believe he's at the pub now, sir.'

'Why don't you join him? Two heads are better than one, and you have a nose for seeing the facts, if that's not a split metaphor. I'm not saying Robbie isn't a good copper, but your experience is needed I think.'

'Thanks for that, sir. I'll go now before Mr and Mrs Makinson get here.'

'They're coming here?'

'On their way, sir. I can't say I blame them. Their son is missing, presumably in Cornwall, so they want to be where the action is. And they have something from the daughter.'

'Right. Well, we'll deal with them when they arrive. Probably better to meet in a hotel or a café. If you're not back, I'll talk to them and contact you, okay?'

'Thanks, sir. I'll get off then, and I appreciate the support.'

'No problem, Cassie, you're doing a great job, I'm sure you'll have a breakthrough soon.'

The Plough was quiet, so Cassie had no problem in spotting Robbie at the bar as she walked in. He turned to see his DI and waved her over. 'Good afternoon, ma'am.'

Cassie acknowledged the barman as she approached and then signalled Robbie over to a table. 'What have you found out so far, Robbie?'

'The barman was on duty on Wednesday. He says it was a very busy night because there was a darts match on, but he did see both Paul and Andy Trevellian at various times during the evening. He thinks Paul was playing pool most of the time and Andy was watching the darts match.'

'Who was Paul playing pool with?'

'A couple of regulars were with him. The barman said they usually get in about now, so I was going to wait for them.'

'Okay, let's have a drink and wait. Mine's a tonic water.' Robbie went off to the bar and Cassie pondered the possibilities of how the brothers could have perpetrated the attack on James Tandy whilst being seen in the pub most of the night. She stood up and went from the bar into the pool room. Strolling around the table, which took up most of the small space, she noticed a doorway at the far end of the room, marked *toilets*. Stepping through, she found herself in a narrow corridor with the gents and ladies toilets facing her. Opposite to these doors were a number of coat hooks, currently free from coats. Carrying on along the corridor, she came to another door on her right. Going through this one, she found herself back in the bar, by the dart board. An idea was forming in her mind. A bemused Robbie watched Cassie as she turned and went back through the door, emerging a little later from the pool room. This time she came over to where Robbie was sitting with their drinks.

'The Trevellian boys are identical twins, aren't they?' Robbie nodded as he sipped his coke. Cassie continued. 'I knew a pair of identical twins when I was a girl and they were always playing tricks on people, pretending to be the other twin.'

'I see what you mean, ma'am, but how does that help us if both boys were seen together?'

'But they weren't seen together the whole evening, Robbie, not by the barman anyway. He said Paul was playing pool and Andy was watching the darts.'

'I still don't get it, ma'am.'

'Bear with me, Robbie. Come with me.' They left the table and followed the path that Cassie had taken earlier. When they reached the toilets, Cassie stopped. What if only one of the twins was in the pub for a period of time?' Robbie listened attentively. 'Wednesday was busy because of the darts match, yes?' Robbie nodded, a puzzled look on his face.

Cassie carried on. 'What if, when they arrived, one of the brothers, let's say Paul, left his jacket on a hook here and then, at the appropriate time, slipped out of the pub? The other brother, who is pretending to be Paul, changed into his brother's jacket and started playing pool, whilst Paul rode to Redruth on his motorbike, attacked James Tandy, then rode back. It would take him no longer than an hour.'

'But the barman saw them both at the time Tandy was being attacked.'

'I'm getting to that. In that hour, Andy, pretending to be Paul, finishes his pool match and says he's going to the toilet. He changes his jacket back to his own and continues on into the bar, making sure the barman notices him – buys a drink perhaps. Then watches the darts for a while, chatting to the barman. Then he does the whole thing again in reverse.'

Robbie blew his cheeks out. 'Let's walk that through if you don't mind, ma'am.'

The two walked on and into the bar. Robbie sat on a barstool. The barman came over. 'Can I get you something?'

'Can you remember if you served Andy with drinks during the hour and a half between seven and eight thirty, about the time you saw him watching the darts match?'

'Oh, let me think. It were very busy, but I do remember Andy ordering two pints, and he was very particular about it, too. He wanted a pint of Betty Stoggs for himself and insisted on a pint of Doombar for his brother, he said Paul never drank anything else.'

'Did Paul join him at the bar? This is very important, so think carefully.'

The barman considered the question. 'Now I think on, he didn't. Andy took Paul's drink through to the pool room then came back for his own. He threw a few arrows on the practice dart board, then went off. To go to the toilet, I expect.'

Cassie had been listening to this exchange and smiling. 'It's possible, Robbie.' She whispered. Turning to the barman, she said, 'And do you remember what Andy was wearing?'

'Let me think. A denim jacket I think, yeah definitely, denim jacket.'

Just then, the barman nodded towards the door. 'There's George and Billy, the ones who played pool with Paul.'

As the two men approached the bar, Cassie walked forward to meet them. Holding up her warrant card she said, 'A few words, if you don't mind, gents.'

George told Cassie that he had played a game with Paul just after seven. 'Paul won then went to the toilet, I think. I carried on playing with Billy.'

'Did Paul come back?'

'Yeah, after a bit, for his game with Billy.'

'Did you see Andy at all?'

'He didn't want to play that night, he was watching the darts match,' said Billy.

George added, 'He popped in with a pint for Paul while he was 'avin a slash. But apart from that, we didn't see him until later on, when the darts had finished.'

Cassie thanked the two men and she and Robbie went back for their drinks. 'Well, I'm gobsmacked, as the saying goes, ma'am. It's practically word for word what you said.'

'Not practically, Robbie. Try exactly.'

'But wouldn't someone have noticed a jacket on the coat hook?'

'It was a busy night, Robbie, there would have been lots of coats on those hooks, easy to hide one.'

'It's still all speculation though, ma'am. Even if they weren't seen together, we could never make that version of events stick.'

'You're right, Robbie. We need something else.' Cassie wandered through to the pool room where George and Billy were playing. 'Can I disturb you for a minute, lads,' she asked returning briefly to the pool room. The men turned and nodded.

'Do you remember anything unusual about Paul that night? Anything at all? What was his mood like?'

Billy looked at George. 'He was a bit excited like, wasn't he, George? Couldn't keep still.'

'He still managed to beat me twice, though,' said George, glumly. 'Even playing left-handed.'

Cassie was interested. 'Doesn't Paul usually play left-handed?'

'Nah, it's Andy who's the kitty paw. When I asked him why he was playing left-handed, Paul said he was trying to copy Ronnie O'Sullivan, you know, the snooker player. Just as good with either hand. Anyway, he was good, better than with his right.'

'Just one more thing. What was Paul wearing?'

'That's easy, his leather jacket. Never had it off since he's bought it.'

Cassie had to stop herself punching the air. 'Thanks, lads. Can I get you a drink?'

'Let's go and pick them up, Robbie,' Cassie said, as they left the pub. 'I think we may have enough to hold them this time and get a search warrant.'

101

Robbie was thoughtful, and as they got into the car, he spoke up. 'There is one thing, ma'am. How did Paul know when James Tandy would be outside the cinema in Redruth?'

'One thing at a time, Robbie. Let's hope we find the crowbar and it's got Tandy's blood and Paul's fingerprints on it. Otherwise we can prove nothing.'

Mr Trevellian was standing in the yard as Cassie and Robbie drove in. He shielded his eyes from the low sun and walked over to the car. 'You still persecutin' us, then?'

Cassie got out of the vehicle. 'We'd like to speak to Paul and Andy, Mr Trevellian. Could you get them for us please.'

The farmer shrugged resignedly, walked towards the farmhouse door and shouted, 'Paul, Andy, get out 'ere.'

The two brothers emerged, chewing a chunk of bread each. 'What's up, pa?' Then seeing Cassie and Robbie, they glanced worriedly at each other. 'What you want now?' said one of them.

Cassie walked up to the boys. 'Which is which?' she said.

Paul sighed. 'I'm Paul and this is Andy.'

Cassie turned to Paul. 'Paul Trevellian, I'm arresting you in connection with the grievous attack on James Tandy. You do not have to say anything. But, it may harm your defence if you do not mention when questioned something you later rely on in court. Anything you do say may be given in evidence.'

Mr Trevellian stepped forward, but was restrained by Robbie. Cassie repeated the caution with Andy and took a pair of cuffs from her pocket. Robbie handed her his pair and she cuffed both boys.

'You can't do this!' shouted Mr Trevellian. 'My lads have done nuthen'.'

As the pair were taken to the car and helped into the back, Mr Trevellian shouted, 'Don't worry, I'll get a solicitor, lads, you'll be out in no time. Bloody scandalous it is.'

Cassie checked her watch as she entered the squad room. Six o'clock already. Peter had left her a note saying that he had gone to meet the Makinsons at the Avalon Hotel. Well, at least she didn't have to fit that into what was rapidly becoming a crowded schedule. She grabbed her phone and dialled Micky's number. He answered right away.

'Hi, mum. You on your way?'

'Hi, love. Are you and Tanya okay? Did you have a good journey?'

'Is this leading to, I may be a bit late?'

'Read me like a book, you can. Just a bit late. Have you had something to eat?'

'After a week of plant-based food, good and healthy though it was, we grabbed a pasty each at Piccadilly station and ate it on the train. All that pastry and meat, lovely.'

Cassie laughed. 'You'll have to tell me all about it later. There's some burgers in the fridge and I'd planned to have them on buns with salad, sorry about the salad, and then some Ben and Jerry's for afters.'

'Sounds great, ma. What time are you back?'

'No later than seven-thirty, I promise.'

Cassie sat opposite Paul in the interview room. He looked relaxed with just a hint of arrogance. He brushed his shoulder length hair out of his eyes and looked enquiringly at Cassie. 'Has dad got that solicitor yet? I'm not sayin' anythin' 'til then.'

'I understand, Paul,' said Cassie. 'You don't have to say anything but, if that's the case, I'm afraid we'll have to hold you until you have representation.'

'You can't do that,' Paul protested.

'I can, Paul.' And with that she left the room.

Walking down the corridor to the next interview room, Cassie thought it might be useful to let the brothers stew overnight, knock some of that arrogance out of Paul. Andy's body language was a bit different, though. As Cassie sat opposite him he looked up nervously, picking at the skin around his fingernails. 'Is dad here?' he asked.

Cassie ignored the question. 'I want you to tell me about Wednesday night. The night you say you were in the pub.'

'We were in the pub,' Andy protested. 'Anyone'll tell yer.'

'So you're saying that both you and Paul were in the pub?'

'Yeah.'

'All evening?'

'What d'yer mean?'

'Were you both in the pub all evening?'

Andy hesitated. 'Yeah, we left at about eleven to go home,' he replied tentatively.

'Neither of you nipped out for a bit?'

'Oh, I know what you're sayin', one of us went out and beat up James Tandy. Well we didn't.'

'Do you like pool, Andy? You know, the game of pool.'

'Yeah, so what?'

'Would you say you're a good player?'

'Not bad. Why you askin' about pool?' Andy was nibbling at the loose skin on his fingers.

'Would you mind writing down the name of the person you were playing with that night.' Cassie slid a piece of paper over to Andy.

He gave a nervous laugh. 'This is daft. It was George and Billy.'

Cassie tapped the paper and handed Andy the pen, which he took up in his left hand.

Sullenly, he wrote the names of his playing partners. 'There,' he said, pushing the paper back.

'I see you're left-handed, Andy.'

Andy blinked rapidly and looked down at the table. 'I'm not sayin' anythin' else,' he stammered. 'My dad said he'd get us a solicitor and I'm not talkin' till he comes.'

'That's within your rights, Andy. We'll be keeping you in the cells overnight and I'll interview you tomorrow with your solicitor.'

'I want to see my dad,' Andy protested.

'That won't be possible. I'll get a constable to show you to the cells. I suggest you do some serious thinking before tomorrow.' It hadn't escaped Cassie's attention that Andy didn't say he hadn't played pool that night. This young man is the weak link, she thought. I'm sure we'll be able to break him tomorrow.

Cassie watched the scared young man being walked down to the custody suite. It's spooky how alike they are on the surface, she thought, but that brother is a lot less confident. I'll start with him tomorrow. I doubt that their dad will be able to afford two solicitors, but we'll wait and see.

Cassie checked her watch. Seven o'clock, good, not too late. She couldn't wait to see Micky and Tanya; suddenly appreciating

104

them more than ever. However, as she entered reception on her way out, Mr Trevellian was waiting. He stood as she approached, fists balled and his face red with anger.

'They tell me I can't see my boys,' he shouted.

'That's right, Mr Trevellian. It's standard practice. Did you obtain the services of two solicitors for Paul and Andy? Or would you like us to arrange for duty solicitors?'

'I didn't know I'd need two. I can't run to that. Bleddy daft, needin' two.'

'They each need personal representation, Mr Trevellian. Now I suggest you go home. There's nothing to be done before tomorrow.' Cassie smiled encouragingly at the man. 'I'll make arrangements for the solicitors.'

Trevellian stood for a few seconds, uncertain about what to do, then turned angrily on his heels and marched out of the station.

Cassie turned to the duty sergeant. 'Get us two duty solicitors for tomorrow, will you. I want to start interviewing at around ten, so tell them to be here in good time.'

'Yes, ma'am. By the way, a message came in for you. About a James Tandy? Apparently, he died at five o'clock. Never regained consciousness.'

Chapter Twelve

Cassie sat at the breakfast table that Sunday morning scanning the headlines. She had taken a phone call from Peter the previous evening and learned that Simon had indeed contacted Suzi. He had confided this to his sister, Claire. This was the information that Mr Makinson was so keen to share with them.

Cassie stared at the newspaper.

Champion of Battered Women Sought in Murder Hunt

There was a picture of Suzi alongside one of Peter and herself at the press conference.

> Police are seeking information as to the whereabouts of Susan Delaney, the well known Women's Aid spokeswoman and feminist writer. She appears to have fled the scene of the brutal murder of Carol Lightfoot on Sunday 7th April. Ms Delaney has not been seen since. Anyone having information. . .*(cont. page 2)*

Page two carried a picture of Simon Makinson, with speculation about his connection with Susan Delaney and the murder. It was standard Fleet Street fodder, but Cassie knew it was necessary to get the public involved after they had consistently drawn a blank. She also knew that the phones would be ringing all day with the usual selection of cranks and attention seekers, but amongst them may lie a clue that would take them to Suzi and Simon. A big part of her hoped that Suzi would heed her personal message and contact her. Cassie had deliberately used the diminutive of her own name to remind Suzi of their friendship and tempt her to call.

As Cassie spread some marmalade on her toast, Tanya came into the kitchen yawning and tying back her long curly hair with a scrunchy. 'You going to work, ma?'

'Yes. Sorry, love, but it's all hands to the pump, I'm afraid. I'll try not to make it a full day and perhaps we can go out to eat tonight, eh?'

'Mmm,' said Tanya, flicking over the newspaper. 'You involved in this?' she said, indicating the headline about Suzi.

'You know better than to ask, Tanny. If you need anything give me a call. I'll let you know when I'll be home later.' Cassie stood and planted a kiss on her daughter's head.

'Okay, ma. Take care.'

Cassie marvelled at how her children took her work in their stride. I'm so lucky that they're good kids, I don't know what I'd do if they threw tantrums or made a fuss. Cassie made a mental note to be back in time to take them out for dinner, come hell or high water.

In reception were two familiar faces. Cassie reflected that she must really be entrenched in the SIS if duty solicitors were becoming well known to her.

'Good morning, Ms Moorcroft, Mr Spruce, thank you for being so prompt. Could you both come into an interview room for a moment before you see your clients.' Cassie led the pair into the comfortable room used mainly for rape victims and children. When they were seated, Cassie said. 'I have to tell you that this is now a murder enquiry. James Tandy, the victim of the assault, has died from his injuries. Paul and Andy Trevellian don't know this yet, so I'll leave it to you to break the news, if you don't mind.'

Sylvia Moorcroft was the first to speak. 'Do you anticipate charging them both with murder?'

'Let's not get ahead of ourselves. I'm telling you this because it will affect your meeting with your clients today. Yesterday they were being held on suspicion of beating someone, today it's a different kettle of fish. Anyway, you'll want to see them now, no doubt. I'll let you know when we're ready to interview them.'

Peter was waiting for Cassie in the squad room. Maggie was updating the white board and Kevin was busy taking phone calls on the dedicated information line. He looked up and rolled his eyes as she entered, indicating his frustration with the public.

Peter beckoned Cassie towards his office. 'D'you want a coffee or anything?' he asked.

Cassie shook her head. 'I'd rather just get on, if that's alright.'

Peter took his seat. 'Just to let you know, Saroj is at the Trevellians' place with some uniforms carrying out the search warrant. I've primed them to look for a crowbar especially, but to make sure they gather the clothes that the brothers were wearing on Wednesday night.'

'There must be hundreds of places to hide a crowbar on a farm. Needle in a haystack time.'

Peter laughed. 'It's going to be a long job, that's for sure, but I'm determined, Cassie. I like these two for this. Snatched conversations about sorting their own problems, sanctioned by dad no doubt, so that's motive. Your brilliant deductions in the pub gives opportunity, and, if Erica saw what she did, namely the crowbar, we've got means.'

Cassie nodded. 'The holy trinity. I think Andy might crack, especially now it's a murder investigation. If I'm correct about the sequence of events in the pub, Paul is the one who did the deed and Andy may blame him for hitting James too hard. Let's see if we can divide and conquer.'

'I'd like to start with Paul, though, if that's all right with you.' Cassie had thought that Andy might be the one to start with and said so.

'I appreciate what you're saying, Cassie, but I'd like Andy to stew a bit longer. Really soften him up. And we can use what we get from Paul as leverage.'

Cassie could see the sense in this so agreed. 'Let's get to it, then,' she said.

Sylvia Moorcroft sat silently next to her client, Paul Trevellian. He too looked somber today, no doubt reflecting on what his solicitor had told him about the death of James Tandy.

Peter and Cassie took their places opposite. After the formalities of the introductions, Peter said, 'Paul Trevellian, I am now arresting you in connection with the *murder* of James Tandy, do you understand the difference from yesterday's caution?' Paul looked up sharply. 'It means, Paul, that this just got a whole lot more serious.'

Cassie took over, as Peter continued to hold Paul Trevellian's gaze. 'The last time we met you said that you did not wish to say anything without your solicitor present. You now have representation, so I'm asking you, where were you on Wednesday night between the hours of seven and eight-thirty?'

Paul glanced at his solicitor, who nodded slightly. 'I was at the pub, The Plough, with Andy. Loads of people seen me there. I was playin' pool with George and Billy.'

Cassie took out a photograph from her file. 'Do you recognise this man, Paul?' The image showed a very battered and bruised James Tandy, as he looked when admitted to A&E.

'I know him, but I didn't do that.' Paul sat back, his eyes darting around.

Peter took over. 'But you see, Paul, we think you did do that, and we are going to prove it, make no mistake.' Peter left the photograph on the table between them. Paul glanced nervously at it. Peter went on. 'You wanted to "sort out" James Tandy, didn't you, Paul? You believed he was responsible for the assault on your sister, Erica. Now, some people might find that totally understandable. Country folks like to deal with their own problems, don't they, Paul? You said as much when DI Wade visited your farm the day after Erica's assault.'

Paul looked up sharply at Cassie, who held his gaze. Peter carried on. 'You and Andy worked out a plan to do just that on Wednesday night.' Paul turned his gaze onto Peter. 'Not too difficult for twins, is it? Now you see me, now you don't.'

Cassie asked if Paul would write down the names of the men he claimed to have played pool with. He looked bemused. 'I told yer, George and Billy.' Sylvia Moorcroft also looked confused. Cassie carried on, pushing a blank sheet of paper towards Paul. She held out a pen. Paul shrugged and took the pen in his right hand, scrawling a couple of names onto the paper. 'Thank you, Paul,' said Cassie. 'I see you are right-handed.' Paul looked suddenly panicky.

Sylvia Moorcroft butted in. 'Detective Chief Inspector Sanders, do you have any evidence to support this speculation? My client has given you an account of his whereabouts on the night in question, and, as he said, there are a number of witnesses who can support that. I suggest you release him, unless you have evidence to suggest his alibi is false, before throwing accusations around.'

Peter took back the photograph and closed his file. 'We will be keeping your client for a little while longer. But for now, we'll draw this interview to a close. I suggest to you, Ms Moorcroft, that you have a serious talk to your client and explain to him the difference between a manslaughter and a murder charge. If he co-operates with us now and shows remorse it could make the difference between a couple of years or life imprisonment.'

Paul's eyes widened to saucers and he looked from his solicitor to Peter frantically. He was about to say something, when Ms Moorcroft laid a hand on his arm. 'We'll see you shortly then, detectives,' she said calmly.

Peter and Cassie left the interview room as a constable entered and led Paul away. Sylvia Moorcroft assuring him that they would talk again soon.

Peter and Cassie went back to Peter's office. 'How do you think that went, Cassie?' Peter said, pouring them both a coffee from his newly purchased machine.

Cassie sipped the aromatic brew. 'Nice coffee. I think we've rattled his cage, and I suspect Andy will be easier to crack. It would be good to know how Saroj is getting on at the farm.'

Peter nodded and keyed Saroj's number into his phone. His DS answered immediately. 'How's it going, Saroj?' he said, without preamble.

We've finished in the house and the outbuildings, sir. Nothing, I'm afraid, except that Mr Trevellian admitted to buying a new crowbar in the last day or so. No explanation except, 'It's always handy to have a spare,' although he couldn't say what had happened to the original. We're just checking the hedges and there's a duck pond which may be worth a look. We've bagged some clothes out of the washing machine, along with Paul's leather jacket. They've been sent to forensics.'

'Okay, Saroj, good work so far, keep on it. Let me know as soon as you turn anything interesting up.'

Peter finished the call and filled Cassie in on the details. 'That's a real pity,' he said.

'The leather jacket won't have been washed, though, so maybe we'll get something off that. By all accounts it was Paul's favourite and I can't see him letting Andy wear it normally. If Andy's DNA is on it we have another link to our hypothesis.' Cassie was feeling buoyant. 'Let's see what Andy has to say for himself, shall we? I'm convinced we'll be charging them by the end of the day.'

'We'd better be, Cassie. We can't hold them without charge for much longer.'

Andy Trevellian looked like he had been crying, his eyes red and his shoulders slumped. Daniel Spruce, his solicitor, was leaning back comfortably in his seat. 'Good morning, detectives,' he said cheerfully. 'We meet again.'

Peter was struck by the difference in the attitudes of the two duty solicitors. Daniel Spruce was older, of course, by quite a few years, but his demeanour suggested he'd seen it all, and that he had little empathy for his client, whoever that happened to be on the day. Sylvia Moorcroft, however, showed a keen interest in her clients. She was clever and determined, qualities that Peter thought he would like to have on his side if ever he was in this position.

Peter nodded gravely at Spruce. 'You've spoken with your client and he understands the situation?'

'Absolutely. I expect we can clear this matter up quite quickly.'

'We'll see about that,' Peter said, as he settled himself at the table. 'This is a grave matter, Mr Spruce, and I do hope your client is fully cognisant of that.'

Andy was watching the exchange nervously, his leg jiggling wildly under the table.

Cassie smiled at Andy. 'Yesterday you told me that you and Paul were in The Plough all evening on Wednesday, that neither of you left at any time until you went home at around eleven o'clock. Is that what you are still saying?'

Andy glanced at his solicitor who was idly examining his fingernails. 'What d'yer mean? I said we were there, and we were.'

Peter then opened his file and placed the photograph of James Tandy in front of Andy. 'Do you know this man?'

111

Again, Andy looked to his solicitor who said nothing. 'I know him. Haven't seen him in ages, though.'

Peter nodded thoughtfully. 'I'm inclined to believe you, Andy,' he said, sitting back.

Mr Spruce looked up sharply. 'Does this mean you are letting my client go, detective?'

'It means nothing of the sort, Mr Spruce.' Then turning to Andy he said, 'I am prepared to believe that you have had no direct contact with Mr Tandy recently. However, that's a long way from saying you had no part in his murder.' Peter waited for this message to hit home. Then he said, 'We know about your little scam on Wednesday night. Identical twins thinking they can fool everyone into believing they are both in the one place when, actually, only one of them was.'

Andy looked around the room as if to find an escape route. He was tensed up and on his toes like he was getting ready to run. His solicitor came to life suddenly and laid his hand on Andy's arm. 'Calm down, Andy,' he said. 'They're just fishing.'

'Is Paul a good pool player, would you say?' Peter said, as Andy sat back into his chair.

'How d'yer mean?'

'Does he play well? Does he win matches?'

'He plays well enough.'

'Is he ambidextrous?'

Andy gave a hollow laugh. 'Like with both hands? Nah, he's useless with his. . . You tryin' to trick me? What's this all about?' Andy looked nervous again.

'We have witnesses who say that someone claiming to be Paul not only played left-handed that night, but that he won the game. What would you say to that, Andy?'

Daniel Spruce whispered something in Andy's ear. Andy said, 'No comment. I'd like a break now.' Peter agreed, collecting his papers and leaving the room with Cassie following.

Peter and Cassie returned to the squad room to find Kevin and Maggie talking excitedly. They both looked up. 'Ma'am,' said Kevin. 'We've had a promising sighting of Simon Makinson's car. It's parked by a caravan at Praa Sands.'

At the same time, Peter was taking a call from Saroj. Cassie was about to respond to Kevin's news when Peter shouted, 'They've found it, Cassie. The crowbar. It was in the duck pond.'

'You should have seen the search team, sir,' said Saroj down the phone. 'Filthy places duck ponds. About a foot of slime and mud at the bottom with old duck eggs embedded in it. Have you ever smelled a rotten duck egg? It's that Hydrogen Sulphide smell, rotten eggs? Only worse than you could imagine. Even though they were in protective gear, the stench that came off them...'

Peter laughed at the image. 'At least we've found what we were looking for. Now we just have to hope that it is the murder weapon and it still has some trace evidence on it.'

'I'll let you know as soon as we get word back from forensics.' Saroj said, and ended the call.

Cassie was anxious to follow up on the information Kevin had just given her about the sighting of Simon Makinson's car. 'Can I have a word, Peter?' she asked.

But before she could speak further, he said, 'I want you to finish these interviews, Cassie.' She started to protest, but Peter held his hand up to stop her. 'I'll follow up the lead on Simon Makinson's car. I know it's not what you want to hear but, if forensics find the evidence we want, you will be able to charge the brothers today.' Cassie looked crestfallen. 'It's your case, Cassie. You've done great work on it. Be in at the finish, it's important.'

Cassie knew when she was defeated. 'You're right, sir. But let me know if you turn anything up, won't you?'

'I promise, Cassie.'

Chapter Thirteen

Saroj joined Peter and the Makinsons on the steps of the police station to make a further appeal to Simon Makinson to come forward. Peter said to the assembled TV and newspaper reporters, 'We have found Simon Makinson's car at Praa Sands, but no sign of him on the holiday caravan site there. Although a man matching his description might have been seen earlier in the week at the campsite shop. I want to stress to Simon that he is not in any trouble as far as we know, but we do believe that he may be able to help with our enquiries into the murder of Carol Lightfoot.' Peter looked over to where Mr and Mrs Makinson were standing nervously, and introduced them.

Mr Makinson stepped forward to the microphone and looked out over the dozen or so reporters in front of him. Peter had told him to look directly into the TV camera when he spoke, so that, if Simon was watching, he would feel more connected to his parents. He coughed slightly and began, reading occasionally from his notes.

'Simon, I hope you are watching this. Your mum and I are very worried about you,' he turned his head towards his wife, who nodded, the tension apparent in her face. 'You don't even have to tell us where you are if you don't want to, but please phone us. You must know that we will help in any way we can. If you're bothered about anything, anything at all, I'm sure we can fix it. Claire is also worried that you have not been in touch. She misses you and wants desperately to know you're okay, as do we.' He folded the paper and put it back in his pocket before addressing the TV camera again. 'That's all I've got to say. We love you son, so please come home.' At this point his voice broke and he turned to his wife, who hugged him strongly.

Peter finished the conference by again appealing to Susan Delaney to make contact, telling the reporters that there had been no sightings of her. He declined to answer any questions but said he would be putting out a press statement later in the week.

Mr and Mrs Makinson left to return to their hotel, and Peter opened the door for Saroj to return with him to the squad room. However, Saroj had spotted a familiar face in the crowd. The man lingered after the reporters had packed up and he waved tentatively towards Saroj.

After telling Peter she would join him shortly, Saroj walked down the steps to greet her brother.

When brother and sister were sat facing each other in Costa, Sanjeed smiled at his sister. 'You look well, Saroj. How long has it been? Six, seven years?'

'Eight,' said Saroj. 'You look older, Sanjeed.'

He laughed. 'Never one to give a compliment, sister.'

'I tell it like it is, Sanjeed.'

'You are harder, though, I can hear it in your voice.'

'If you mean I don't defer to you like I used to, then you'd be right.' She sipped her coffee. 'Why are you here, Sanjeed?'

He bent forward over the table. 'Our father is ill. He is in the hospital and wants to see you.'

'What is the matter with him?'

'He has cancer… er, in his male parts.'

'Testicular or prostate?'

Sanjeed gave a hollow laugh. 'You're very direct.'

'I have a medical degree, so why would I use terms like 'male parts'?'

'They were always disappointed, mum and dad, that you didn't make more of yourself. Become a doctor.'

'They were more than disappointed, Sanjeed, they tried to smuggle me to India to marry an old man.' Saroj felt the old anger return. 'Well? The cancer?'

'Testicular,' whispered Sanjeed. 'He may not have long to live.'

'Then I will visit him. Give me the details.'

'We could go now,' he said hopefully.

'I am busy now. We have two murder investigations on the go, so I will have to see when I can make it.' She looked at her brother, his face showing disappointment and confusion. It must be a shock to him that a female would not simply comply with his wishes. 'Thank you for letting me know, Sanjeed. I promise to visit dad as soon as I can. Now I really must get back.'

As she watched Sanjeed disappear into the distance, Saroj stood thinking about what he had said. She had been determined not to accede to his demand that she go straight away to see their father, mostly to establish the fact that she was now her own woman, not to be ordered about by men. However, it may be the last chance she had to see her dad if he was as gravely ill as Sanjeed had hinted. Making her mind up, she went into the reception and asked the duty sergeant to notify DCI Sanders that she was taking a couple of hours personal time, and set off for the hospital.

The cancer ward was like an oasis of calm. Saroj had marvelled at this when she did her medical training. Perhaps it was the fact that the patients were resigned to their fate and demanded less urgent attention. No matter what the reason, the hushed calm atmosphere was welcome, giving the impression to visitors that all was well with their relatives. Saroj spotted her father at the far end of the ward. He looked just the same as the day she left except for the grey in his long beard. Checking in with the nurses Saroj asked how Mr Kapoor was today. 'Peaceful,' was the reply.

'Hello, papa,' Saroj said to the figure dozing in the bed. He looked up sharply.

'Saroj? Is that you?' His voice trembled a little.

'It's me, papa. How are you feeling?'

'Get a chair daughter, sit with me.' Saroj pulled up a chair.

'You look well, daughter. Tell me about yourself. Are you married? Children?'

'Papa, I'm here to see how you are,' she said, shaking her head. 'But no, I'm not married.'

'A woman should be married,' he said, some of the old strident

116

tone returning to his voice. 'You are handsome enough, why would someone not want to marry you?'

'Ha!' Exclaimed Saroj. 'Papa, I have never met anyone I want to marry. I am happy with my independence and my career.'

Mr Kapoor shook his head sadly. 'I'll never understand you, my daughter. But no matter, perhaps all to the good actually.'

Saroj looked quizzically at her father. 'How do you mean, all to the good?'

'I do not have long to live, Saroj. My Mina is not a well woman, she will need care when I have gone.'

'You can't mean for me to look after mama,' said Saroj incredulously, 'after all this time? And this is why you wanted to see me?'

'Sadly, you have not been a very dutiful daughter, Saroj, but now you must be. Your mother is in need of someone to care for her and you are her daughter. A good Muslim daughter would want to do this.'

'It may come as a shock to you, papa, but I am not a Muslim anymore. And I am far too busy to be a housemaid for anyone. You are not short of money; get someone in. Get Sanjeed's wife to do it, anyone but me.'

The old man shook his head angrily. 'Pha! You are a cold-hearted woman, and no daughter of mine. You reject your family and your faith, and for what? To be a policewoman? Not even got the gumption to be a doctor.' He waved his hand dismissively. 'Go! Get out of my sight.'

Saroj stood and gazed down at her father. 'I hope you have a peaceful end, papa. I won't be seeing you again. Goodbye.' The old man closed his eyes as Saroj walked away.

Chapter Fourteen

Cassie was not pleased. 'Where's Saroj?' she asked to no one in particular. Maggie, Kevin and Robbie gave a collective shrug. Knocking and entering Peter's office, she asked the same question. 'No idea, Cassie. She was with me at the press conference, but I've not seen her since. Have you tried phoning her?'

Cassie gave Peter a look. 'Of course I have, but her phone's off.'

'Can't help you then. Is it important?'

'I hoped she might join me interviewing the Trevellian twins. I've had word that blood has definitely been found on the crowbar and it's the same group as Tandy's, but it'll take a while to be DNA matched. They've found fingerprints, too, despite the bar being given a somewhat cursory wipe with what seems to be an oily rag. I've asked for the oil to be analysed. We might be able to match it to something at the Trevellians' farm.'

'Good thinking, Cassie. When will you get to know about the fingerprints?'

'Any time soon, but I want to start on the interviews. Saroj led the search on the property so she would be the best one to put any questions to them arising from that.' Cassie looked at her watch for the umpteenth time. 'Could you step in if she doesn't appear, sir?'

'Try her phone again. If she doesn't answer I'll join you in the interview room, but, if I get any word about Susan Delaney or Simon Makinson, I may have to duck out.'

Cassie tried Saroj's number and this time it was picked up. 'Where the hell have you been?' she shouted.

118

'Very sorry, ma'am. I got word that my dad was in hospital and he'd asked to see me. It took me longer than I thought. I'm not far away. Didn't you get my message?'

'No, Saroj, there's been no message. I'm sorry about your dad. Do you need time off?'

'Oh no, ma'am. I'll be with you in ten minutes. I'm annoyed that the duty sergeant didn't pass on my message, I'll have a word with him when I get back.'

Cassie cancelled the call. 'I thought Saroj was estranged from her family,' she said.

Peter looked up. 'Something wrong?'

'Her dad's ill, in hospital she said. She's been to see him.'

'Perhaps it'll break the ice. It's been several years since she's had contact. Is she okay to interview, do you think?'

'Says she doesn't want time off, so I presume so. I think the solicitors have been with their clients long enough anyway, so I'll get ready for when she arrives.'

Saroj was her usual professional self when she and Cassie faced Andy Trevellian and Daniel Spruce across the table. After setting up the recorder and making introductions, Cassie addressed Andy.

'We found the crowbar,' she said simply.

Andy looked at his solicitor for guidance but received none.

'In the duck pond. Did you think we wouldn't look there?' Saroj said. 'It was a bit messy alright, but the attempts you made to wipe it weren't good enough.' Saroj took a photograph of James Tandy's head injury out and slid it over to Andy. She pointed with her pen. 'You see here?' Andy turned away. 'Look at it, Andy.' He reluctantly looked. 'Our forensic people just love this sort of injury. A very clear indent which matches exactly the part of your crowbar with the blood on it. James Tandy's blood.'

Now that he had looked at the image, Andy couldn't pull his eyes away. 'Is that what he died from?' He said quietly.

Cassie answered. 'The blow caused a massive sub-dural haematoma. That's a bleed to the brain. The pressure from that bleed caused irreversible brain damage. And, yes, death eventually. He never regained consciousness.'

Andy looked like he was about to say something when his

solicitor spoke up. 'That's very sad indeed, detective, but I hope you've got more than a crowbar with blood on it before you accuse my client. Anyone could own a crowbar like that and fling it over a hedge into a duck pond.'

Cassie ignored the comments, but was irritated by the solicitor's interruption. She was sure Andy was about to say something incriminating. 'Andy, we have found fingerprints on the crowbar which are, as we speak, being compared with the one's you gave earlier.'

'You forget, detective inspector, that my client has a twin, an identical twin.'

Cassie raised her eyebrows and smiled slowly. 'As you don't seem to know, I'll let you into a secret about identical twins. Almost everything about them *is* identical, but not their fingerprints. They are unique to the individual.'

Andy looked sharply at his solicitor, who looked down at his notebook. 'So I... Andy stammered.

'So you what? Couldn't be blamed by your brother?'

'Now you're putting words into my client's mouth.' Daniel looked at the two detectives. 'Would this be a good time to stop? I would like to consult with my client.'

Cassie agreed and ended the session. Andy Trevellian and Mr Spruce were escorted out by the constable to another room. 'Offer them some tea, would you?' Cassie shouted after him.

When they arrived back in the office, Cassie asked Saroj to check up the forensics. 'I'll simply have to go to the loo,' she said as she rushed from the room. Maggie was in the ladies-room when Cassie rushed into a cubicle. 'Excuse me talking to you this way, ma'am,' said Maggie, 'but I thought you'd like to know straight away, we've had some forensic results back. The fingerprints on the crowbar from the Trevellians' farm are a match for Paul Trevellian, and they have James Tandy's blood on them so there can be no mistake. He's the assailant.'

'You beauty!' Cassie shouted, her words echoing around the room.

Maggie laughed at the slightly comic situation. 'Only too glad to help, ma'am.'

* * * *

Paul Trevellian was looking a little less cocky today. His shoulders were slumped, and he looked nervously at the detectives as they entered. Sylvia Moorcroft was the first to speak. 'Before we begin, DI Wade, do you have anything new to put to my client or are we going to rehash the speculation we endured earlier?'

Cassie chose to ignore the solicitor and prepared the recorder for the interview. When the four had introduced themselves, she turned to Sylvia Moorcroft. 'To answer your question, Ms Moorcroft, we now have irrefutable evidence that your client dealt the blow that caused James Tandy's head injury.'

Paul looked up suddenly. 'You've got nuthen!' he shouted. 'Because I didn't do it. You're just, you know, speculating, like she said,' nodding towards his solicitor.

Saroj opened her file and took out two photographs of the crowbar. One a full shot and the other a close up of the bloodied end. She passed them over the table. 'Do you recognise this implement, Paul?'

'It's a crowbar, so what?'

'It's more than that. It's *your* crowbar and it has James Tandy's blood on it.'

Paul leant over to Sylvia and she whispered something to him. He nodded and carried on. 'Even if it was my crowbar, and I'm not saying it is, someone must have stolen it from the farm. I had noticed ours had gone missing as it 'appens, and dad bought a new one.'

Paul looked smug, thinking he had scored a point against the detectives.

Saroj continued by placing a further photograph in front of Paul. 'Have a close look, Paul. Do you see those fingerprints? The ones on the surface of the blood? They are a match for yours. How do you suppose that happened?'

Sylvia touched her client's arm and whispered to him.

'No comment,' said Paul.

Saroj took another photograph out of her file and placed it on top of the others. 'This is a close up of a hair found on James Tandy's body. It looks a lot like one of yours, don't you think? Long and sandy-coloured.'

'Lots of people have hair like that,' Paul scoffed, 'doesn't mean it's mine.'

'We will have the DNA analysis of that hair back soon. What do you think that will tell us?'

Paul shook his head. 'No comment,' he said.

Sylvia Moorcroft made the same observation as Daniel Spruce had made in Andy's interview. 'My client is an identical twin, detective. If there is a match it could be either one of them.'

This time, the solicitor had made a valid point, but Cassie wasn't going to allow her a victory. 'The evidence is stacking up, Paul. Your fingerprints – and they are yours. You and your brother may share identical DNA, but not fingerprints; your probable absence from the pub at the time James Tandy was attacked; you being overheard to say you would sort out Tandy for the attack on your sister. In fact, the only thing we don't know at the moment is how you lured James Tandy into the alley by the cinema in Redruth. So why don't you tell us about that, Paul?'

'No comment.'

'I'd like some time with my client, DI Wade. But you will have to charge him or let him go in a few hours, as we both know.'

Cassie packed up the photographs and closed her file. 'And that charge may be murder, Ms Moorcroft. Please give your client time to think about that. We'll see you again in an hour.' And with that, Cassie turned off the recorder and she and Saroj left the room.

Kevin had helpfully gone out for sandwiches which were very welcome. As Saroj and Cassie sat at Cassie's desk they ate hungrily and thought about the interviews. 'So how did Paul get Tandy to meet him?' Cassie said, her mouth half full of ham and tomato.

'Tandy would have no reason to trust Paul enough to meet him alone. In fact, he was probably expecting some kind of retaliation so would have avoided the brothers all together.'

'So who would he have trusted?'

Saroj stood and walked over to the coffee machine. Pouring two large mugs she speculated, 'What about Erica? She might have said she wanted to meet him. We know she didn't blame him entirely for the rape, so he would have been inclined to believe she was genuine.'

'But why would Erica do that knowing what her brother's intentions might be?'

'It's easy enough to check her phone. It's a long shot but worth a try.'

Chapter Fifteen

Saroj arrived at the Trevellians' farm on the Monday morning to find no one but the old lady, who was asleep in the chair by the range. Knocking again on the door to rouse the woman, Saroj shouted, 'Mrs Trevellian! It's DS Kapoor.'

The old lady looked up blearily. 'Who's that, yer say? Saul's out down fields wi' sheep.'

'I was looking for Erica, Mrs Trevellian. Is she about?'

'Erica? She'll be at school or down at that interferrin' busybody's.'

'Do you mean her other grandma?'

'Aye. Spends more time there than her ought. Should be 'ere, seein' to us.'

'Thank you, Mrs Trevellian, I'll see if I can find her there.'

'Tell 'er to come 'ome if her's there!' The old lady shouted after Saroj.

Not likely, thought Saroj, further away from here the better.

Mrs Trevose's house was a deal more cheery than the farm. The smell of freshly baked scones met Saroj as the door was opened by a smiling old lady in an apron. 'Mrs Trevose? It's DS Kapoor.' Saroj held out her warrant card. 'I'm looking for Erica, is she here?'

'Come in, sweet'art. Erica should be home any time.'

Saroj was surprised to realise that it was nearly four o'clock. 'Thank you, I will wait if that's all right.'

'Some tea, me dear? And there's some scones if you've a mind.'

'That would be lovely, Mrs Trevose.'

123

'Call me Annie, sweet'art', they all do.'

As Annie went into the kitchen to make the tea, Saroj looked around the pretty sitting room. There were wildflowers in a jar on the table, which was free from clutter unlike her son-in-law's place. A smell of lavender, partly from the flowers and partly from furniture polish, pervaded the room, competing with the scones for dominance. All together cosy and cared for. A small bookcase held a range of detective novels. Saroj recognised Peter Robinson, Lynda La Plante and Val McDermid amongst others. On top of the bookcase were framed photographs which drew Saroj's attention. She picked up one of a young woman, smiling as she held the head of a large shire horse.

'That's Angela, Erica's ma.' said Annie, as she came back with the tea tray. 'Saddest thing in me life that. When she went.'

Saroj put the picture down. 'Do you not hear from her, then?'

'Don't know if her's alive or dead, sweet'art. Just upped and left one day without tellin' a soul. It wer 'is fault though, I'm sure of that.'

'Mr Trevellian?'

'Aye. 'e's a cruel one that. Knocked 'er about you see. I think she'd had enough. Hard on Erica, though.'

'What's hard on Erica?' a voice called from the doorway.

'Nuthen', love. You 'ad a good day?'

Erica noticed Saroj. 'Oh, hello,' she said, dropping her backpack to the floor and taking off her coat.

'There's tea and scones,' said Annie. 'Get yerself a mug and plate.'

'Lovely, gran. I'm starvin'.'

'She's a different maid when she's 'ere,' said Annie to Saroj. 'Away from them menfolk and that sour faced nan of 'ers.'

'What about school, Annie? Is she managing to get there more often?' Saroj hoped that the girl was attending regularly and not being drawn into looking after the family. A poignant thought considering her own situation with her dad.

'When her's 'ere she is. Bin stayin' wi me since them lads were arrested. An' all the better fer it.'

Erica came back in. Saroj noticed that she was neat and clean and quite a pretty girl with her long hair shining as it caught the light. 'I just wanted to ask you something, Erica,' said Saroj.

Erica nodded as she poured some tea. 'Could I have a look at your phone?' asked Saroj.

'My phone? Why?'

'It's just part of our enquiry. Do you mind?'

Erica took the phone out of her pocket. 'I've only just found it again. Dad went mad when I lost it, said he wasn't gonna buy me another. But then it turned up at the back of a drawer.' Erica rolled her eyes and shook her head. 'No idea how it got there. Must have put it there sometime. Daft.'

Erica handed Saroj the phone. 'Could you key in the PIN, Erica,' said Saroj handing it back. Erica quickly pressed some keys and returned the phone to Saroj, who deftly found the text history. 'You seem to have wiped all your texts,' she said, looking up at Erica.

'I know,' said the girl incredulously, 'they were just gone. Don't know how that happened.'

'Was this while your phone was lost?'

'Yeah, when I found it they was just gone, like I said.'

'Do you mind if I take it away? I'll bring it back quickly. I'd like one of my colleagues to look at it.'

'Yeah, that's alright.' Erica looked thoughtful. 'Is it to do with Paul and Andy?'

'I'm sorry, I can't say anything about that. It would just be helpful in our enquiries.'

Erica shrugged, and continued to help herself to a scone, piling jam and cream onto the cut surface.

'Jam first?' said Saroj, smiling.

'Always jam first, miss. It's the Cornish way.'

'You're good with phones, Robbie,' said Saroj walking into the squad room to find Robbie and Maggie eating doughnuts. Robbie held out the box. 'Want one, ma'am?'

'No thanks, Robbie,' she replied patting her stomach. 'I've just had the best Cornish cream tea ever, and I've got Erica Trevellian's phone. Do you think you can retrieve the deleted texts? If I send it to the tech department, it'll be away ages.'

Robbie held out his hand. 'I'll give it a try,' then mischievously, 'if you tell me where you got the cream tea?'

Saroj patted the side of her nose. 'Some secrets are not for sharing, Robbie.'

Very quickly, Robbie pulled up some texts. 'Not securely deleted, ma'am, easy to retrieve, actually.' He passed the phone back to Saroj.

'Well, well, that's interesting. Looks like we've hit the nail on the head, Robbie. Thanks for that.'

'No problem at all, ma'am. Helpful in the Trevellian case?'

'Very helpful, Robbie. You seen DI Wade?'

'She's with the Chief, ma'am.'

Cassie and Peter bent and looked into the screen of the phone that Saroj handed to them.

I want to be friends again. I don't blame you for anything that happened. Meet me on Wednesday at 7.30 in the alley by the cinema in Redruth. E x

'It was sent to James Tandy's phone, sir, but Erica didn't write that,' said Cassie. It's the missing piece, Peter.'

'Just to be certain,' he replied, 'get Erica to confirm that she didn't write it, will you, Saroj. And let her know that we'll have to keep her phone for the time being.'

'I'll do that now, sir. She's going to know what it means for her brothers, though. It might not be easy for her.'

'I understand that, Saroj, but I know you can convince her to do what's right.'

Saroj found Erica crying when she stepped into the cottage behind Annie. Mr Trevellian was standing with his back to the fire grate, arms folded across his chest. 'An' 'ow am I supposed to manage on me own?' he shouted at Erica. 'Eh? Tell me that.' He glanced up at Saroj but didn't stop his tirade. 'You're part of a farmin' family, and that means responsibility, girl. Wi' the boys away, I'm gonna need you more than ever.'

Annie Trevose puffed herself up. 'Now you listen 'ere, Saul Trevellian, that maid's needin' an education. She's too young to take Angela's place an' you know it.'

Saul bridled at the mention of his estranged wife's name. 'You know nuthen about it, old woman, so keep that out.' He pointed to his nose.

126

Saroj thought she'd better intervene before things got more heated, and, in any case, she wanted to prevent Erica going back to the life of a drudge if she could. 'Mr Trevellian,' she said calmly. 'As you are aware, the multi-agency meeting held about your daughter concluded that she must attend school regularly, she's already behind her classmates and needs time to catch up.'

Saul sneered at Saroj. 'An' what would you an' them do-gooders know about anythin'? She's my girl and she'll do as she's told by me, not you, or folks like you, an' there's nuthen you can do about it.'

'I wouldn't be so sure about that, Mr Trevellian,' said Saroj, desperately trying to remain cool headed. 'You have a legal responsibility to send your child to school or to provide equal and varied lessons for her at home. Can you do that?'

'All she needs to know is runnin' a household an' tendin' to hens and such. An' helpin' wi' lambin' when it's time.'

'I'm afraid that is not what the education department requires, Mr Trevellian. Erica needs access to the whole curriculum. Until you can demonstrate that she will receive that at home, she has to attend school.'

'An' if she doesn't? What's thee gonna do about it?' Saul looked aggressively into Saroj's eyes.

Undeterred, Saroj continued. 'There are legal avenues we can go down. For one, Erica could be made a Ward of Court, and the court would effectively become her parent. But I hope it won't come to that. Now, it might be helpful if you went away and thought about what I've said. But I'm warning you, if any harm comes to this child, I'll make sure the full weight of the law is brought to bear. Do you understand?'

Saul Trevellian slammed his hand on the table with such power that the jug of flowers jumped and toppled over. He looked at Erica who was cowering in her chair. 'This ain't over, girl,' he said menacingly, and stormed out of the door.

Annie Trevose rushed to Erica and cradled the girl in her arms. 'There, there my lovely, 'e's gone, an' this lady will make sure he can't bother you, that's right, isn' it, miss?'

Saroj smiled at the old woman. 'I think we need some tea, don't you?'

Annie scuttled off to the kitchen, glad to have something to do,

127

and Saroj pulled up a chair to sit by Erica. 'Thanks for sticking up for me, miss.' Erica said, wiping her eyes. 'He gets like that sometimes, shoutin' and that, but 'e's never hit me.'

'Let's just take things one step at a time, Erica, shall we. He'll probably calm down and see that what I've said is true. But, at the end of the day, he's not your responsibility, you know that, don't you? You have a responsibility to yourself.'

'How d'you mean?' asked Erica.

'To do what you want to do in life, sometimes you have to make a break with those who would stop you. Do you know what I'm saying?'

'I think so. I want to go to school and dad's trying to stop me. Is that it?'

'That's a big part of it, yes. But we'll see what happens. For the moment do you want to stay here with your gran?' Erica nodded. 'Well do that for as long as you can. If your dad tries to make you go home against your wishes, you can call me or the school, okay?'

Erica seemed to be brighter when Annie came back into the room with the tea. 'Now then, that's better. Dry yer eyes and have a cuppa. The cup that cheers, eh?'

Erica accepted the tea with a warm smile at her grandma. Turning to Saroj, she said, 'What did you want to see me about? Have you brought my phone back?'

Saroj took Erica's phone out of her pocket. 'There's something I'd like you to look at.' Switching the phone on, Saroj scrolled to the text and showed it to Erica.

I want to be friends again. I don't blame you for anything that happened. Meet me on Wednesday at 7.30 in the alley by the cinema in Redruth. E x

'Did you write that?'

Erica's eyes widened and she looked up at Saroj, puzzled. 'No, I didn't write that.' She paused as she took in the full implications, then cautiously asked, 'do you know who did?'

'I'm sorry, I can't discuss that with you, Erica. But do you have any thoughts about who it might be?'

Erica looked at her grandmother, tears springing again to her eyes. 'Gran, did James say he was meeting anyone on Wednesday night?'

'He only said he had to go out for a bit. He dressed up, mind, right smart he looked.'

'What time was this, Annie?' asked Saroj.

Oh, let me think. Be about a quarter afore seven. Spotlight was still on and that's six-thirty to seven. So about then, I think.'

Erica cried for real now, sobbing into a tissue. Annie was by her side in a flash. 'There, there lovely, don't take on.'

'But don't you see, gran?' Erica said between sobs, 'somebody pretending to be me got James into that alley so they could beat him up, and now he's dead!' Her whole frame shook as she gave way fully to her grief.

Chapter Sixteen

Monday 22nd

Cassie was tidying her desk, which had become messy with notes and jotted down phone numbers, when her phone rang. 'Now, gorgeous, when are you going to let me take you out again?'

'Mark!' she said delighted that he had rung. 'I'm in the office at the moment, just let me take this outside.' As she manoeuvred her way to the door, Maggie and Kevin gave each other a knowing look.

'That's better,' Cassie said, as she leaned against the stairwell bannister. 'How's my favourite man?'

'Dying to see you, that's how. Please tell me you're available this weekend.'

'It's only Monday, Mark, so at the moment I don't know. I'm dying to see you too, but with two murder cases on the go... well, you know how it is.'

'Okay, I do understand, really, but let's be hopeful and pencil something in. I could be with you by five-ish on Friday and take you and the kids out for dinner. I really want to meet them, Cass. Have you told them about me yet?'

'Not really had time yet, Mark, but I intend to as soon as I get a minute to sit down with them. They'll be fine about it, though. Always pestering me to get a life, you know, so I think they'll welcome the news. It's you I'm concerned about. Who wants to be grilled by a pair of cheeky teenagers?'

'Don't worry about me, just work your little socks off and be free on Friday, then we'll see where we are. Okay?'

'Okay, you've got a deal. And I'm so glad you rang, I have something to look forward to now.'

As Mark continued to whisper endearments, Cassie glanced up the stairs to see Saroj waving to her.

'Have to go, Mark. See you Friday... Yeah, me too.'

'We're good to go with the text message, ma'am,' said Saroj, noticing the silly smile on her boss's face. 'Erica has confirmed that she didn't send it, and knew what that meant. That girl's got so much pressure on her at the moment, what with James's death, her brothers arrested and her dad trying to force her home to look after him. Thank goodness she's got her grandma.'

'All the same, Saroj, we need to keep an eye on her. I'll get Robbie to call his contacts on the multi-agency panel and mobilise some support, and a heavy hand if necessary. It's not strictly our department but I don't want to see this girl go under.'

Andy Trevellian looked forlornly at his solicitor. Daniel Spruce was in full flow. 'In situations such as these, Andrew, my strong advice is to think about yourself. Loyalty is fine, but when it means you putting yourself in harm's way, namely a prison sentence, well you just have to be sensible.' Andy looked at his feet and sighed. Daniel carried on. 'I'm sure that your brother wouldn't want you to sacrifice yourself for him.' He paused. 'It's certain that Paul is going to get a prison sentence, maybe a very long one, you could be more help staying free. What about your dad and the farm? He'll need help if he's going to carry on – think about that.'

Andy only heard, Paul is going to prison for a long time, the rest of what his solicitor was saying was just so much white noise.

Daniel continued, trying to get through to this young man who seemed set to throw his life away for his brother. Twins or not, this was a disastrous course of action. 'You told me that the scam was Paul's idea?' Andy nodded. 'And that you thought it would be a laugh to fool everyone like that?' Andy simply stared at Daniel. 'You also said that you didn't know that Paul was taking the crowbar. You thought he was simply going to rough him up a bit, is that right?'

The photograph of James Tandy's head injury flashed before Andy's eyes. Why did Paul have to do that? he thought, and the kicks to his balls, that was unnecessary. What he said to his solicitor was, 'Can we wait and see what happens to Paul? I'll think about what to say then.'

'We can't really control that, Andy. DI Wade will probably interview you first and, depending on what you say, she'll charge Paul as she sees fit. I suggest that you make a statement now and get it over with. You'll almost certainly get bail, and then you can go and help your dad. I'm sure he doesn't want both his sons in prison. What do you say?'

Sylvia Moorcroft was also having a stern word with her client. 'They have all the evidence they need to charge you with murder, Paul. I may be able to commute that to manslaughter at some point, but that will be up to the CPS. What you do and say now will have an effect on that, do you understand?'

'What does that mean exactly? A confession?'

'A statement, along with an expression of remorse. You will say that you had no intention of causing such harm as was inflicted. You simply wanted him to be hurt the way he hurt your sister.' Sylvia paused to let her words sink in. 'Of course, there is the issue of the crowbar, why you took it with you. What would you say to that?'

'I took it to threaten 'im. But he tried to run off, so I swiped out.'

'That's logical, if a little tenuous. What about the kicks to his genitals?'

'So he couldn't do it to anyone else, what he did to Erica. He's an animal.'

'A jury might go for the 'avenging your sister' defence. Play that part up, play down the construction of the plan involving your brother. That could have occurred to you at the last minute, before you left for Redruth. By the way, how did you know that Tandy would be where he was?'

As Daniel Spruce predicted, Andy was the first to be interviewed that day. Cassie and Saroj were confident that they would be charging the brothers by the end of the morning. After the formal

132

openings, Daniel Spruce said, 'My client would like to make a statement.' This was music to Cassie's ears as she knew she would get to the truth now, at least Andy's version of the truth.

'Go ahead, Andy,' she said.

Andy took a deep breath. 'We all knew, that's dad, Paul and me, that James Tandy had raped my sister Erica, she's only fourteen.' He let that fact sink in. 'Dad said he shouldn't get away with it and that the police would do nothing.' He paused and looked at his solicitor, who nodded encouragingly. 'Paul said we should sort it. Rough him up a bit, see how he liked it.'

'So you are saying it was Paul's idea to rough James up?'

'Yeah, but I agreed he needed a lesson.' Daniel Spruce frowned.

'What happened next, Andy?'

'Paul worked out this plan so he could get Tandy on his own and do 'im.'

'By, do him, what exactly did he mean?'

Daniel Spruce chipped in. 'I think that's a question to put to Paul Trevellian, detective.'

Cassie nodded acceptance of the point. 'Tell me about the plan, Andy.'

'Paul said I should stay in the pub and pretend to be him. We've got away with stuff like that before. I should wear his leather jacket and play pool with Billy and George like he usually does. Then put my own jacket back on and watch the darts for a bit. It was crowded so it worked well.' Andy smiled at the thought. 'It was a bit of fun, we fooled them all.'

'Not quite all, Andy. You see, you played pool left-handed, whereas Paul is right-handed, George was suspicious of that.'

'Aye, we never thought of that.'

'Then what happened?'

'Paul came back, and dad came into the pub for the last hour. That couldn't 'ave been better, him bein' there to see us both. Paul was really wired at how we'd got away with it. He said that Tandy wouldn't be messin' with little girls anymore.'

'He said exactly that? That James Tandy wouldn't be messing with little girls anymore?'

'Aye, more or less. Then we had a couple of pints and went home.'

'What about the crowbar, Andy? How did that feature?'

Andy glanced at his solicitor who nodded. 'I didn't know about the crowbar, that he'd taken it. When we got back on his bike…'

'Paul's bike? Who was upfront?'

'Paul, of course. He wouldn't let me near it except as a passenger. Anyway, he showed me the crowbar then, waving it about like a sword he was, swishing, you know. Then he went into the barn with it, and I went in the house. That's all.'

'Thank you, Andy, you've been very helpful,' said Cassie. 'We'll stop there. Would you like anything?'

Andy nodded. 'Some water please,' and hung his head. He felt exhausted and guilty. No matter how often his solicitor told him he'd done the right thing, he knew he had betrayed his twin, and that felt awful.

Saroj started the interview with Paul Trevellian by showing him the text on Erica's phone. 'Who sent that text, Paul?'

'That's not my phone, it's Erica's. She must have sent it,' he said.

'Did you take Erica's phone and send that text?'

'No comment.' Sylvia looked sharply at Paul. They had agreed that there would be no, no comment, answers.

'What if I told you that your fingerprints are on the phone?'

'That's easy. It's always around the house. I probably picked it up.'

'Our technicians are very good, Paul. They can show whereabouts the thumb prints have been on the phone, and yours correspond with the message typed out here.' Again she showed Paul the text.

Sylvia spoke up. 'My client has answered the question, can we move on.'

Cassie placed her palms down on the table. 'Let me spell it out for you, Paul. We have a statement from your brother that you, Paul, devised a plan to allow you time to go to Redruth, meet with James Tandy at an arranged time, as shown in this text, attack him and get back to the pub before you were missed.' Cassie took out the photograph of the head injury to James Tandy. 'This indentation in James Tandy's scull, matches exactly the profile of the crowbar you took with you that night.' Cassie took out a forensic report. 'This is the result of an analysis of oil found on a piece of cloth in the barn on your farm which is an exact match to oil found on the crowbar recovered from the duck pond on your farm.' Another photo was slid across the table. 'This image is of two fingerprints found in James Tandy's blood which was on the crowbar at the spot where it hit his skull. Those fingerprints are an exact match to yours.'

She showed him another photograph, this time of the hair found on the body. 'This is a photograph of a hair which has a DNA profile consistent with yours. It was found on James Tandy's body.'

Paul was slumping in his chair, wondering what Andy had said in his statement. Had his brother dropped him in it? He couldn't quite believe it. His eyes raced from side to side and his breathing became erratic.

Sylvia Moorcroft took this opportunity to call a halt to the proceedings. 'I think my client is unwell. He needs a break.'

'Of course,' said Cassie. 'Do you need a doctor, Paul?' she asked kindly.

Paul shook his head and then rested it on the table on his folded arms.

'We'll leave it there then, let me know if anything changes, Ms Moorcroft. I'll have some tea sent in.' Cassie was determined to play this by the book. No cock-ups.

Back in the squad room, Peter looked up expectantly. 'Nearly there,' said Cassie. 'We have a statement from Andy and I'm confident we will have one from Paul in the next hour or so.'

'Well done, Cassie and Saroj,' said Peter. 'Great teamwork. The usual celebrations will be in order later, and I'll get the first round in.'

'Do we have anything on Simon Makinson's car yet, sir?' Cassie's mind was always straying into concern for her friend.

'It's been taken to the forensic laboratory. There was no body in the boot, if that's what you're concerned about, just a small suitcase with men's clothes. Both Simon and Susan are still 'whereabouts unknown'.'

'No sightings of them at all at the campsite? That's hard to believe.'

'Uniform are doing a house to house, or van to van, right now, but the site is sparsely occupied at this time of the year, straight after the Easter holidays, so we may not get much.'

'If they've been staying in a van all this time, sir, they would have to get food.'

'There's a small supermarket on site with a self-checkout, so the staff say customers often come and go without contact with them. None of the staff we have spoken to accurately recognised the photos of Susan or Simon. Though one woman thought that she saw a man similar to Simon, but he was wearing a hoodie so she couldn't be sure.'

Cassie was thoughtful. 'Do we know who owns the van, sir?' she asked.

'Not yet. Maggie is doing a search.' He called over to his DC. 'Maggie! Any luck with the owners?'

'Just now, sir. It's owned by Women's Aid. They use it to give families a break. It's a well-guarded secret.'

'If they've been there for a week, they'll have left a mountain of evidence. Let's hope SOCO have come up with something definitive. The murder weapon, perhaps.'

'What would we do in their place?' Cassie mused out loud. 'They've left the car, presumably because it would be picked up.'

'Then they'll be walking. The coast path is the most likely as it avoids CCTV, but which direction?' Peter picked up his phone and spoke to the duty desk, arranging for search teams to go along the coast path in both directions from the campsite.

'They can't get far on foot,' he said.

'What about a helicopter, sir?' asked Cassie.

'I can ask the Chief Super. Let's give the ground teams a couple of hours, though, and see where we are. I'd hate to incur the expense of a 'copter unnecessarily.'

'Chief Super on your back, sir?'

'Always, Cassie. He's asked to see me, but I've managed to avoid it for a few days. He's bound to be concerned about our lack of progress in the Carol Lightfoot case and I guess I'm putting off the moment. If we could locate Susan Delaney and Simon Makinson and bring them in, I would at least have some positive news for him. And let's get this James Tandy business boxed off. I want them charged by the end of today, Cassie, then I can tell him that at least.'

'Yes, sir. I'm on it.'

Chapter Seventeen

Sunday 7th April – Susan Delaney's flat

'Come on, lazy bones, just because it's your birthday doesn't mean you can hog the sofa.' Suzi laughed at Carol wrapped up snugly in the blanket.

Carol chuckled. 'I might get up if there was a cup of tea in the offing.'

'Well, there's tea but no milk I'm afraid. You get up and get dressed and I'll pop out to the shop. Don't open the door to anyone.' Suzi reminded Carol.

'Okay, mother,' Carol said sarcastically. 'I know.'

'Can't be too careful,' shouted Suzi as she left the flat.

Just as Carol was about to go into the bathroom, there was a light tap on the door. 'Forgotten something, then?' she laughed, expecting a shamefaced Suzi at the other side of the door.

As Carol opened the door it was slammed violently open, trapping her against the wall. She screamed loudly and tried to run. She was grabbed by strong arms and flung on to the sofa, still screaming.

'Shut up you bitch,' said a familiar threatening voice. 'Get dressed now.'

Carol felt the old panic rising in her throat and realised that she had peed in her pants. 'Get away from me! Help, help!' she shouted, but he was on her in a flash, his hand over her mouth.

Seeing the urine patch on the sofa, he said, 'You dirty bitch. Get yourself cleaned up.' He grabbed her by the hair and pulled her off the sofa. Carol twisted frantically and headed for the window, either to raise an alarm or throw herself out, she didn't mind which.

Before she reached her destination, the man brandished a knife. He waved it at her. 'Get dressed or get cut, it's up to you.'

Carol suddenly went calm. She stood facing her tormentor. 'Kill me then. It's better than being with you.'

He lunged, hatred in his eyes. Instinctively, Carol held up her arms in defence but the knife blows kept coming, slashing through the skin, and Carol was forced to drop her arms. Seizing his opportunity, Penworth thrust the knife deep into her chest. 'You ungrateful cow,' he sobbed. 'I gave you everything.' He stared at Carol's lifeless body for a moment, then stood and fled. He bumped into someone as he reached the street but carried on running away from the flats.

Arriving at the same time, Simon Makinson shrugged off the collision with the man and continued his examination of the buildings, holding his phone to check the address. Realising he had gone too far past, he turned back to Manor Court. The street door was ajar, so he entered and started walking up the stairs. 'Flat eight,' he said to himself, looking at the numbers on the doors as he went.

When he reached the second landing, he saw it. Again, the door was ajar. 'Does no one lock their doors here?' he muttered. 'Hello!' he shouted. 'It's Simon Makinson. You said for me to call anytime.' He stepped cautiously into the room. A shiver ran up his spine and his senses were assailed by a smell he couldn't quite place. Then he saw her. Legs first, sticking out from halfway behind the sofa. Then as he neared, the full horror of what he was seeing hit home.

Simon forced back the vomit rising in his throat. 'Susan?' he said hoarsely. 'Mother?' Then he knelt shakily to see if she was still alive. He had seen this done on TV but never had to check for signs of life before. Forcing himself to look into her face, he was puzzled. One eye was closed and scarred, and her jaw was misshapen. The white-blonde hair was the same as her Facebook photo, and her size seemed about right, but Simon hardly recognised the woman who he believed was his birth mother. Putting his finger on her throat, he felt for a pulse, but there was nothing. He knew she was dead even before he had done this, as

138

her good eye stared sightlessly upward. Noticing the knife for the first time, he grabbed it and pulled it out. A weak spurt of blood hit his shirt and he recoiled in horror.

Just then Simon became aware of another person in the room. He turned to see a blonde woman holding a wine bottle above her head, ready to bring it down on him. 'No!' He shouted. 'I didn't...'

Suzi relaxed her grip on the bottle, and it fell to the floor. Walking forward a few paces she saw her friend on the floor. The man stood over her, with the knife still in his hand. Suzi looked at him and knew instantly who it was. If this had been a better meeting, she would have exclaimed how like the handsome singer from twenty plus years ago he was. Now, her mind was working overtime. Knowing that any commotion would alert her ever-watchful neighbours, Suzi sprang into action.

Many years' experience of rescuing women and children from violent homes had equipped her for this moment. Taking the knife gently from Simon, she dropped it into the plastic grocery bag she was still holding. 'Come with me,' she said, drawing him away from Carol's lifeless form. 'We have to go now.'

Suzi knew that Simon was in a state of shock, but didn't at this moment understand what had happened here. She just knew that she had to have some breathing space to figure things out. This young man was her son – her son! And it seemed like all her protective motherly instincts came into play instantly.

Leading him gently away, Suzi reached the doorway. She glanced onto the stairwell but saw no one. 'Come on, love,' she coaxed, and quietly closed the door behind them. Once on the street, Suzi became all action. 'How did you get here, Simon?' she asked urgently.

He shook his head as if to clear it. 'Car. I came by car.'

'Okay, that's good. Give me the keys.' Simon rummaged in his pockets and came up with a bunch of keys. 'Good. Now where have you parked?'

Simon pointed along the road. 'Side street,' he said.

'All right, let's go.' Suzi pulled him faster along the street, aware that they might be stopped at any moment.

'Which car, Simon?' Suzi asked urgently, as they turned the corner into the side street. 'Which car, Simon?' she repeated.

'White Fiesta. There.' He pointed again.

They reached the car and Suzi opened it with the key fob. Pulling the passenger door ajar, she ushered Simon in and closed the door firmly. She ran around to the other side and jumped in. 'Seatbelt, Simon,' she instructed, and he complied automatically.

'Right, don't worry, we'll sort this out,' she said, a plan forming in her mind.

'Give me your phone, love,' Suzi said gently, putting the car in gear and moving off slowly. Simon automatically handed his phone over. 'That's good,' said Suzi, looking down at it for a moment and then switching it off.

She carried on to the A30 until she reached the Long Rock roundabout, glancing every now and then at the still figure in the passenger seat. Turning right, Suzi drove into the Morrison's car park and parked in a deserted corner.

Turning to Simon, she said kindly, 'Take your shirt off for me, will you.' He started to unbutton his shirt. 'D'you have any clothes in the car?'

He looked at her, then: 'Hoodie, back seat.'

Suzi grabbed the hoodie, taking the blood-stained shirt from Simon and balling it up. 'Here, put it on,' she said, passing him the garment. 'How you feeling?'

'I don't know,' Simon stammered. 'Numb, I guess.'

'Okay, I hear you, but I want you to do one more thing, then we can relax for a bit. Do you think you can do something for me?'

Simon looked over at the strange woman next to him who seemed to be in control of the situation. 'I'll try. What do you want me to do?'

'I bet you've got a credit card, haven't you?' Simon nodded. 'Okay, I'm going to drive over to the ATM and I want you to get some cash out. What's your credit limit at the moment?'

'I don't know.'

'Try to draw out three hundred then, or as much as you can.' Suzi was aware that she was pushing Simon into action but told herself that it was necessary. There'd be time for gentle conversation later. At least, if the police were looking for her, they wouldn't find any action on her card.

Simon nodded. Suzi drove to the area of the car park by the ATM and parked as near as she could. 'Okay, love?' she prompted.

Simon got out and went over to the machine. Acting automatically, he keyed in his PIN and ordered the cash. After collecting it, he walked back over to the waiting car. He passed the money to Suzi.

'That's great, sweet'art.' Suzi had noticed some chocolate bars in the glove compartment and took one out. Passing it to Simon, she said, 'Here, eat this and then try to sleep for a bit.' She knew he was in shock and was concerned. There was a blanket on the back seat, the sort used by posh families for picnics, she thought. Grabbing it, she wrapped it around Simon's shoulders. 'Now just rest. Everything's going to be okay.'

Suzi had one last thing to do before leaving the car park. She picked up her phone and keyed in a familiar number. When the call was answered, she simply said, 'It's Suzi here, code name Sparkle. Is the van free?'

'Hi, Suzi. Let me check,' was the friendly reply. 'Yeah, as it happens it is.'

'That's great. I'll be using it for a week.' This arrangement wasn't questioned, and her Women's Aid colleague simply said, 'Okay, take care, Suzi.'

Suzi then turned her phone off. 'Right,' she said out loud. 'Let's go.'

Simon dozed fitfully in the passenger seat as Suzi concentrated on manoeuvring back onto the A30. She carried on the few miles to the next roundabout where the road split into two lanes. Taking the right-hand lane towards Helston, she drove straight on and joined the A394. Glancing over at Simon, she saw him twitch jerkily as he slept, a small moan escaping from his lips. 'It's going to be okay, love,' she whispered. 'I'll take care of you.'

Signs to St Michael's Mount at the next roundabout reminded her of happier times and the Women's Aid barbecue at a rented cottage in Marazion. She had only recently come to Cornwall and was entranced by the view of the Mount with the impressive granite castle and chapel on the summit. After the food, the group of slightly tipsy women had walked over the man-made granite causeway which links the Mount to Marazion, only passable at low tide. Suzi remembered the giggling as the women rushed back along the slippery rocks as the tide started to turn and their feet got wet.

Simon woke briefly. He looked over at Suzi and couldn't quite place where he was or with whom. Then the morning's events came slowly back. This woman was probably his birth mother. His determination to find her had led to an event too awful even to think about. He realised that he had simply allowed her to take him away, insisting that he followed her instructions. She seemed caring though. No. More than caring. Protective, that was it, the feeling of being protected.

Suzi became aware of Simon watching her. 'Okay, love? We'll soon be there. Here, have some water.' Suzi handed Simon the water bottle and he took it, his eyes never leaving her face.

'Where are we going?' he asked, as he unscrewed the cap.

'Somewhere where we can have some time to think things through.' Suzi slowed her speed to pass through the small hamlet of Rosudgeon. 'Just a few more minutes.'

'That woman, the one who… you know, who was she?'

'I don't want you to think about that now, Simon. We'll have plenty of time to talk in a bit. Trust me, love, we need to make sure you're alright first, okay?'

Simon gazed out of the window, aware that Susan was indicating right and turning onto a side road. Driving slowly down a hill, she turned right again into what looked like a holiday park. Simon missed what was written on the sign at the entrance, but they were soon passing rows of holiday homes, large caravans he supposed they were, but he'd never had an experience of seeing one close up. Eventually after a few twists and turns, Susan pulled in between one of the caravans and a tall hedge. The car only just squeezed in, and Simon hoped that the bodywork wouldn't be scratched. As if that matters, he thought glumly.

Susan unfastened her seatbelt and turned to face Simon. 'We're going to stay here for a while, just so that we can sort things out.' He nodded. 'You'll have to get out this side as I'm jammed up against the hedge on your side.' Simon unfastened his belt and threw off the blanket, flinging it onto the back seat. Squirming around, he lifted his long legs over the steering column and shifted over into the driving seat. Susan was bending down over by the hedge, lifting various stones. 'Why can't they leave it in the same place each time?' she muttered to herself. 'Ah, here it is.' She waved a set of keys triumphantly.

Simon wriggled out of the car, arching his back and breathing in the cool air. He could smell the sea and hear the distant sound of waves crashing against a shore. 'Come on,' said Susan. 'Let's get you in.' Simon walked around to the other side of the caravan, pausing to take in the view of the sea. 'This is a lovely spot,' he said. 'Is this yours?' indicating the van.

'No, it belongs to friends. We'll be quite safe here, don't worry.'

Simon realised that he wasn't worried, and that surprised him. The events of the morning had been so shocking that he ought to be concerned at least. By this time, Susan had walked up the few steps leading to a wooden deck and the entrance door. 'Come on,' she smiled.

Simon's holidays since he could remember had usually been abroad somewhere. A French holiday villa, sailing off a Turkish island, SCUBA diving in the Caribbean. Never would his parents have dreamt of staying in a caravan. They'd been to Cornwall a couple of times, though. He remembered a hotel on the Isles of Scilly, the helicopter flight was exciting and moving between the islands on little boats was fun. They once went to St Ives because mother had wanted to visit The Tate and Barbara Hepworth's garden, but she didn't like the crowds, he remembered. Then there were the sailing holidays in Falmouth. He and Claire had taken a few lessons at the sailing club.

Following Susan through the door, Simon was taken aback by the spacious interior of the holiday home. It's bigger than my flat in London, he thought, and better appointed. 'It's lovely,' he said.

Susan took his arm and led him to a comfortable armchair. 'You just sit there while I check things out. I'll put the kettle on as soon as I've turned on the gas. Are you warm enough?'

Simon hugged himself. 'A bit chilled.'

'That's probably still the shock. You're looking a lot better though, some colour in your cheeks.' Susan disappeared through a doorway and came back with a blanket, which she wrapped around Simon. 'There, we'll soon get you warm.'

Simon watched Susan as she flitted around the space, opening cupboards, checking the fridge, turning on the heater. 'There's lots

143

of food, bless Christine for stocking up after the last lot left.' She waved tins, jars and packages at Simon. 'Pasta, minced beef, tomatoes – that's a spag bol for tonight. Chicken in sauce, tinned new potatoes, peas, carrots, no end of goodies.' She reached into the back of a high cupboard. 'Aha! This is just the thing.' Holding a half full bottle, she grabbed a couple of glasses. 'Brandy is what you need, and me too, if I'm honest.' Pouring two large ones, she finally settled in the chair next to Simon and passed him one. 'I won't say Cheers, but I'll drink to you and how glad I am that you found me.'

Simon sipped the brandy and felt the warmth as he swallowed the fiery spirit. He coughed lightly. 'Susan? Why haven't you called the police?'

'Okay. I don't know what happened yet, but I know what it would look like to the police. D'you see what I mean?' He nodded. 'I want to hear from you how you came to be in the flat with Carol as she was when I came home.'

'You mean dead,' Simon said flatly.

'I mean dead, yes. And why you were holding that knife.' Simon put his head in his hands. 'We don't have to get into it yet, though. But I want you to know that I can see no reason why you should harm Carol, and I've been doing a lot of thinking about it while we've been on our way here. She had one real enemy, someone who would have attacked her like that, but I can't get my head around how that could have happened, not yet.' Susan put her hand on Simon's arm. 'Look at me, love.' He raised his head. 'That's why we're here. To find out what happened without the police jumping to conclusions. Believe me, I've been down that road.' Simon's eyes widened. 'Oh, not on my own account, love. I've represented women who wouldn't be believed when they say their fine upstanding partner or husband has controlled them all their lives, or pushed them down the stairs, claiming their clumsiness. So, I don't fully trust the police.' Susan smiled. 'I do have a good friend who's a detective inspector, and I have thought of contacting her, but even she is bound by rules and regulations. Better that we take our time and understand what happened ourselves before involving the police.'

'Can we talk about it later?' Simon said wearily. 'My head aches and I feel so muddled. I wouldn't mind another one of these, though,' he said, holding up his glass.

*   *   *   *

The spag bol wasn't restaurant quality exactly, but it was hot and tasty. Susan had discovered bars of chocolate in a drawer, and they ate their fill of these for afters. The sun was beginning to set so Susan dropped the blinds and turned on the table lamps, creating a warm and cosy atmosphere.

They were sharing yet another brandy, this being the only alcohol in the place, when Simon asked the question that had been on his mind ever since he had seen his birth certificate. 'Will you tell me who my dad was?'

Susan blew her cheeks out. 'Phew. You want to talk about that now?' Simon nodded. 'Okay. He was a singer in a band. Johnnie was his name, the band was called Subliminal. And it was what you might call a one-night stand.' A question formed on Simon's face. 'Before you ask, I tried to find him to at least name him on your birth certificate. You have to remember that this was before Google, and I didn't have a computer, anyway. In the end, I thought that if he'd wanted to find me he would have.'

'He knew where you lived then?'

'Not exactly. I gave him a phone number, landline, no personal mobiles then. Anyway, he could have found me, that's what I'm saying, and he didn't.'

Simon didn't push the point. 'What was he like?'

'What don't you get about a one-night stand?' Then more gently. 'You look just like him, though.' She smiled. 'Handsome.' Susan took in Simon's dark curls and brown eyes fringed by long lashes. 'Yes, very handsome.'

Simon was a bit drunk but he was still aware that these were sensitive issues. The drink emboldened him though. 'You could only have been fourteen, you were just fifteen when you had me.'

Suzi had always known that she might have to answer these questions one day, in fact, she thought she would welcome it, but now she felt embarrassed with this young man, her son, opening up feelings that she had buried long ago. 'I was fourteen but looked and acted older. I'd had a bit too much of this,' she raised her glass, 'Vodka though, not brandy, and one thing led to another. My friend Cassie tried to tell me it was rape, but it didn't feel like that at the time. Now I know different.'

145

'He was a sort of Jimmy Saville character? Preying on young girls.'

'I don't think so, Simon, I really don't. But who actually knows. I'm sure that sort of thing was rife in the music industry, may still be. All I can say is that I don't think he was aware of my age.'

'I bet I can find him,' Simon said. 'Search engines are so sophisticated, I've found a lot of obscure stuff about minor politicians from the 80s and 90s and even further back, for my research. I could track him down.'

Susan saw the determination on Simon's face. 'It's that important to you? You have a dad. Johnnie was just a sperm donor.'

'People track down their sperm donors, I've heard. And there's the genetic thing. Does he have an incurable disease or a hereditary problem of some kind?' He shrugged. 'Oh, I don't know Susan. Just because I can? Is that good enough?'

Chapter Eighteen

Cassie and Saroj spotted the two solicitors in conference in the corridor. Sylvia Moorcroft was in full flow. Cassie couldn't make out what she was saying but there was a lot of arm waving and her tone was strident.

'Are we ready to continue?' Cassie asked, approaching them. 'Shall we take Paul first this time?'

Sylvia Moorcroft seemed pleased, 'Delighted, DI Wade,' she said. 'Room two?'

'I'll get the duty sergeant to bring Paul up and see you in there.'

As soon as the four were settled and the tape had been re-started, Sylvia Moorcroft began. 'My client would like to make a statement.' She looked over at Paul who was looking tired and defeated.

'Can I see my brother first?' he asked.

'You know that's not possible, Paul. Your statement?'

Paul sighed. 'Okay, I did beat up James, he had it coming for what he did to Erica.'

Sylvia Moocroft caught Paul's attention and gave him a meaningful stare.

'Well, he did,' Paul said stubbornly. 'Anyhow, I did it, Andy wasn't involved.'

'Tell me how you planned it, Paul.'

'I knew we could play the twin scam, we've done it before. Got away with it, too. Well nearly. Bloody left-handed business, didn't think of that. We did it like you said, Andy wore my jacket when he played pool and then put his back on to watch the darts, simple. I rode to Redruth, met Tandy and... Well, you know the rest.'

147

'How did you get him to meet you?'

'I took Erica's phone and texted him. It was easy. He's so stupid, I knew he'd think she wanted to be friends. As if she would, after what he did.'

'What about the crowbar?'

Paul looked at his solicitor, who nodded encouragingly.

'I took it along to threaten him with. Never meant to use it, but he started to run away when he saw me and I just lashed out. Didn't seem to hit him hard, I think he hit his head on the floor. It's probably that that did the damage.'

Cassie raised her eyebrows at this. 'And the rest? The kicking?'

'Yeah, well, he shouldn't go around doin' that to girls. It was just a kick where it hurts.'

'His penis and testicles were crushed, Paul. More than a kick where it hurts, wouldn't you say?'

Sylvia Moorcroft spoke up. 'My client has given you his statement, detective.'

'Stand up, Paul,' Cassie said, acknowledging the solicitor's point. 'Paul Trevellian, I am charging you with the murder of James Tandy on Wednesday night the tenth of April. You do not have to say anything. But, it may harm your defence if you do not mention when questioned something which you later rely on in court. Anything you do say may be given in evidence. Do you understand, Paul?'

Paul looked at his solicitor. 'You said it would be manslaughter!'

'I advise you to say nothing, Paul. We'll speak later about the charge, okay?'

The interview with Andy Trevellian went very much as expected. Cassie told him that they had charged his brother with murder and were treating his role in that as accessory to murder.

Daniel Spruce objected, saying that his client's statement would make his role clear, without making any assumptions at this stage.

Andy told them that Paul had planned the whole thing and he simply went along, seeing it as a game. He realised that Paul was going to rough James up a bit, but didn't know about the crowbar, and never wanted any real harm to come to James. 'Just teach him a lesson. Like dad said he deserved.'

Cassie charged Andy with perverting the course of justice.

148

Speaking to Peter later, Cassie reflected that Mr Trevellian senior had probably initiated the attack on James Tandy with his comments about teaching the lad a lesson, but that would be difficult to prove.

'Well, Cassie,' said Peter, 'he'll suffer if both his sons go to prison, and we'll have to be satisfied with that. Anyway, you've done a great job and I've got some positive news to share with the Chief Super, so a good result all round.'

'Do you want me to concentrate on finding Susan Delaney now, sir?'

'Naturally, Cassie. I want to be kept fully informed remember, and I'll be interviewing her when we have her in custody.'

Cassie was itching to get involved again in the search for her friend. She returned to the squad room for an update.

'We have officers on the ground, ma'am,' said Kevin, 'but no sightings yet.' By the way, ma'am, he continued, 'there's that file that you asked for.'

Cassie went over to her desk and picked up the manilla folder labelled *Carol Lightfoot Assault*. It had been marked, 'No Further Action' in red lettering. Sitting down, she turned the pages and read the reports outlining the case. The police had been called by Mr Ali Kamal, the shopkeeper that Cassie remembered speaking to. He had been putting some plants out on the pavement when he saw Carol running towards the shop from the direction of her home, covered in blood. He took her in and called for an ambulance and the police.

That ties in with what he said to me, Cassie thought. Reading on she got to the interview with Matthew Penworth. He said that he saw Carol in the garden with blood on her clothing. He said that he thought she had had an accident of some kind, but saw a man running away. When he realised that Mr Kamal had taken Carol in, he took off in the direction that he saw the man running, thinking he had something to do with it.

The paramedic's report said that Matthew Penworth had wanted to ride with Carol to the hospital but that she had not wanted him to. He did have a private word with her, presumably to reassure her, the paramedic said, and then left.

149

The police report from the hospital said that Carol told them she had been attacked in front of her home by a man she didn't recognise. When interviewed, Matthew Penworth supported this version of events, saying he was sorry that he hadn't been able to catch the man he thought responsible. He gave a vague description of the said perpetrator, but enquiries failed to find anyone.

Carol stuck to her story despite the suspicions of the A&E doctors that this was a case of domestic abuse.

The investigating officer reported that Matthew Penworth made several attempts to visit his girlfriend, but she refused to see him. Concerning the visit where he allegedly tried to force her to come home with him, Penworth had blamed the Women's Aid workers who had poisoned her against him because they all hate men.

The case was closed and tagged for no further action.

Cassie was furious. The incident had been given a very cursory investigation as far as she could see. The woman was running away from her home. Why would anyone do that? Surely, she would have sought help from her boyfriend if she was attacked in her own garden. This didn't seem to have been questioned, however.

The discussion Cassie had had with Mr Kamal revealed that Matthew Penworth had been a good customer before the incident but now didn't use his shop at all. This fact was surely significant but there was no indication that Mr Kamal had been interviewed beyond his original statement.

Despite the A&E doctor's concerns, Carol's story of a random attack had been accepted, even though in cases of domestic abuse it is known that women often lie about the cause of their injuries through fear of reprisals. The conversation Penworth had with Carol in the ambulance could have been significant. He may have threatened her not to tell the police what actually happened, and told her to say she was attacked by someone else.

This was as clear a case of domestic abuse and coercive control that Cassie had experienced. If there had been a more thorough investigation of this case, Matthew Penworth would be behind bars, Carol Lightfoot would not be dead, and Susan Delaney would not be a suspect in her murder.

Cassie threw the folder down onto her desk, causing heads to turn. 'Well, he's not getting away with it this time. I'm convinced that Penworth murdered Carol Lightfoot, and I'm going to prove it.'

Chapter Nineteen

Tuesday – 9th April
Praa Sands

Suzi made some coffee. Simon was still sleeping as far as she knew, and she thought she would let him rest. Suzi had insisted that they have a day off from digging into the past after the evening's conversation had caused her to toss and turn all night, and she had awoken early with a pounding headache. They would have to tackle what happened in the flat, though, if she was going to get to the bottom of why Carol had died in this awful way. A headache still throbbed behind her eyes, a sure indication of a migraine, which she suffered from occasionally, especially when stressed. Finding a supply of paracetamol in the bathroom cabinet, she took two and wandered out onto the small deck with her coffee to get some fresh air. It looked like it was going to be a lovely day. There was a fine mist over the sea through which the sun shone weakly. The gulls were wheeling overhead, chasing off a buzzard that was looking for an opportunity to steal a chick. The noise was quite deafening, and she tried to tune it out as she reflected on the last couple of days.

Her memories returned to that night at the club in Liverpool, singing on the stage, Johnnie's interest in her, the vodka, the sex. It had been a remote dream for so long and when Simon questioned her about it, she was made to confront the reality all over again. She now accepted that Johnnie had sexually abused her. He should have asked her age or realised that she was not an adult, but, looking back, she concluded that he had only been concerned with his own pleasure, knowing that he would never see her again.

That one catastrophic event had culminated in the situation they now found themselves in. What do they say, the beat of a butterfly's wings in China can lead to a hurricane in Peru? Something like that, anyway. All actions have consequences, surely that was what it meant. And certainly, hers and Johnnie's actions that night did.

Suzi shook herself out of her reminiscence. Wallowing in the past was not going to help. She must discourage Simon from asking any more about that period, and deal with the present.

Just then a voice came from the van door. 'Do I smell coffee?'

Suzi looked up. Her heart lurched at the beauty of him. Tousled hair, slim toned body, sleepy eyes. She had called him Adam when he was born. Nobody knew that, only her, but this morning he was her Adam, not someone else's Simon.

'Have a seat and I'll get you some,' she said.

'No, you've looked after me enough. Shall I get you a top up?'

Suzi handed Simon her mug. 'Just milk with mine, please,' she said, feeling a rush of maternal love for this young man who had returned to her life after twenty-one years. I will not believe that this boy is capable of what happened to Carol. Today we will solve this riddle together. Then I'll be able to phone Cassie. Not before.

Risking a walk after being cooped up in the van for a day, Suzi suggested that they take a look at the beach. 'It's so busy today that no one should pay us any attention. Have you got anything suitable in the car for you to wear?'

'I've got a couple of T shirts and another pair of jeans, clean underwear, that sort of thing.'

'T shirt and jeans will be acceptable at this time of year. Want to get them and change?'

'Pity I've no swimming things. A dip would be nice.'

'Do you know how cold the Cornish sea is at this time of year? Ankle numbing, that's what.'

Simon laughed. 'I'm not a wimp, you know. I get wet plenty when I'm sailing.'

'Well, I'm just paddling, and that's bad enough.'

Simon appeared from the van with pale blue denims, a white T shirt and sunglasses. 'Will this do?' He joked, giving a saucy twirl.

152

'Perfect,' said Suzi. She had found a bag of assorted clothes meant for women and children who might have left home in a hurry, and found a pair of cut offs and a check shirt which fitted well enough. 'Now we both look like holiday makers.'

Mingling with the small crowd of people heading for the beach, they didn't draw any attention towards themselves. Walking through the already packed car park, they went down some wooden steps and past a beach café, where the smell of bacon frying was tempting. Thinking that eating out would be just too public, Suzi and Simon carried on down the steps and onto the sand. The beach was strewn with boulders and smaller stones, especially near the water's edge, but it was wide and long and fringed by dunes, so altogether attractive. Suzi and Simon decided to walk towards the less populated area away from the café and beach shops, and slipped off their shoes to test out the water.

Simon was the first to get his feet wet. He shrieked and laughed. 'I see what you mean. Not exactly tropical. Come on, Susan, don't be nesh.'

Suzi hadn't heard that word since she left Liverpool. 'And what would you know about nesh? Being a posh boy and all that.'

'Less of the posh. My folks may be well off, but they came from working class backgrounds. I know a lot of interesting lingo.' He grabbed Suzi's hand and pulled gently. 'I thought they were all *dead hard* up north. Get your feet in.'

Suzi gasped as her toes hit the cold water. 'Oh, Adam, it's freezing.'

'What did you just call me?'

Suzi skipped away from the water. 'Sorry. It's what I named you when you were born, that's all. It's how I think of you. It just slipped out.'

'No, it's okay. It's nice that you named me.' They were still holding hands and he smiled warmly at her.

'Come on,' she said, 'let's find a rock to sit on. We've got a lot of talking to do.'

When they were perched on two slab-like granite rocks at the back of the beach, Suzi started the conversation about the morning Carol was killed. 'Let's go through it from the time you arrived at the flat. Try to remember the details, that's important.'

Simon gulped. 'This is so hard, Susan, every part of me simply wants to forget it.'

'I know, love, but we can't. Come on, you found the flat…'

'I found the flat. But wait a minute, just as I came near to the door on the street, someone pushed past me. I remember because he almost knocked my phone out of my hand. I was using Google Maps.'

'Can you remember what he looked like?'

'No, not really. I thought he was a runner, though. I think he had shorts on, you know, those lycra ones. Dark colour, maybe black or dark blue. I think his T shirt was paler, could have been white, no, wait a minute, yellow. It was yellow with some writing on the back. That's why I thought he was a runner. You know, with the running club name on the back of his shirt.'

'You're doing really well, Simon. Did you see where he went?'

'No. I'd gone past the door by then and had to double back. That's when I noticed that the door was open.'

'The door was open? I definitely shut it when I went out. Sorry, carry on.'

'I went up the stairs looking for flat eight, and saw the door open there, too. I remember thinking that you must be very trusting to leave doors open. Wouldn't happen in London.'

'Okay, was the door broken in any way?'

'I didn't notice, but I'd say not, probably. Anyway, I went in, I shouted first, I think. Susan? or something like that, could have been hello! And there was this awful smell, like a lavatory.' Simon looked down on the ground as if seeing the awful image again. He spread his hands. 'She was just there. Lying on her back half behind the sofa. I presumed it was you and, what a shock, you know, her face all damaged like that, and that one eye staring at the ceiling. It was terrible, Susan.' He winced and looked up at Suzi.

'That must have been awful for you, love, but we have to carry on. Can you tell me what happened next?'

Simon sighed and nodded. 'I felt for a pulse. Not that I knew what I was doing but… Anyway, I knew she was dead. That eye, you know. Then I pulled the knife out. I know I shouldn't have done that, but I couldn't stand it, it looked so grotesque sticking out like that. Then the blood spurted out of her. I nearly vomited.' He took a deep breath and swallowed as if reliving that feeling. 'Then you arrived.' He looked up at Suzi. There were tears in his eyes.

Suzi put her arms around him and held him tightly. This was the first time she had had such close contact with her son and, despite the awfulness of the circumstances, she luxuriated in the feel of his arms around her. My boy, she thought, how I've missed you.

Eventually she let him go. 'Shall we walk back?' he said. 'I'm suddenly very tired.'

Back at the van, Suzi made some tea and a sandwich with some tinned tuna she found in the cupboard. Simon took the tea into his bedroom but refused the food. 'I might have it later.' Was all he said. He looked thoroughly miserable, such a contrast from the morning's joviality.

Suzi was mad. It's that Penworth character, I just know it is. The way Carol talked about him, how he treated her. She knew he wouldn't let go easily, but I persuaded her she'd be safe with me after the refuge became too much. But then she saw him.

Carol had heard that Penzance was to have a farmer's market on Market Jew Street and she wanted to go. Suzi had been careful not to have too many outings, super cautious, was what Carol called her. So Suzi relented and they walked the short way into town, up through the main street, until they came to the narrow shopping street that was Market Jew Street. The stalls were crowded and there was a good turn-out. They bought home baked bread from Baker Sam, some fresh mackerel and organic veg. Working their way up the street, Suzi paused to taste some cheese, Carol walked a little way ahead picking up some scarves and laughing with the stall holder.

Suzi noticed him first. A man was walking towards Carol, determination in his stride. Suzi acted quickly. She ran to Carol and grabbed her arm. Carol looked round in panic and she spotted Matthew Penworth bearing down on her. Setting off like a frightened rabbit, Carol sprinted down the street dodging around shoppers. Suzi was hard on her heels and the two met up at the end of the street. Suzi pulled Carol into a shoe shop on the corner. The shop assistant looked up shocked. Suzi shot behind her and into what looked like a stock room. 'You can't go in there!' the girl shouted, and followed them in.

'Is there a back way out,' Suzi said pleadingly. 'Her boyfriend's after her.'

The shop assistant appreciated the situation immediately. 'I know all about that. Here, this leads to the alley. And good luck, nasty bastards they are, men.'

Safely back at the flat, Carol couldn't stop shaking. 'He'll never give up, Suzi. I'd rather kill myself than have him get to me again.'

Now Carol was dead, and Suzi knew Penworth was responsible. It was just a matter of proving it. He had got away with beating her and nearly blinding her, and Suzi was very afraid that he would get away with her murder as well. She was going to have to be as devious as he was. A plan began to form in Suzi's mind. There would be a risk and it would take courage, but she'd never been short of that. Especially now, she felt like a lioness defending her cub. They would not pin this on her Adam, she'd defend him or die in the attempt.

Chapter Twenty

Peter was on the phone as Cassie knocked. He beckoned her in and then finished his conversation. She waved the slim folder at him. 'I've been reading this, sir. It's the file on Carol Lightfoot's assault from seven months ago.' Peter raised his eyebrows quizzically, noting the NFA stamp on the file. 'I think it's relevant, sir,' Cassie persisted, hoping her boss wouldn't tell her to leave old cases alone and get on with the priority of the day, finding Susan Delaney and Simon Makinson.

'Take a seat, Cassie.' Peter could see that his DI was wound up, and thought again about the wisdom of having her on the case. 'How is that going to help us now?'

'It was a shambles sir – the investigation. The way it went down, it was obvious that Penworth had attacked Carol Lightfoot in their home and that she had managed to escape and run for help.'

Peter held up his hand to stop her. 'Obvious? Was there any forensic evidence to back that up?'

'They never got that far, sir, but I'd bet anything that there would have been blood in the house, considering her injuries and what the shopkeeper said.'

'What are you asking for, Cassie? Do you want to reopen this case, is that it? Because I'm telling you now that it's not a priority at the moment, and cold cases are not our responsibility. Unless it has a more than good chance of providing hard evidence in the murder we are currently investigating, it will have to wait. We'll discuss how we might get someone to reinvestigate if appropriate when that's over and done with.' Cassie's mind was working overtime, so much so that Peter thought he could hear cogs turning. He caught her attention. 'Evidence, Cassie! I don't want conjecture. Penworth's a slippery character, and it wouldn't do our current case any good if there was even a sniff of a witch hunt.'

Cassie nodded glumly. 'Sir.'

'You're not going to make me regret having you on this case, are you? You seem determined to deflect suspicion from your friend and on to Penworth. He may be a very nasty individual, but at the moment, there's nothing to tie him directly to the murder of Carol Lightfoot.' Peter paused for that to sink in. 'Now, where are we up to? Any luck finding the murder weapon or blood-stained clothing? How's the house to house on the caravan park going? Bring me something I can use, Cassie, and leave that,' indicating the file in her hands, 'alone.'

Cassie stood. 'Yes, sir. And I am open minded, honestly. It would be the same if it wasn't my friend who was implicated. I have a feeling about Penworth.'

'Okay, I get that, Cassie. You're a good detective and I know what it's like to have a feeling about someone, and they can sometimes be right. Just keep the victim in mind and get justice for her, that's all I ask.'

Cassie smiled and nodded. 'That's all I want, too, sir.'

Cassie returned to the squad room. Seeing just Kevin at his desk, she wondered where Saroj and Maggie had got to.

'Maggie's joined Robbie on the coast path search, ma'am, and Saroj is over at the Trevellian's farm, boxing that off.'

'Anything from the caravan, Robbie?'

'SOCO's going over the van that Susan Delaney was staying in. They've taken Simon Makinson's car away for inspection.'

'What about house to house?'

'Most of the holiday makers had gone home now, ma'am. No one noticed a pair matching their descriptions, not definitely anyway. One woman said she remembered a blonde woman with a dark-haired lad young enough to be her son. A toy boy, she concluded. Not able to describe either one of them beyond that.'

'Well, we know they were there, so we don't really need confirmation of that beyond what forensics find. It's where they are now that's important. Why has Maggie gone to join the search? I thought she came out in a rash if she left the office.'

Kevin laughed. 'She knows that part of the coast path really well, ma'am. She was born in Rosudgeon. Thought she could be of help.'

Maggie sat on a wall, her back to Acton Castle. Robbie was stood facing her admiring the large granite building. 'I never knew this was here,' he said, checking out the ramparts with the Cornish flag flying. 'What was it, a fort of some kind?'

'It was built by a botanist called John Stackhouse, the cove below is Stackhouse Cove. He studied the marine environment, specifically seaweed. He named the castle after his wife Susana Acton.'

'How come you know so much about it, Maggie? Don't live here do you?'

'I wish. It is apartments now, though, not that I could ever afford one, but it's been a hotel and even a smugglers' den, so the story goes.' Maggie smiled up at Robbie. 'I did it as a project for school. Prussia Cove, just by here, was named after the smuggler nicknamed the King of Prussia. He excavated tunnels from the castle down to Stackhouse Cove to get the contraband up.'

'We could do with being up on those ramparts. Maybe we'd be able to spot Susan Delaney and Simon Makinson from there. We've been walking for an hour or so now and not seen hide nor hair of them.'

'They've possibly gone in the other direction, Robbie. Maybe the other team are having better luck.' Maggie stood and dusted herself off. 'It could be time to call in the helicopter, what d'you think?'

'Let's contact the other crew and, if they've drawn a blank, we'll ask the Chief.'

Saroj pulled into the courtyard in front of the farmhouse. The old lady, Saul Trevellian's mother, was sitting outside on a chair, dozing in the sun. As Saroj got out of the car, the old dog came bounding up, its tail between its legs. It darted about from side to side as if rounding Saroj up, then let out a snarl and a bark.

'Margo!' shouted the old lady. 'Get by 'ere.' The dog obeyed immediately. The old lady squinted up at Saroj. 'An' who might you be?'

Saroj marvelled that the old lady didn't remember her recent visit. She held out her warrant card and re-introduced herself. The woman snorted. 'Bleddy foreigners get everywhere.'

Trying to keep her temper, Saroj asked, 'Is Mr Trevellian about?'

The old lady stood shakily, leaning on a stick. 'What you done wi' them lads? Them should be 'ere, 'elpin' out on farm. They's done nuthen' wrong.' She waved her stick at Saroj. 'If they's not with yer, yers can get off my land.' Wobbling a little, old Mrs Trevellian sank back into her chair.

Saroj tried again. 'I need to see Mr Trevellian.'

' 'E be down at that interferrin' busybody's. Gone to fetch Erica back.'

Saroj knew immediately that the old lady referred to Erica's other grandma, and was afraid for the girl if her father had gone to get her. It couldn't end well for her. Saroj turned and jumped into her car. Driving down the lane, she was almost run off the road by Saul Trevellian's Land Rover. Just managing to avoid skidding into the ditch, Saroj stopped and looked back at the speeding vehicle. I do hope Erica's not in there with him, she thought, but, rather than follow, she imagined she'd learn more from Mrs Trevose, so carried on down the road.

Pulling up at Mrs Trevose's front gate, Saroj saw a man of about fifty handing a paper of some kind to Erica. At least the girl seems safe, she thought. The pair stopped and looked down the path as Saroj walked towards them. The man smiled and held out his hand. 'Hello, I'm Geoff Sayer, Education Welfare Officer.'

Saroj shook the man's hand warmly. 'DS Kapoor. Didn't I just see Mr Trevellian driving away from here?' she said, as she showed her warrant card to the welfare officer.

'I'm afraid I've had to come down hard on Erica's father. He is adamant that Erica should be at home, and as much as said that he had no intentions of letting her go to school. He knows now that he faces prosecution if he attempts to keep her away.' Geoff smiled. 'It seems he took exception and left, but I don't think he'll be causing any more trouble.'

Erica gave a rueful grin. 'You don't know my dad,' she said, shaking her head.

'We'll cross that bridge when we come to it, Erica. In the meantime, you have all the information you need, and you can contact me or anyone on that list any time there's a problem. Okay?'

Erica looked over to Saroj. 'D'you want to see me and gran?' Saroj nodded.

'I'll be off then,' said Geoff. 'I'll see you in a couple of weeks, Erica. Nice to meet you, DS Kapoor.'

Inside the cosy living room, Saroj filled Erica and her grandma in on the outcome of their interviews with Andy and Paul.

Erica's face crumpled, and she started to weep quietly. Mrs Trevose patted the girl's shoulder. 'Don't take on, lovely. They boys did wrong and they 'ave to pay fer it. That's justice for James.'

'I know, gran, but it's all such a mess.'

Saroj left Erica and her gran to come to terms with things. A whole family shattered, she thought. But Erica's safe for now, at least. Saroj drove back up the lane to the farm. She had one more unpleasant task to perform then she could put this case to bed. Mr Trevellian wasn't going to take the news well.

Chapter Twenty-one

Friday 12th April
Praa Sands

Spending time with Simon had been wonderful and Suzi was reluctant to end it. She had seen the coverage of Carol's murder on the TV in the bedroom she was using, and had somehow kept Simon from taking an interest. He seemed content to read from the selection of books left in the caravan, or simply sit and doze on the deck. They spent their evenings talking and getting to know each other. Suzi had learned about Simon's ambition to be a politician or at least a government advisor, with the intention of improving the lives of those less fortunate. Suzi had expressed her surprise. Had thought he would be a true-blue Tory, but Simon told her that his parents were not like that. They had money, but also a social conscience, and had brought him and his sister up to understand inequality and social depravation. An idealist, she thought, but she was impressed by his determination. When she was young, she had had no idea where life would lead her, but had somehow landed where she could do some good. It seemed like her son was following in her footsteps. Perhaps it's genetic, she mused, not really believing that. It sounded like his adoptive parents had set a good example. The nature, nurture debate, she thought casting her mind back to her social work degree. Still, it was lovely just to sit and listen to Simon. His knowledge astounded her, and she was so proud to be associated, even peripherally, with this impressive young man.

Thinking back to the TV and Cassie's appeal to her to get in touch. Suzi knew it was personal. Using the name Cassie was designed to speak directly to her, and she was tempted. It would have been easy then to phone her old friend and ask for help, but Suzi knew that Cassie was a detective first and a friend second. She had to be. Suzi understood about putting emotions to one side and doing what the job demanded. She had no doubt that Cassie would do the same. So far, she and Simon had evaded the police, but Suzi knew it couldn't last. It was time to put her plan into action. They would have one more evening together and then Simon must be re-united with his family and she would do what she had to, in order to keep him safe.

Suzi looked up from her reverie as Simon called from the kitchen. 'We've got tinned ham, pasta, a jar of cheese sauce and some dried oregano. And there's a tin marked, sticky toffee pudding, we could give that a go too if you like?'

Suzi laughed. Simon had turned out to be a good cook, at least good with improvisation. 'I'd say it sounds like a feast.'

Simon started to take the ingredients out of the cupboard. 'Should we leave some money for these things to be replaced. It seems rude to use everything and not give back.'

'If you'd like to, we can,' Suzi said. 'Women's Aid is a charity, and we get donations, fortunately, but every little helps. I'll be contacting someone there tomorrow so I can pass it on.'

Simon stopped and stared at Suzi. 'What's happening tomorrow?'

Saturday came, and Suzi and Simon had been walking for an hour when Suzi stopped. She had only told Simon half of her plan, and that was that he should contact his sister to collect him, and give her a couple of hours before handing themselves in. The conversation had been hard for Suzi as she wondered if it would be the last time she had Simon all to herself, or even the last time she would see him.

'And what will you be doing?' he said.

'I'll be okay. I have a friend from WA picking me up. I just have a bit of business to see to before I contact the police.'

'You won't do anything stupid, will you?'

How well he seemed to know her after just a week. 'No, love, I just want to sort something out. Trust me.'

Now Suzi handed Simon his phone. 'Call Claire. Tell her we're in Perranuthnoe, she'll be able to Google it.' Suzi had already spotted Christine Taylor's van on the roadside. She went over to Simon and hugged him. He hugged her back, holding on tightly. Suzi held back a sob. 'I know I can't make any claim to you, but I love you, don't ever forget that.' Then she was off and running towards where Christine waited for her, not looking back for fear of changing her mind.

Chapter Twenty-two

Whilst Suzi and Simon were enjoying a makeshift carbonara on their last evening in the caravan, Mark and Cassie were sitting opposite Micky and Tanya sampling the real thing. Cassie had not been able to find a good reason for Mark not to come over that Friday, and was feeling more and more glad that she hadn't.

The Lightfoot case had stalled, and Peter told everyone to go home and get a good night's sleep. He was happy that the Erica Trevellian case had been put to bed and invited everyone to the pub for a celebratory drink before they went home. Cassie had declined, saying that she had promised to spend time with her kids, not letting on that she had a date with Mark, which would have led to some good-natured teasing that she wasn't ready for yet. She had rushed home to shower and change, and was just spraying a mist of perfume over herself as the doorbell sounded.

'I'll get it,' shouted Tanya, rushing to be the first to set eyes on mum's new man. Opening the door, she registered a little surprise as Mark was not what she imagined. She supposed that she had always thought that mum would be attracted to someone just like her dad, tall and distinguished looking. But here was a guy only just a little taller than her, with a shaved head and glasses. He was dressed fashionably in grey trousers and a black leather jacket with an open neck white shirt underneath. His glasses were designer by the look of it and drew attention to his startling dark blue eyes. He smiled, showing even white teeth. 'You must be Tanya,' he said, his voice warm and friendly.

Tanya pulled herself together. 'That's right, and this,' stepping back to reveal the other interested party, 'is Micky.'

Cassie's voice sounded from behind them. 'Are you going to keep the poor man on the doorstep, then?' she joked. 'Come in, Mark, it's great to see you. Let's have a drink. Micky, can you see to that? Mine's a G&T and Mark? What will you have?' She was aware that she was prattling on, and Tanya's face confirmed it, as she looked incredulously at her mother, who was normally the most together person she knew.

'Coming up,' said Micky. 'G&T for you too, Mark?'

Mark smiled and nodded. 'That would be great, thanks. It's good to see you, Cassie. You look lovely.' And he produced a bunch of red roses from behind his back.

Cassie moved towards him and accepted the flowers. 'They're beautiful, Mark.' And she kissed him on the cheek. Her two kids were watching transfixed. 'Drinks, Micky,' she said over her shoulder without looking round.

'Coming right up, ma.'

'Tanya, close your mouth.'

'Yes, ma. Sorry. It's really nice to meet you, Mark,' she said, finding her manners.

After the stuttering start to the evening, everyone was getting along swimmingly at the restaurant. Mark showed a great interest in what Micky and Tanya had to say, teasing out their ambitions for the future and asking what they thought of Cornwall. He seemed genuinely interested in their opinions, treating them as young adults and not kids. Micky asked about Mark's life and was particularly fascinated by the rugby stories, finding out that Mark had once had ambitions to be professional, but a neck injury had put pay to that.

'I never knew you wanted to play professionally, Mark,' Cassie had said.

'You never asked,' was the reply.

Turning to Micky she showed that she wasn't completely ignorant of Mark's passions. 'Mark played rugby with Peter. They have some fascinating tales to tell about locker room banter and tattoos.'

Mark shot her a glance. 'For another time, though, I think,' he said. 'Now, who wants dessert?'

By the time Cassie, Tanya and Micky were getting into a taxi, they were all getting along like the proverbial house on fire. Talk had been about what they could do the following day, and Mark had agreed to come over after breakfast to discuss a coastal walk. Cassie had kissed Mark briefly before climbing into the car. He held onto her hand and squeezed her fingers lightly. 'Tomorrow then. I've had fun tonight, your kids are great.'

'Don't tell them that, they're big-headed enough,' she quipped. 'I'll see you tomorrow.'

But, like with all best laid plans, the next day's events would change everything.

Chapter Twenty-Three

Saturday

Claire screamed to a halt on the gravel path which led out of Perranuthnoe and towards the coast. She was out of the car almost before it had stopped, running to her brother with her arms outstretched.

She grabbed hold of him, tears springing from her eyes. 'Simon, we've been so worried.' She held him away from her. 'Let me look at you, are you okay, where have you been?'

Simon hugged his sister to him. 'So good to see you, sis. I'll tell you all about it soon, but I don't really want to talk at the moment. Is that okay?'

'Whatever you say, Si. I'm just glad to see you alive and well. Shall we call the folks now? They're out of their minds with worry.'

'Not just yet.' He caught the surprised look on Claire's face. 'I know, and I will call them, but not just yet. Trust me,' he said, echoing what Suzi had said to him just a while ago.

Claire nodded. 'Okay, if that's what you want. I passed a café just now. Shall we grab a coffee?'

The conversation in Christine's car was intense but business-like. She knew that Suzi could be impulsive, and was quizzing her about the details of her plan before agreeing to go along with it.

'So, let me get this straight. You want to go into the lion's den with the intention of implicating him in Carol's murder. Do you know how mad that sounds? Matthew Penworth is a violent and unpredictable man. He put Carol in hospital, and she was lucky to have survived that attack. Now you want to confront him. Are you out of your mind?' Christine waited but Suzi said nothing. 'If you've got evidence that it was him who killed Carol, why can't you just give it to the police and let them arrest him?'

Suzi smiled over at her friend. They had been in a few sticky situations together and she was used to this sort of debate. It was good to have someone question her proposed actions. It would help her firm up the plan. 'I have evidence but I'm not sure it's good enough. I won't tell you any more than that, though, Chris, because I want you involved as little as possible. If all goes to plan, the police will never know about your part in this.'

'And if it doesn't go to plan?'

'Then you'll play a small part, but have no knowledge of my intended actions.'

'You know I trust you, Suzi. But I want you to promise me you'll be careful. Don't take risks with a man like Penworth, it's not worth your life.'

Suzi smiled. If I thought that's what it would take to save my Adam, it would be.

Claire was both fascinated and shocked to hear that Simon had spent a week in a caravan with his birth mother. He hadn't told her anything about the events that brought them to that point, but had dwelt on the feeling of connection he had with the woman he had thought about for so long. 'She's strong and organised, protective and just a little bit crazy.'

'Sounds like you're a bit in awe of her,' Claire said, showing her mistrust of the woman.

'She's amazing, Claire. She survived things that we couldn't even dream of experiencing. We've been lucky to have the parents we have. A safe and stable upbringing, good schools, all the advantages. She had to make her own way, but still managed to make something of herself, she became a hero to a lot of people, Claire.'

'Aren't you a bit starstruck? Alright, she is a big noise in women's issues, I know that. I've even read her stuff before I knew who she was. But was her life all that bad? She was able to make choices, after all. University, good job, appreciated for her talents, whatever they are. We'd do well to have all that.'

Simon squirmed a bit, not wanting to be seen as gullible, but he knew what he knew. 'You don't really know her, Claire. She didn't choose to be raped when she was fourteen. She didn't choose to have her baby snatched away from her. She didn't choose to be beaten by some smack head…'

'Okay, Simon. Have it your way. All I'm saying is you spend a week with this woman, and she tells you a sob story. How do you know it's even true?'

Simon stood up, almost knocking his chair over. 'You're jealous. I can't believe it. Just wait till you find your birth mother …'

'Never, Simon. I've got a mother and a bloody good one. I don't need to idealise some woman who's only connection to me was to give birth.' Claire was shouting now and drawing attention to them.

Simon walked away and out of the café, leaving Claire to pay the bill. He looked out over the sea and thought about Suzi. Where was she? What was she doing? He wanted more than anything to be with her. He was afraid that she was putting herself in harm's way to get him out of this mess. Claire would never understand that feeling of being protected against all odds that he had experienced with Suzi. He knew that there was nothing she wouldn't do to keep him safe, and that's what he was afraid of.

Cassie was luxuriating in the shower, thinking of the night before. She couldn't have hoped for a better meeting for Mark with her kids. They certainly took to him and he handled their good-humoured banter beautifully. In the taxi Tanya had even said, 'He's a keeper, ma, don't do anything to mess it up.' Micky had laughed, but essentially agreed with his sister. Over breakfast this morning they had repeated their endorsement of mum's new man and said they were looking forward to seeing him today. Mark had planned a coast walk and lunch at a beach café. Cassie was pleased that the weekend was going so well, she even forgot about Suzi for a few hours.

As Christine drove Suzi to what she thought of as a disaster waiting to happen, she decided that her colleague and friend needed some sound advice.

'I'm sorry Suzi, but I'll have to stop off here. I desperately need the loo, must be all the excitement.' As Christine walked down the steps to the public toilets, she took out the card that the police officer had given her, with a personal mobile number written on the back. She quickly keyed it in.

As Cassie stepped out of the shower her phone rang. Not recognising the number, she answered cautiously. Listening to the hurried message she said, 'I'll be half an hour, don't let her do anything stupid.'

'That's better,' Christine said, as she rejoined Suzi. 'Now I can wait for you without needing a pee.'

'Always practical,' laughed Suzi. 'I can remember your advice from when I first met you. *When you are going to get a woman and her kids, make sure there's fuel in the car and you've been to the loo.*' The atmosphere in the car had lightened, but Suzi remained silent for the rest of the journey.

After about half an hour, Christine pulled up on the roadside at the entrance to a small modern estate. 'He lives here?' she said incredulously. 'It looks a bit up market for someone like him.'

Suzi looked over at her friend. 'Aren't you the one who reminded me that abusive men could be from any background? Doctors and lawyers as well as brickies and druggies.'

'Very true, Suzi. Which only goes to my point of being careful around him. He's not a thicky, he'll suss you out in no time.'

'He won't even see me, Chris. I'll be in and out before he gets home. It's Saturday, a busy day on the market, so I think he'll be tied up there for a while.'

Just then, the driver's side door opened, and Christine got out. Suzi looked over wondering what could be happening, when Cassie slid onto the seat.

'Oh, for fuck's sake, Chris, what have you done?' Suzi exclaimed.

'The right thing,' said Cassie, holding her gaze on the agitated Suzi. 'What were you even thinking of? Or were you not thinking, as usual?'

Suzi held up her hands to ward off any further admonishments. 'Don't pre-judge me, Cassie, wait till you've heard what I have to say.' Suzi told Cassie about her plan to secrete the murder weapon in Penworth's house. She explained what had happened on that Sunday when Carol was killed, laying out Simon's actions and the fact that he had seen a man that she was sure was Penworth, running from the scene. 'But I know how it looks, Cassie. Simon's fingerprints will be on the knife as well as Penworth's, and he could have been wearing gloves, which means Simon's may be the only ones...' All this came out in a rush as Cassie listened calmly.

'I'll stop you there, Suzi,' said Cassie, taking her friend's hand. 'If what you tell me is true...' Suzi opened her mouth to speak but Cassie stopped her. 'If what you say is true,' she repeated, 'and we find the murder weapon in Penworth's house, how could Simon's fingerprints be on it?'

Suzi thought for a moment and then her shoulders sagged. Cassie carried on. 'Simon wouldn't have seen the knife at all, would he? Penworth would have taken it with him before Simon got there.'

Cassie saw that her friend was deflated and so treated her gently. 'I know you're only trying to do the best for Simon but really, Suzi, you should leave this sort of thing to us. If you had come to me with Simon as soon as you met him, instead of playing detective, we would have got to this point sooner. Now, if Penworth is our killer, he will have had time to cover his tracks and cement his alibi.'

Suzi shook her head sadly. 'I know he's the killer, Cassie. Carol told me how he had beaten her and almost blinded her. She was terrified that he would find her. I think he knew where she was staying...'

Cassie stopped Suzi from saying any more. 'Save it for the formal interview, Suzi. Right now, I have to arrest you in connection with the murder of Carol Lightfoot. You don't have to say anything. But it may harm your defence if you fail to mention

172

when questioned, something you later rely on in court. Anything you do say may be given in evidence. Do you understand?'

Cassie then took out her cuffs and put them onto a shocked Suzi's wrists. 'Come on, it's time to sort this mess out.'

Claire wasted no time in contacting her parents after Simon had stormed out of the café. The relief in her father's voice was the only vindication she needed. 'We'll be right there.' He had said. Now all she had to do was delay Simon until they got here. Paying the bill, she looked out of the window to see her brother standing, staring out to sea, his whole body looked tense.

Approaching him, she said, 'I only want to help, Si. I'm just worried that you are in over your head.'

Simon turned around. He loved his sister and knew that she had always looked up to him, believing that he could do no wrong. This time, however, she had challenged him, questioning his judgement. 'Let's have a little walk down to the sea,' she said, taking his hand, 'and you can tell me more about your birth mother if you want to. I promise I'll listen.'

They walked towards the sound of the crashing waves, coming eventually to a small stone jetty. The tide was well out but the sound of the water on the gravelly beach was soothing. They sat on a stone wall and Simon talked about his week with Susan, telling Claire how funny and intelligent his real mother was. Claire had balked at the choice of the word *real*, but said nothing. She glanced at her watch wondering just how long it would take her parents to arrive.

Noticing this, Simon said, 'I think we should be off. Susan said to give her a couple of hours, and I think that's just about up now.'

They stood and walked back up the slope and met their parents coming down towards them. Turning to his sister, Simon said, 'You phoned them, after I asked you not to. Well thanks very much, sister, I'll be sure not to ask you for a favour in future.'

'It's for the best, Simon. We can sort this out now, as a family, just as we always do.'

He pushed past her, bypassing his parents and ignoring their calls for him to stop. Eventually though, he came to a halt, realising that he had no choice now but to go with them. He only hoped that Susan had done what she wanted to do. He longed to see her again but knew that, once they got to the police station, that wouldn't be possible until they had sorted things out.

Mr Makinson caught up with his son. 'Simon,' he called. 'I spoke to our solicitor last night and he's on his way. Maybe even here by now. Everything's going to be alright. Just do what he tells you and all will be well, I'm sure of it.'

Mrs Makinson joined them and put her arms around Simon. 'It's all that woman's fault. She's obviously unstable, you shouldn't have gone with her…'

Simon threw his mother's arms off and turned to face her, anger in his eyes. 'You know nothing about her,' he shouted. 'Now just leave me alone.'

The car journey to Truro was tense. Mrs Makinson sobbing into her handkerchief and Simon staring blankly out of the window. Mr Makinson said nothing, but hoped that, when they got this thing sorted, their family could get back to normal. Glancing over at his son, he wondered if this would be possible. We'll go away somewhere, he thought, a family holiday may be just the thing we need. I'll get Avril to book. South of France, maybe. A villa for just the four of us, no pressure, just R&R.

Simon's thoughts were only about Susan. Now that he had found her, he wanted to spend more time in her company. Once we get all this business out of the way, I'll suggest we have a break together without the hassle of the last week. Simon was supremely confident that Susan would be able to convince the police that he was not responsible for her friend's death. He could almost see the pair of them walking out of the police station hand in hand as the real killer was taken below to the cells. Wishful thinking, maybe, but the thought cheered him and, for the first time since they left the caravan, he felt optimistic.

Chapter Twenty-four

Suzi had been placed in a cell awaiting interview. She looked around the bare room and still couldn't quite believe that her oldest and best friend had arrested her and brought her here. Surely, they could have talked about things a bit more. Suzi was convinced that, if Cassie had heard all the details of the day Carol was murdered, she too would be sure that Simon was simply in the wrong place at the wrong time. Then she could fight his corner with her superiors. It was essential to Suzi that Simon had someone in his corner. She had had some bad experiences with the police when the culprit had walked free, Matthew Penworth being one such. She was sitting with her head in her hands when a constable opened the cell door and entered.

'Would you like some tea, Ms Delaney?'

Suzi was on her feet in a shot. 'No. No tea, thank you. I want to see Cassie, er, DI Wade. It's important.'

'I'm afraid that won't be possible. You'll be called for interview in a short while and you will be able to speak to the detective in charge then. Now, are you sure about the tea?'

Suzi shook her head sadly. 'Can you at least tell me if Simon Makinson is at the police station.'

'I'm afraid I can't discuss the case with you, madam. My advice is to try and relax and wait calmly.' With that the cell door banged shut and Suzi was once more alone.

'Relax and wait calmly,' Suzi muttered as she flopped down onto the hard bed. 'How is that even possible?'

*   *   *   *

Peter was with Cassie in his office. He had received a call from Mr Makinson to say that he was bringing Simon in and that their solicitor was on his way. In fact, the solicitor, Allister Bradbury, was already here and making his presence felt. Clearly an experienced criminal lawyer, he had made it clear that he would be seeking the immediate release of his client unless the police had compelling evidence that Simon had committed a crime. Peter had assured him that he would furnish him with all the relevant details in due course but, as Simon wasn't even in custody yet, they should all wait and see what happened next.

'You did well bringing Susan in, Cassie,' said Peter, 'that couldn't have been easy for you.'

'It's my job, sir,' Cassie said, a little stiffly.

'No need to be prickly, Cassie. I know you always put the job first, that's not what I'm saying. It's just the way you go about it that I sometimes have a problem with.' He paused and took in the tension on his DI's face. 'This has been a frustrating investigation so far, but we're getting somewhere now. We have two suspects in custody, and we are in possession of what we believe is the murder weapon. Now we just have to wait for the forensic results and find out what each of them are saying.'

Peter gazed steadily at Cassie who was nodding in agreement. 'However, I don't want you to have any part in the interviews.' Cassie made to protest but Peter held up his hand to stop her. 'I can't let you take any further part in this investigation, Cassie, you must know that.'

Cassie pursed her lips. 'I could observe, sir, give you some insights, especially with Suzi.'

'I'd rather not at this stage. I want you to go home now. I'll call you if I have anything to report, or if I think you can assist me.' Cassie didn't move. 'That's all, DI Wade.'

However, Cassie wasn't happy to do just nothing, so she decided to get the ball rolling with the new information she had got from Suzi concerning Matthew Penworth, despite Peter's warning. He would be pleased if she managed to make progress on that score, wouldn't he? She knew that Saroj would be with Peter on the interviews so, as soon as they had left the squad room, she collared Robbie and Kevin to help her.

'We have new witness information that a man wearing running gear was seen leaving the vicinity of Susan Delaney's flat around the time that Carol Lightfoot was murdered.' Cassie wrote the description on the white board as she spoke. 'A man of about six foot wearing black or dark blue running shorts, of the lycra type, and a yellow T shirt with an emblem on the back. Our witness says he was in a hurry, but he could have just been running for exercise. We need to eliminate that man.'

'It's all a week too late, ma'am, isn't it?' said Kevin. 'People's memories aren't the best after all this time.'

Trying not to be dismissive, Cassie agreed. 'Very true, Kevin, but it's all we have. The T shirt may be connected to the area, though, and could be a running club. So as well as door to door enquiries and CCTV, let's check out local clubs.'

Robbie chipped in. 'It could also be cycling clubs, ma'am. They run for fitness as well as cycle.'

'Good point, Robbie, check them out as well. The clothing would almost certainly have blood on it, so, if our man had any sense, he would have wanted to dispose of it quickly. And before you make the point again Kevin, I know this is a bit late in the day to be searching dumpers, but let's give it a try. Also, find out when the bins were emptied and on what part of the landfill they would have been deposited.' Kevin wrinkled his nose at the thought of sifting through landfill.

Looking over towards Maggie, Cassie asked, 'Can you do the CCTV, Maggie? If our man wasn't a genuine runner, he probably had a car in the vicinity.'

Maggie nodded. 'On it, ma'am.'

'Oh, and can you let me know when the fingerprint analysis on the murder weapon comes in? See if we can tie it to our mystery man.'

'Okay everyone, keep in touch. I have to pop home first but let's agree to meet up later, say three o'clock in Penzance. Where's a good place to meet, Robbie?'

'Sainsbury's supermarket has a big café, ma'am.'

'Okay, we'll meet there. But don't forget, contact me anytime if you have a lead.'

Chapter Twenty-five

'We'll take Susan Delaney first.' Peter was talking to Saroj in the corridor. 'She either abducted Simon Makinson or removed him from the scene for another reason, which might make her complicit if he turns out to be our murderer.'

'Her being his mother is interesting. Do you think she was expecting him? Maybe he interrupted an argument between Susan and Carol Lightfoot, witnessed something, so she had to get him away.'

'Mmmm. We could do with the fingerprint results on the knife, but I don't want to delay the start of the interview.' He made a quick call to Maggie. 'Chase up forensic would you, Maggie, and interrupt the interview when you get something.' Maggie said she would, and quickly decided to keep Cassie's interest in the fingerprint analysis to herself for now. She was sure there was some tension between her two superiors, and she didn't want to get in the middle of it.

As the pair entered the interview room, Susan was already in deep conversation with her solicitor. Peter recognised the young woman. 'Ms Moorcroft, spending a lot of time here recently.'

'Good morning, Detective Chief Inspector. My client has a reasonable explanation to the events which took place on Sunday 7th April, so I'm sure we can resolve this matter quickly.'

Peter smiled at the expected introduction by Sylvia Moorcroft. She was a sharp cookie and was aware of the benefit of stating her case as soon as she could. But Peter was too experienced to be influenced by her bravado. 'Let's see what the next hour or so brings, shall we.'

Turning to Saroj, he signalled for her to start the recorder. Peter checked the time and introduced the session, asking each person to say their name for the record.

'Do you mind if I call you Susan?' he said to the tense looking woman sitting opposite. She shook her head.

'Okay, Susan, I want you to talk me through the events of the morning of Sunday 7th April. Don't leave anything out.'

Susan looked over at her solicitor for reassurance, then began. 'It was Easter day and we, that is Carol and I, were just about to have breakfast. It was more special because it was also Carol's birthday.' Susan paused as she remembered how she wanted to surprise Carol with a cake. 'Carol had never had much fuss made of her birthday and I wanted to give her a day to remember. Anyway, when I checked the fridge, I realised we were out of milk and short on bread, so I nipped out to the local shop.'

'What time would this have been?' asked Saroj, making a few notes.

'Oh, just after nine-thirty, I'd say. I told Carol not to answer the door and I made sure it was closed firmly behind me.'

'Why did you think it necessary to take these precautions?' Peter said.

'Carol had escaped a very violent man. He had already shown that he was capable of hunting her down.'

Peter stopped Susan there. 'Are you saying that this man knew where Carol Lightfoot was staying?'

Susan told the detectives about her and Carol being spotted and chased by the man, who she now named as Matthew Penworth, at the farmer's market. 'I thought that we had evaded him, though, but he must have seen us come into the flat. That's all I can imagine.'

Saroj got them back on track. 'So you left to get supplies.'

'Yes. I was gone about fifteen minutes, I suppose. When I got back, I noticed first that the street door was open, which was unusual. One of the other tenants must have failed to shut it, is what I thought. Anyway, I was cautious and crept up the stairs. My flat door was also open. I peeped in and saw...'

'Go on, Susan.'

Susan cleared her throat. 'I saw a young man standing near the sofa, looking down behind it. He was holding a knife. Then I saw

Carol's legs sticking out. It looked like she was lying down behind the sofa. The young man turned and looked at me.' Susan took a deep breath. 'I recognised him.'

'Can you tell us who the young man was?'

'When I say I recognised him, that's not quite right. I had spoken on the phone to a young man who thought he might be my son. You see, I had a child when I was young, and he was adopted. Simon had sought me out and we had spoken a few times, but I had never met him.'

'Yet you were sure it was your son?'

Susan smiled ruefully. 'He was the spitting image of his father and he had said when we spoke that he would come to see me. I'd put him off until the Monday, but he must have disregarded that.'

'What happened next?'

'I realised that Simon was holding a knife and I walked towards him to see what had happened. That's when I saw Carol. She was obviously dead, but I did check for a pulse. Simon was clearly in shock. He was trembling and saying mummy or mum, I can't remember exactly. I believed he thought that Carol was his mother. We're both slim and blonde.'

'Then what?'

At this point Sylvia Moorcroft touched Susan's arm and whispered something to her. To Peter she said, 'I would like a moment to consult with my client, chief inspector.'

Peter nodded and announced that the interview had been suspended before switching off the recorder.

Leaving the room, Peter almost collided with Maggie. 'Two things, sir,' she said. 'The forensics are back, and Simon Makinson has arrived and is with his solicitor.'

Peter and Saroj were meeting in his office discussing the new evidence. 'So that's interesting, Saroj. We have both Simon Makinson's and Matthew Penworth's prints on the knife. Susan Delaney's are there too, but then it was her flat, so that means nothing.'

'Do we know the order in which the prints were left, sir?'

Peter gave a hollow laugh. 'That would be helpful, wouldn't it? But, no, apparently there's no way of telling. Both sets are bloodstained.'

Peter continued to read the report. 'There are traces of blood on a shirt and jeans found in Simon Makinson's car. The clothes had obviously been washed but the blood was found in the seams. It is a match for Carol Lightfoot's blood group, but DNA analysis will take a couple of days, even though I've fast tracked it.'

'All things considered, sir, can we assume the blood is hers?'

'We can work on that hypothesis, yes. What we have been told so far is that Simon Makinson was found by Susan Delaney standing over the body with the knife in his hand.'

'That's pretty incriminating, but what would be his motive for killing Carol?'

'Susan Delaney said that she and our murder victim looked superficially the same. Simon hadn't actually met the woman he believed was his mother, so he could have mistaken Carol for Susan.'

'So are you saying he might have come with the intention of killing his birth mother? That seems a bit extreme.'

'I'm not saying that, Saroj. He didn't bring the knife with him. We know that because it had Susan Delaney's prints on it. So it could have been that they had an argument and he lost his temper, picked up the knife and stabbed her.'

'But if they had time for an argument to develop, wouldn't Carol have identified herself? I don't buy it, sir.'

'I admit it's a bit thin, but we can put these questions to Makinson himself and see what explanation he comes up with.'

'Then there's Penworth's prints to explain. If Susan was away for only fifteen minutes or so and Makinson was holding the knife when she came back, how did Penworth's prints get on the knife?'

'Okay Saroj, are you saying that Penworth must have been in the room before Makinson arrived? Susan Delaney was convinced that Penworth had discovered where Carol was living, so he could have been there to persuade her to come back with him.' Saroj nodded. 'So the sequence of events was – Penworth stabbed Carol and Makinson burst in on them?'

'Or the other way round. Makinson could have stabbed Carol and Penworth burst in on them. He pulled the knife out of her body and Makinson picked it up.' Saroj held out her hands in a who knows gesture.

'It's time we interviewed Makinson. He's had enough time with his solicitor.'

Allister Bradbury was an impressive sight. Immaculate in a dark pinstripe suit, crisp white shirt and blue silk tie. He was a black man, around six foot two with neatly cropped hair, slightly greying at the temples. Saroj put him at about fifty but he could have been older. His smile revealed even white teeth as he stood to shake hands with Peter and Saroj.

'Allister Bradbury,' he said in a deep strong voice. 'I've spoken to my client and I'm sure we can clear up this misunderstanding quickly.'

Peter smiled and said, 'We'll see, shall we?' then took his seat opposite Simon Makinson, noticing the young man's body language. His shoulders were slumped and his head bowed. Not the demeanour of an innocent man, Peter speculated. Saroj took the other chair facing the solicitor.

After Peter had started the recorder and everyone had introduced themselves, he turned to Simon. 'Do you understand why you are here, Simon?'

Allister Bradbury spoke up. 'We have a prepared statement, chief inspector,' he said passing a neatly handwritten sheet of paper to Peter. 'I believe that explains everything you want to know.'

Simon was deep in thought. He had heard from his solicitor that the police had found his fingerprints on the murder weapon. This wasn't a surprise, but he had suddenly become acutely aware of how much trouble he was in. He couldn't explain how the woman had been killed before he found her, and Mr Bradbury told him that it wasn't necessary for him to. That was for the police to determine. Still, it remained a mystery. Casting his mind back, the events of that morning were hazy to say the least. He had a clear memory of the excitement he felt at finally getting to meet his birth mother. He had deliberately not told her of his visit as he wanted to surprise her. He remembered later, when he and Susan were in the caravan, that he told her of the man he bumped into. He had also told Mr Bradbury about the man, and felt that the solicitor laid great store on this information, seizing on it as what he called an alternative suspect, which gave room for reasonable doubt. The police must be persuaded to search for this man at all costs.

Simon became aware that the detective was addressing him. 'May I call you Simon?'

Simon nodded, then said, 'Yes, I don't mind.'

'Okay, Simon, it's good that you have prepared a statement, but I'd like you to tell me in your own words, what happened on the morning of the 7th April.'

Simon looked at his solicitor, who said to Peter, 'You have the statement, detective.'

Ignoring this, Peter repeated, 'In your own words, if you please, Simon.'

Allister Bradbury nodded. So Simon cleared his throat and began.

'I'm adopted. I've always known this, my parents never hid a thing from me or my sister. So, a couple of years ago I started to look for my birth mother. It was surprisingly easy. I had my birth certificate and just searched for her online.' He smiled then at the memory. 'She was a little bit famous. A writer and champion of women's rights. I felt proud of her, if that doesn't sound silly. I knew she was very young when she had me and I suppose I had always thought that she must have been a tearaway, you know, a bit wild. Anyway, my adoption certificate led me to the adoption society, and I found that Susan had left a letter and phone number for me if I ever wanted to contact her. I didn't act on it for a while, a bit scared I suppose, and I was busy with uni. Anyway, long story short, I eventually phoned her. She told me she was living in Cornwall and was happy for us to meet.'

'When did you arrive in Cornwall?' Saroj asked, preparing to make a note of the answer.

'I left London on Good Friday, it was the start of my Easter holidays. I booked into a Premier Inn in Camborne and got there about six on Friday evening.'

Saroj made a note to check out the booking. 'When did you make contact with Susan Delaney?'

'As soon as I arrived. I was excited. I was getting to meet my birth mother at last and I didn't want to wait.'

'But you didn't go to see her until the Sunday.'

'No. She said she would be busy on Saturday and it was her friend's birthday on Sunday. She said she wanted to spend the day with her. She told me she would ring me on the Monday, and she gave me her address.'

'But you didn't wait until Monday.'

'I spent Saturday driving around. I went to Falmouth because of the sailing connection. I'd sailed there before, you see, and Falmouth has a lot of maritime history. I enjoyed the trip but I couldn't get Susan off my mind. That night I decided to surprise her, I couldn't spend another day wandering about, it would have driven me mad. So I set off early the next morning. The roads were busy, holiday traffic I supposed, and it was about nine-thirty when I arrived in Penzance. The SATNAV told me I had arrived at my destination, but I was on a busy road, so I pulled into a side street and got Google Maps to take me the rest of the way on foot.'

Allister Bradbury tapped Simon on his arm to stop him. 'Chief inspector, I really do believe that the statement adequately covers the events. Do you really need to put my client through this?'

'I do, Mr Bradbury.' Then to Simon he said, 'Are you okay to carry on or would you like a break?'

'No, I'm okay,' said Simon, glancing apologetically at his solicitor, who shrugged and leaned back in his chair.

Simon thought for a moment, then continued. 'I was looking at my phone, not taking notice of people on the street. Isn't that what people say about mobiles? They make you blind and deaf. Anyway, as I approached the building I was after, a man bumped into me. I got the impression that he had come from a house, not from along the pavement. He almost knocked the phone out of my hand. I glanced down the street at him and thought that he was a runner, you know, out exercising.'

'Can you describe the man, Simon?' Saroj said.

'I've thought a lot about it since. He was about six feet tall, I think, with lightish hair, he may have had a pony-tail, but I can't be sure. I thought he was a runner because he had those lycra shorts on, black or a dark colour, and a yellow T shirt with writing on the back. Not like from a pop concert, more like a club logo.'

'Did you notice anything else?'

'No, he was running away from me.'

'Which direction?'

'Er, opposite to the way I had come, so I'd say towards the town. I could see the railway station in that direction too.'

Saroj made a note. 'Okay, then what?'

184

'Well, I realised that I'd missed the flats, probably because of the man distracting me, so I walked back a few paces to find it. The door to the building was open so I didn't have to ring. I went up to flat eight where Susan lived, and the door was open there too. I remember thinking that she must be very trusting, leaving her doors open like that. I went in and called out but there was no reply. Then I saw someone lying behind the sofa, just their legs sticking out.'

'What did you think had happened, Simon?'

'I don't know, an accident or something.' Simon took a deep breath and sipped some water.

'Take your time,' said Peter. 'This is important. What did you do next?'

'I went over and looked. There was a woman just lying there, face up.' Simon swallowed hard. 'It was horrible. She was covered in blood but that wasn't the worst part, her face... it was terrible, all disfigured with one eye closed, missing I think, and the other just staring upwards. Then I saw the knife. It was in her chest.'

'What did you do?'

'I pulled it out. Oh, I know that's not what you're supposed to do, you see it all the time in crime dramas on TV, but you don't think, do you? Blood spurted out a bit and ran down her top. I wanted to see if she was still alive, but I was shaking so much I couldn't do it properly. I thought it was her, you see, my mother. I think I said something like mum? But I can't be sure because just then Susan came into the room.'

The solicitor was about to speak when Peter held his hand up to stop him. 'Okay, Mr Bradbury, I'll leave it there for now. You've been very helpful Simon. I'll get someone to take you back to your cell and arrange some refreshments for you.'

'Can I see my parents now?'

'That won't be possible. I'm sure Mr Bradbury will be speaking to them. And he'll let them know you're okay.'

Simon nodded glumly. 'Is Susan alright?'

Peter simply shook his head. 'We'll see you in a little while.'

When Peter was alone with Saroj in the interview room he said, 'What do you make of that?'

'If he's telling the truth, it could be like we said. Someone, perhaps Penworth, was in the flat just before Simon. He stabbed

Carol when she refused to come with him and then ran, bumping into Simon on his way out.'

'Mmm. I'll get Cassie on to it. She'll not thank me for spoiling her weekend, but we need to follow up on this mystery man straight away.'

Chapter Twenty-six

But of course, Cassie was already on to it, and her weekend was well and truly spoiled. She had called at home to find her two teenagers playing a video game. They looked up as she came in. 'You're in trouble,' said Micky smirking. 'Mark stayed for a while, then he left saying to tell you he'd be in touch.'

Tanya chipped in, 'He didn't look too pleased, so I'd say don't hold your breath for a phone call.'

Cassie swore under her breath. 'When did he leave?'

'About half an hour ago,' said Micky checking the time on his phone. 'He got a cab to the station.'

Cassie was out of the house in a flash. There was no room on the small station car park, so she left her car in the pick-up area. She spotted Mark on the far platform. He saw her too but didn't wave, he simply looked at his feet. Cassie ran to the bridge and crossed over the railway line. Approaching Mark, a bit breathless, she said, 'I'm so sorry. Really, Mark, it's just that everything kicked off at once. We've got two suspects in custody and I'm hard on the heels of another, it's mad but the time just flew. I know I should have phoned but…'

Mark stopped her. 'I understand, Cassie. Really I do. But I'm realising that this might not work. You'll always be needed elsewhere.'

'That's not fair, Mark. Have you forgotten us spending the night together? And don't forget, it was your idea to come down this weekend. I told you we had a big case on the go, but you insisted. You can't blame me for doing my job.' Cassie was getting angry at the unfairness of Mark's stance.

Mark shuffled his feet. 'No, you're right, Cassie, I did want to see you this weekend and get to know your kids too, but don't you see how impossible it is? My work is going through a quiet period at the moment, that's why I have time to do training and stuff, but sooner or later I'll get busy when you're free. Everyone I know in the force says that relationships between cops don't work. Perhaps they're right.'

'You sound like a petulant schoolboy.' Cassie was really angry now. 'You want to pack it in because of one missed arrangement? Well, go ahead, call me when you see sense.' And with that barbed comment, she stalked away.

As Cassie was climbing into her car, her phone vibrated. 'Yes!' she shouted.

'No need to bite my head off, ma'am,' said Robbie. 'I've been up to my armpits in dumpers and a skip for the last hour.'

'Okay, Robbie, spare me the sob story. What did you want?'

'Only to tell you that I think I've found the clothing we were looking for. Well, part of it anyway. There was a skip outside a domestic dwelling. The man who opened the door said the skip hire people had been delayed collecting it due to the Easter weekend. Anyway, I've got a pale-yellow T shirt with blood stains on it. It's a Penzance Cruisers' shirt, they're a cycling club.'

'Yes!' Cassie shouted. 'That's great, Robbie. Sorry for snapping, you've done a good job. Get it over to forensics, will you.'

Cassie had forgotten about Mark completely. She was back on the trail and feeling excited. Keying in another number, she connected with Maggie. 'Any news on the CCTV front, Mags?'

'Yes, I have got something,' she replied tentatively. 'But the Chief wants to see you urgently, he's none too pleased by the looks of him.'

'Righto, I'm on my way. Tell him five minutes will you?'

Cassie spoke out loud to herself as she drove. 'So we've got Penworth's fingerprints on the murder weapon and a blood stained shirt which could be his. He certainly has motive and opportunity.' She wondered if she should call and arrest him on her way to the station, but decided she should speak to Peter first. He was sure to be pleased about this development. And Maggie said she had something from CCTV. Hopefully Penworth running away from the scene. Screeching to a halt in the car park, Cassie wasted no time in getting to the squad room. Spotting Maggie at the photocopier, she went up to her. 'What have you got then, Mags?'

Maggie's eyes flashed over to Peter's office where he was waiting at the open door. 'In here now, DI Wade,' he said. 'If you don't mind.'

Cassie was no sooner through the door than she started to tell Peter about the new evidence, but he stopped her in her tracks. 'What was my last instruction to you, DI Wade?'

'What, sir? Oh, you mean telling me to go home and enjoy my weekend, something like that.'

'Yes, exactly like that. So why have you been carrying out investigations of your own and involving three members of my team to help you? When we already have two suspects being interviewed for this crime.'

'Look, sir, I know what you're saying but Penworth is a suspect too, at least in my books. He's had more than enough time to cover his tracks, so I thought it was vital to get onto it as soon as possible. And, as you didn't want me involved in the interviews with Suzi or Simon Makinson, I thought it would be a good use of my time.'

'You thought, did you? What don't you understand about the chain of command? I decide what investigations are carried out and, as it happens, I do have my suspicions about Penworth's role in this, but I can do without you going off half-cocked. If we are to arrest him, I don't want him walking away again.'

'I haven't approached him, sir,' said Cassie, now thankful that she hadn't arrested him, 'but I do have some new evidence that could be important. Robbie has found a blood-stained T shirt near the scene, one that matches the description Suzi gave me.'

'The description Suzi gave you? And just when did you receive that information? Under caution? In interview? When?'

'Not exactly, sir. I mean I did caution her, but she gave me the information before that, if we're being technical.'

'Oh, I think we have to be technical, don't you? Penworth's solicitor could insist that the information gained in that way was inadmissible.' Peter thought he'd made Cassie suffer enough. 'Fortunately for you, Simon Makinson gave up that information in interview so we can legitimately follow it up. We also have Penworth's prints on the murder weapon.'

'Yes!' shouted Cassie. 'It's him, I know it is sir.'

'Okay, DI Wade. I think you might be interested in something that Maggie has found. But I want you to listen to me. Stay out of this investigation until I ask you to get involved, okay?'

'Yes, sir. And I'm sorry for the misunderstanding.'

'Go, before I decide to discipline you.'

Cassie left the office and went straight over to Maggie's desk. 'You okay?' said Maggie quietly.

'I'm fine, just got our wires crossed.'

Maggie was sure it was more than that but wasn't going to pry. Instead, she brought up an image on her computer. It was of a man in running gear on the road near Susan Delaney's flat, just his back view unfortunately, but he had the same hair colour and build as Matthew Penworth. Maggie switched screens and the image became one of a side street, with the same man getting into a car. The registration was clear. 'It's Penworth's car, ma'am,' said Maggie smiling.

'Great work, Maggie.' Aware of doing things by the book and checking with Peter before she did anything, Cassie said, 'We'll wait for the blood analysis on the T shirt, then I think it might be time to bring him in.'

Chapter Twenty-seven

Gerald Makinson was pacing. His wife Avril sat, wringing her hands, a box of tissues on her lap. 'It's all that woman's fault,' she said, not for the first time.

'Give it a rest, Avril,' Gerald said sharply. 'Let's hear what Allister has to say before we say anything else on the subject.'

'Well, you have to admit that if Simon hadn't gone chasing off after his birth mother… birth mother, ha! What did she ever do for him? Pushed him out, that's all. Then abandoned him. Now she's the best thing since sliced bread. After everything we've done, Gerald.' Avril started sobbing again.

Just then there was a sharp tap on the hotel room door. 'That'll be Allister,' said Gerald, walking quickly over to let him in.

Allister looked grave, and Avril's sobbing increased. He looked at the pair of them and felt heartily sorry for his old friends. 'Sit down, Gerald. I'll go through things as I see them at this point. And I don't want you to worry, I believe that he's done nothing wrong, apart from leaving the scene of a crime, and that's a misdemeanour.'

Gerald sat facing Allister. 'Go on. Tell us the worst,' he said gloomily.

'They have his fingerprints on the murder weapon.' Avril let out a cry. Allister cut in quickly. 'He has an explanation for that, which I accept. He is sure that Susan Delaney will back him up, too. He said that she believes the murderer is an ex-partner of Carol Lightfoot, that's the victim. He was violent to her in the past, apparently. I understand that the police are looking into him as a possible suspect. They won't tell me more than that.'

Gerald wanted to know more. 'So what's his explanation for having a murder weapon in his hand?'

'He found the woman, Carol, dead, stabbed. The knife was in her chest and he pulled it out. I think he thought it would help.'

'The bloody fool,' said Gerald. 'Why didn't he just get out of there? Call the police?'

'I believe he thought that the dead woman was his birth mother.'

Avril let out another cry. 'I told you, Gerald, it all comes back to her. If only he'd let things lie. He had such a promising future, and now what? Prison?'

'Don't get yourself het up, Avril.' Gerald went to her side and put his arm around her. To Allister he said, 'So what's next?'

Allister checked his watch. 'I'd better get back. They want to start the second interviews soon.' He shook Gerald's hand. 'I'll keep in touch.'

'Sylvia Moorcroft is asking what the delay is, sir.' Kevin said, as he looked in on Saroj and Peter.

'Let her wait,' said an irritated Peter. 'No, on second thoughts, you can tell her that we're looking into something which may be of benefit to her client. That should keep her quiet. If she wants to leave, she can. We may not get round to second interviews today if we bring Penworth in. Don't mention that, naturally.'

Kevin gave a rueful smile. As if I would, he thought. The chief's a bit jumpy about this case since Cassie went AWOL.

Passing Maggie's desk, he checked on progress with the blood stain. 'I wish everyone wouldn't keep asking me about that. I'll tell the Chief as soon as I have something, okay?'

Lordy, Kevin thought, everyone's a bit touchy. 'I'm going to the canteen. Anyone want anything?' he said, trying to bring a bit of normality back into the squad.

'Cassie's there at the moment, she's organising sandwiches,' said Maggie without looking up.

'Sweet,' said Kevin. 'It'll probably be a long day.'

Suddenly Maggie jumped up and almost ran to Peter's office. Kevin stayed where he was. 'We've got the blood result, sir,' said Maggie to Peter. 'It's the same group as Carol Lightfoot, DNA to follow as soon as they can, they know it's fast tracked.'

192

'I think that's enough. Come with me, Saroj, we'll pick the bastard up.'

Cassie heard the last part of the conversation. 'You're picking Penworth up? Shouldn't I be in on that, sir?' she added as an after-thought.

'I don't mind, sir,' said Saroj. 'DI Wade is the senior officer.'

Peter nodded. 'Okay Cassie, get your coat, you've pulled.' Cassie smiled at the joke. Things were back to normal for the moment.

Penworth wasn't at his home. Peter called for a constable to stand guard outside and let them know if he turned up. Meanwhile, he and Cassie drove off to Truro and parked by the Pannier market. Arriving at Penworth's stall, they saw him in conversation with another stall holder, seemingly sharing a joke. He turned and saw the two detectives bearing down on him and, for a moment, it looked as if he might make a run for it. However, he stood his ground and faced Peter and Cassie, hands on hips. 'What do you want with me now? It's police harassment, that's what. I may make a complaint.'

Peter ignored the barb. He simply took out a pair of handcuffs and read Matthew Penworth his rights. He followed up with, 'You're nicked son, and this time you won't be coming back.'

The market was busy on this Saturday afternoon and the incident had caused a small crowd to gather. Penworth turned and snarled at them. 'What are you looking at?' He turned to his neighbouring stall holder. 'Lock up for me, Ted, I'll see you later.' Then, straightening his shoulders, he allowed Peter to lead him from the market.

Back in the squad room Peter faced the team. 'Let's take stock of where we are,' he said, sitting on the edge of a desk. 'I think we can release Susan Delaney for now, but keep Makinson until we've interviewed Penworth.'

'Simon Makinson's solicitor is here, sir, and demanding we either charge or release his client,' Saroj said. 'And I think he has a point. Simon's come up with a reasonable explanation as to why he was at the murder scene, and Susan Delaney's statement backs him up. With what we have on Penworth, it's looking likely that we'll be able to charge him with murder, then we'd be looking at a lesser charge for Makinson.'

Cassie agreed. 'I think we should release him to his parents' custody with the condition that he stays at the hotel with them.'

Peter held his hand up to silence his team. 'Alright, I hear what you're saying. Here's what we'll do. Saroj and I will interview Delaney and Makinson one more time, then, if their accounts are consistent, we'll let them go.'

There were nods of agreement around the room. Then Cassie raised her hand as if in a classroom. 'I'd like to join you for Makinson's interview, sir. I understand why I can't be involved with Susan but there's no reason I can't be useful with the boy.'

Peter wanted to be fair to his DI. 'What exactly did Susan Delaney tell you when you picked her up?'

'I didn't question her, sir, and I stopped her and cautioned her when she wanted to go into detail. I can be objective, really.'

Peter pondered for a few seconds. The whole team seemed to hold their breath, hoping that the rift that seemed to have developed between the Chief and Cassie had been healed.

'Okay, Cassie, you and I will take Makinson first as his solicitor is already here. Saroj, get Sylvia Moorcroft back if she's left, and find a duty solicitor for Penworth. Obviously, it can't be Moorcroft.'

Cassie was delighted but tried not to show too much elation. She and Peter retired to his office to discuss tactics. 'I think you should start, Cassie. This young man is vulnerable and might respond better to a female. You've read Saroj's notes but what I want is an account of how things were left after Susan found him at the scene, you can start there. I'll jump in if I need to.'

'Right, sir, and thanks again for this.'

'Just do a good job, Cassie.'

Allister Bradbury started by asking for his client to be released, which wasn't a surprise. Cassie acknowledged his request and said that she just had a few more questions to put to Simon. The solicitor nodded. Cassie continued, addressing herself to Simon. 'And I advise you to be completely truthful, Simon.'

Simon straightened his back and looked directly at the imposing black woman facing him. Susan had described her lifelong friend to him, and he wondered if this was she. 'I haven't been lying,' he said. 'I've got nothing to hide, I didn't kill that woman.'

'Okay,' Cassie said gently. 'Let's pick up from when Susan came into the room. You were standing with a knife in your hand. What happened next?'

Allister Bradbury nodded, so Simon began talking. 'I think I was in shock because everything moved slowly, like a dream. Susan took the knife off me and I think she checked the woman for a pulse. Then everything speeded up. It was like being drunk, you know, when you only partly realise what's happening. I was leaving, going down the stairs to the street and Susan was leading me. She was talking but I can't remember what about. She asked about my car, I remember that, and I gave her my keys.'

Simon had been looking at the table while he spoke but suddenly looked up, straight at Cassie. 'She was protecting me. I don't know… I felt that I would be okay as long as I was with her, d'you understand? I just let her take control, it was easy.'

'Carry on, Simon, you're doing very well.'

He shrugged, 'Well, she asked me to get cash from the ATM…'

'Can you remember where that was, Simon?'

'Er, a supermarket, I think. Yeah, a big car park and a supermarket.'

'That's good, Simon. What happened next?'

'I slept. I can't believe that now, after what had happened, but I fell asleep. When I woke up there was a blanket over me, and we were arriving at the caravan site.'

Cassie glanced at Peter, a signal that she had finished, and he should take over. Peter addressed Simon. 'Okay, I'm going to leave it there for now. You can go and be with your parents, but I want you to stay with them. I will almost certainly want to see you again tomorrow, so no leaving Cornwall, okay?'

Simon looked relieved. 'Thank you. I won't go anywhere, I promise.'

Cassie and Peter watched Allister Bradbury and Simon walk away. 'I believe him,' said Cassie. 'Poor lad was in the wrong place at the wrong time.'

'Perhaps if your friend hadn't been around, he would have done

195

the right thing and called the police. We could have had Penworth charged by now. She's got a lot to answer for.'

Cassie remained silent. She was just protecting her son, she thought, what would you have done? But she just shrugged and said, 'Who knows?'

Sylvia Moorcroft burst through the station doors and strode over to reception. 'Back so soon?' said the sergeant smiling, 'we'll have to get you a desk.'

Sylvia smiled back, liking the cheeky sergeant despite her mood. 'Always happy to help. Now could you tell DCI Sanders that I'm here.'

'No need,' said a voice from the doorway. Cassie shook hands with the solicitor. 'I apologise for the inconvenience, Ms Moorcroft. DCI Sanders is ready for you, if you'll follow me.'

'I'd like to see my client first, DI Wade.'

'Naturally. How is she holding up?' Cassie couldn't resist finding out a little about her friend.

'She's fine,' said the solicitor. 'There really isn't a case to answer so I'm fully expecting her release.'

'Here we are,' said Cassie, indicating a doorway. 'I'll have Ms Delaney brought up.' Cassie wondered if Suzi really was fine. She knew her friend's first thoughts would be for Simon and Cassie hoped that Suzi wasn't going to sacrifice herself for him. She was quite capable of such a gesture, and, not knowing about the situation with Penworth, she could still believe that Simon was in danger. To Sylvia she said quietly, 'Simon Makinson has been released for now and we have another prime suspect.' Sylvia looked round shocked. 'You didn't hear it from me, though.'

The solicitor inclined her head. 'Thank you, DI Wade. It's good to know.'

Sylvia Moorcroft sat at the side of her client. Smiling, she tapped Susan's arm. 'I think it's time to make a statement.'

Susan looked at her solicitor. 'What's happening to Simon? Is he alright?'

'I understand that Mr Makinson has been released for now and

196

they are holding a new suspect.' Susan gasped, and Sylvia continued. 'The police will almost certainly want to speak to Simon again, but it seems they have decided not to hold him for the moment.' She studied Susan. 'It's a good sign.'

Susan nodded, looking relieved. 'That's good news. Now, what do you want from me?'

Formalities concluded, Saroj started the interview. 'Shall we begin where we left off, Susan? You had entered the room and saw Simon Makinson holding a knife.'

Susan checked with Sylvia, who nodded. 'I want to make a statement,' she said.

'Go ahead,' said Saroj. 'We're listening.'

'After I saw Simon with the knife, I went over and saw Carol lying there, behind the sofa. She was obviously dead, but I checked for a pulse anyway. Things sort of accelerated from then on.' She took a deep breath. 'Immediately I saw Simon I knew he was my son. He looked just like his father.'

'Can I stop you there, Susan,' said Saroj. 'I understand you became pregnant after you were raped when you were fourteen, is that correct?'

'Yes,' said Susan hesitantly.

'How can you be sure, after all this time, and considering the trauma of that event, that you would recognise your assailant again?'

'I definitely would, and I wouldn't call him an assailant. It wasn't like I was attacked in an alley or something. I spent time with him, and he was kind. I know it was rape, technically, but I didn't see it like that at the time. He was handsome and talented, and I thought he was really interested in me. With hindsight, I know that was silly, but then I was young and foolish.' She gave a wry grin. 'But, to answer your question, I will never forget his face, ever. And Simon is the image of him.'

'Okay, so you knew Simon was your son,' Saroj prompted.

Susan started cautiously. 'You have to understand, detectives, I have grown used to crisis situations. Over the years I have rescued women and children from violent situations more times than I could mention, so I sort of went into rescue mode. All I could think of was getting Simon away from that room to somewhere safe where we could talk.'

Peter spoke then. 'But, for all you knew, Simon could have just stabbed your flatmate.'

'I'm not saying it was entirely logical, but even in my panic, I never believed that. I always intended to call the police when I knew more, but I could see how it would look to an outsider. Above all, I wanted to protect him.'

'Is that why you took the knife?'

'Yes, I suppose. It was a reflex action.'

'So you were sure that Simon hadn't stabbed Carol. What did you think had happened?'

'The very thing Carol feared would happen. Her ex-partner, Matthew Penworth, had found her and killed her.'

Susan went on to describe the chance encounter she and Carol had had with Matthew Penworth in Penzance. 'He was obsessed with getting Carol back, and he was very resourceful. I believe he followed us that day and saw where we were living. He knew me from Women's Aid and hated me. I think if I'd been there when he arrived, he might have killed me too.'

Susan leant forward and put the palms of her hands on the table. 'I can't stress enough how dangerous this man is, detective inspector. He will find another victim and kill again if he's not stopped. He almost killed Carol a few months ago, but somehow walked away from that. If you allow him to walk away from this…'

Peter stopped her flow. 'Okay, Ms Delaney. Tell me what happened next.'

Susan settled back in her seat. 'I drove Simon's car. He was in shock and didn't really understand what was happening. I knew you would be looking for me so I stopped and asked Simon to get some cash so there wouldn't be a trace on my card.'

'Where was that exactly?'

'Morrison's car park.'

'Go on.'

'I phoned Women's Aid and asked to book the caravan for a week. Fortunately, it was free. Then I turned off my phone, I had switched Simon's off earlier. I drove to the caravan at Praa Sands and looked after Simon.'

'You seem to have thought of everything, Susan.'

198

'Like I told you, it's been my life for a long time. I know how to escape detection.'

'Why didn't you call the police straight away? You spent a whole week with Simon, time when we could have been looking for the murderer.'

Susan thought for a few seconds. 'I can't really answer that logically. I suppose I thought if we stayed away you would find out that Matthew Penworth was responsible, and then we could come out of hiding. Ultimately, I wanted to spend time with my son.'

Peter nodded. 'Thank you, Ms Delaney. I'm going to release you for now, but I want you to stay in the vicinity and don't even think of contacting Simon Makinson.'

Susan sighed, clearly relieved to be let go. 'It's okay for me to go home?'

Peter nodded. 'It may still be a bit of a mess, but I believe our forensics team have finished.'

Susan thought briefly about the room where Carol had been killed and imagined the blood stain which would still be on the carpet. She could soon clean that up, but the events of that day would be forever etched on her mind. The twist of fate that led Mathew Penworth to her home at the same time as her son. It seemed bizarre now, but she was strong and would get over it. She wasn't as sure about Simon.

Chapter Twenty-eight

Back in the squad room Peter was briefing the team. 'We've let Susan Delaney and Simon Makinson go for now. We will probably charge both of them with perverting the course of justice, but I am quite sure that neither of them committed the murder of Carol Lightfoot.' He looked around the room and noted the collective nods of agreement. 'I am confident that we have enough to charge Matthew Penworth with the murder. That should happen today. Well done everyone for the excellent work in bringing this to a conclusion. The first drinks will be on me tonight.'

A muffled cheer erupted from the team. Peter continued, 'But the second will be on DI Wade,' he laughed.

'Too right,' she said, her Liverpool accent coming out.

'Now, Cassie, let's go and nail the bastard.'

Before they could leave the room, Kevin came in, obviously with news. 'I went back to Penworth's lock up ma'am,' he said, 'and found this.' He showed Peter and Cassie a photograph on his phone. It was of a box of yellow T shirts with the Penzance Cruisers logo on the back. 'Penworth must obviously be the club's supplier.'

'That's good work, Kevin,' said Peter. 'He can't claim that he didn't have access to the shirt, and it's one more thing to tie him to the murder scene.'

Matthew Penworth had taken up his usual pose, relaxed and arrogant. The duty solicitor was Daniel Spruce and he looked none too pleased at having to represent such a reprehensible human being as Penworth. However, he began by saying that his client would not be making a statement today, and that he maintained his innocence.

Peter faced Penworth. 'That, of course, is your right, Matthew. Is it okay if I call you Matthew?'

'It's my name,' said Penworth with a shrug.

'I thought you might like to know that we're releasing Carol Lightfoot's body today, her parents are taking her home.'

'Her parents!' shouted Matthew. 'They didn't care about her. Why should they have her body? I should be the one burying her, she's mine!'

Peter was pleased that his ploy to rattle Penworth was paying off. 'So she was yours, you say?'

'She belonged to me, you know? Like the songs? They all say, *she belongs to me…*' He sang the last bit. 'It was like that with us.'

'So you had a loving relationship?'

Matthew looked stunned. 'Of course. She was nothing when I got her. I gave her everything she could want.'

'You gave her everything,' echoed Peter, 'but was she satisfied?'

'Now you've hit the nail on the head, mate. They're never satisfied, are they? They take from you and then want to leave. Ungrateful, that's what I call it.'

'Carol was ungrateful,' echoed Peter.

Matthew backtracked. 'Well, no, not exactly. She had her head turned, watching these TV shows, you know *Loose Women* and the like. Thought she could do without me. I put a stop to that, though; no more TV.'

Daniel Spruce laid a warning hand on Penworth's arm, but he shrugged it off.

Cassie took over from Peter. 'But she did leave you,' she stated quietly.

Matthew swung his head round to face Cassie. 'What would you know about it? She had her head turned, like I said. It was them cows at the women's place, they wouldn't let her come home.'

'You mean after you beat her up?' Cassie knew she was sailing close to the wind but thought that Peter was being too subtle.

'I didn't do that,' he sat back smugly. 'It was never proved that I did.'

'But she left you and went to live with a woman. Perhaps she preferred women.'

'Don't be daft, she wanted me, she was likely teaching me a lesson, but I knew she'd come home if I wanted her to.'

'But you couldn't get to her, could you? You didn't know where she was.'

'Oh, I knew.' Daniel tried to speak to Matthew, but he ignored his solicitor. 'She was with that Women's Aid tart. Filling her head with feminist rubbish. I just had to see her, and I knew she'd come home.'

'So you went to see her?'

Daniel Spruce couldn't hold back any longer. 'My client retains the right not to answer your questions.'

'Shut up, you,' said Matthew. 'Yes, I went to see her. She'd completely changed. You should have seen the nightdress she was wearing, like a tart she looked.'

'And you didn't like that, did you, Matthew. You liked her in pink. Pretty things.'

'I told her to put something decent on and come home with me. I said I wouldn't punish her, and we'd put it behind us.'

'What did she say to that?'

'It just shows how they had brainwashed her. She said she'd rather die.'

'Then what happened?' Cassie was getting excited, but her voice remained calm.

'She went for the window. I thought she would jump out or something stupid. Not in her right mind, see? When I pulled her back, to save her like, she grabbed a knife.' Matthew's face crumpled and tears welled up in his eyes. 'She pushed me away, said she hated me. Me! She wasn't herself, she kept pushing and struggling. The knife just slipped into her.'

'Where did Carol grab the knife from, Matthew?'

'Matthew looked puzzled. 'How d'you mean?'

'It's a simple question. Carol was going towards the window. Where was the knife?'

'I don't know. She just had it, like I said. But I took it off her so that she couldn't use it on me.'

202

Daniel Spruce sat back and sighed, running his hand through his hair and closing his eyes. If only they'd listen, he said to himself.

Peter asked Matthew to clarify. 'You were holding the knife and it slipped into her?'

'Yes, I took it off her. Silly cow, why would she do that? She could have just come home with me and everything would have been alright.'

Daniel Spruce spoke up then. 'I'd say my client was defending himself, wouldn't you, detective inspector?'

Peter didn't respond but simply set out some crime scene photographs of Carol Lightfoot's arms. 'See these cuts here Matthew? They are defensive wounds inflicted at the time of her attack by you.' Matthew and his solicitor stared silently at the images. 'There was only one person defending herself here, Matthew, and that was Carol Lightfoot, trying to ward off a vicious attack from you.'

'I think, Mr Spruce, that a jury would have no hesitation but to come to the same conclusion. Right now, I'm charging your client with murder.'

Kevin, Maggie and Robbie were waiting apprehensively when Peter and Cassie returned to the squad room. They both walked in solemn faced, then, not able to keep up the pretence, Cassie cracked a smile and waved her hands in the air. 'We got him!' she shouted, and a cheer rose up from the team.

'Well done everybody,' said Peter. 'I just have to make a phone call and then it's the pub.'

'Not before you have one of these,' said Robbie, and he popped a Champagne cork.

'It'll have to be mugs,' said Maggie.

'I don't care if it's a sweaty wellie, Maggie,' Cassie said. 'Bring it on!'

Chapter Twenty-nine

Simon hugged his mother and his dad patted him on the back. 'It's so good to have you back, son,' he said. They were in Mr and Mrs Makinson's hotel room. There was a bottle of Champagne in an ice bucket on the desk with four glasses. 'We're expecting Claire sometime, but I think we can open this now,' Mr Makinson said, picking up the bottle.

'It's not over yet, dad,' said Simon, 'the police want me back.'

'Yes, but they've let you go,' said Mrs Makinson, 'that must mean something. They've obviously realised that you couldn't have done such a terrible thing. Allister said so.'

Mr Makinson was pouring the wine, but Simon didn't feel like celebrating. He was concerned about Susan. Had they let her go too? He really wanted to speak to her, but he knew that wouldn't go down well with his mother. 'Did you get me a room, dad?' he asked.

'I did, son, it's just down the corridor. Here's the key.' He handed Simon the key card.

Simon took his chance. 'I'll just freshen up if that's okay. Then I'll have that drink.'

As soon as Simon was alone, he called Susan's number. It rang several times, and he was just about to give up when a quiet voice said, 'Hello.'

'Hi, it's me,' Simon knew that she would recognise his voice. 'Are you okay?'

'Simon, I've been so worried, but we shouldn't be talking. The police warned me not to contact you.'

'Well, you haven't, I've contacted you,' he joked. 'It's so good to hear your voice. They've let me go for now, but I can't figure why. The worst part, though, was not knowing what was happening to you.'

'My guess is that they've got a much more likely suspect. I told you about Matthew Penworth, didn't I? Well, I think Cassie, my friend, was following that up.'

'Is that DI Wade?'

'Yes, Cassandra Wade, she's a good mate.'

'She interviewed me with the chief inspector. I was shit scared I can tell you.' There was no reply from Susan. 'What do you think will happen next?'

Susan hated to think about her son being scared. 'Try not to worry, Simon. They might charge us with perverting the course of justice, and that may be a just slap on the wrist.' She didn't tell him that it could also mean a prison sentence. Susan was aware that the police may be tracing their calls so wanted to cut the discussion short. 'Look, Simon, I should go. We'll speak again soon, but for now you should try to relax with your family, okay?'

'Alright, I'll try,' he said quietly. 'I'm glad I found you, you know. I hope you don't regret it.'

Suzi was touched. 'Never. I loved our time together. And we can have other times, in better circumstances.' Simon said goodbye and there were tears in Suzi's eyes as she finished the call. She feared that their relationship had got off to such a dramatic start, thrown together as they were by the awful events of that day, that normal life would be too ordinary. He had needed her then, depended on her, perhaps the reality when it came could never match that.

After the excitement of the previous week, Saroj was not able to settle. Taking the day off, she decided to pay another visit to her father. She wasn't quite sure why, especially as the last one had ended badly. However, she was tormented by the thought that there was unfinished business between them. One bone of contention had been her not taking up medicine after she finished her degree. At the back of her mind there had always been the nagging feeling that she had only refused to become a doctor to spite her father. She loved her job and felt she was a good detective, but had no interest in progressing up the ladder. She was a hands-on person. For a while now she had been thinking of changing direction and, albeit unwittingly, her father had reminded her of her love of anatomy. A seed had been germinating in her mind and, now that she had time to think, it had developed into an idea. Perhaps her father would die easy if she told him. Maybe she owed him that.

The other person that had been lurking at the back of Saroj's mind was Erica Trevellian. Without fully understanding why, she had taken a keen interest in the girl and had been thinking how satisfying it would be to care for and shape a young person. A child of her own might still be possible, she wasn't too old, but the long hours and erratic nature of her job with the police meant that she had never got to know anyone well enough to want to start a family with. The job she had in mind, though demanding, would give her more stability.

All of these thoughts were racing around her mind as she pulled up at the hospital car park. Taking the ticket from the machine, she wound her way around the rows of vehicles looking for a space, thinking how much easier it was when she was on police business and could leave her car more or less where she wanted to. Finding a small space at the end of a row, she squeezed in, having to contort her body to exit from the car.

Saroj found the ward easily but stopped at the doorway, slightly surprised to see the family gathered around her father's bed. As she approached, her mother looked up, tears in her eyes. She held out her hands towards Saroj in a begging gesture. 'My child!' she said. 'Come, come.'

Saroj went to her mother and took her hands. 'Mama,' she said, 'how are things?'

Mrs Kapoor swept a hand over towards the figure in the bed. 'As you see, my Saroj, he is dying.'

Saroj looked then at her father. He was pale and even more shrivelled looking than the last time she came. His breaths were ragged, occasionally stopping altogether, then shuddering to a start again. She knew he didn't have long.

Saroj looked at her brother across the bed and noticed the woman who must be his wife by his side. A small figure in a sari who kept her eyes lowered. 'Sanjeed,' Saroj said and bowed her head in greeting. 'It's good to see you again. Have you spoken to the doctors?' Saroj knew that this task would always be left to the man of the house and not the wife.

'They say his time is very near. He may not wake again.'

'Hmm. Shall I stay with him while you take mama for a drink. It does no good to sit and wait like this. I'll come and get you if there is a change.'

Sanjeed's wife looked up at Saroj, a shocked expression on her face, wondering how this woman had the nerve to tell Sanjeed what to do. And even more shocked that he was about to comply.

'Come, mama,' said Sanjeed. 'What sister says makes sense. Let us walk a while.'

Alone with her father, Saroj pulled her chair nearer to the bed. 'Well, papa,' she whispered, 'I believe that you may be able to hear me even though you can't wake. I wanted to tell you that you were right, not in your choice of husband for me, I could never concede that, but in saying I should stay with medicine. I have decided to take your advice now, but you may be shocked at the direction I want to go in.

Saroj left the hospital and, on impulse, decided to visit Erica Trevellian. Her mind had been on the young girl and her relationship with her dad. Much like Saroj's own daughter/father relationship, she felt it would be difficult for the girl to break away and become her own person. It perhaps wasn't her place to interfere, but she had felt a strong pull towards Erica since they met, maybe missing having a child of her own? Whatever the reason, she wanted to follow her feelings and make sure that Erica was okay.

It was Monday and Saroj knew that Erica would be at school, but it was nearly four o'clock so she should be home by the time Saroj arrived at Mrs Trevose's cottage. As she neared the familiar row of granite houses, she spotted Erica walking down the edge of the narrow road.

Pausing to let the car go by, Erica didn't look up until Saroj had stopped. 'Want a lift?' Saroj said cheerfully.

Peering through the car window, Erica recognised the police detective and smiled. She nodded enthusiastically and jumped in. 'I thought the police were finished with us,' she said.

'We are but I just wanted to check that everything was alright. Your family has had quite a time of it.' Saroj had reached the house, and pulled up. 'How are things going at school?'

'Okay,' said Erica. 'I've had a word with our career's tutor, and he reckons I could go to college if I work hard in the next couple of years.'

'I'm sure you could, Erica,' replied Saroj. 'What would you study?'

'Don't laugh, will you, but I'd like to go to agricultural college.' She looked over at Saroj who was smiling broadly. 'I know a lot about farming and, if I was qualified, dad might let me be more involved, maybe make some changes too. Anyway, that's what I think.'

'It sounds like a good plan. Have you talked to your dad about it?'

'Yeah, he thinks it's worthwhile going to school now.' She laughed. 'Anyway, he said he'd teach me a few things himself, about the livestock and that, and I can help Andy out at the weekends. He's been very quiet since what happened with the boys. I think he realises he needs me, and not just as a skivvy.'

Saroj felt immensely proud of the girl. 'Sounds like you know where you're going, Erica. That's great.' Saroj patted Erica's hand. 'Now you'd best be off, and give my regards to your grandma.'

Saroj watched Erica skip up the path and wave as she reached to door. Then she drove off to put her own plan into action.

Chapter Thirty

Peter and Cassie were busy tidying up the paperwork that came with a murder investigation. 'The Chief Super's pleased,' Peter said, signing off his report. 'Two murders cleared up and the budget not overstretched. However, I'm still not as pleased as I should be. You and I need to get a few things straight.'

Cassie was a little preoccupied. 'Sorry, Peter, what were you saying?'

'Sit down, Cassie. You must know I've been less than happy with the way you've conducted yourself lately. You go off on a tangent and treat investigations as if they were your sole responsibility. At the end of the day, it's down to me – I'll carry the can if anything goes wrong. Any actions carried out need to be with my express approval, that's what the chain of command is all about.'

'I know, sir, and I'm sorry.' Cassie felt mentally exhausted. She had not been able to speak to Suzi and was concerned about how her friend was coping, and, to cap it all, she knew she had messed things up with Mark. Now Peter was intent on giving her a dressing down. It was the last thing she needed.

Peter leaned forward and looked Cassie in the eye. 'You're a good detective, Cassie, and I'd like to depend on you more. My plan is to take a less hands-on role for a while, and I need to know you're up to taking more responsibility. At the moment I'm not convinced.'

'I am up to it, Peter, really. I relish more responsibility.' Cassie didn't want this conversation, but she needed to convince Peter to put their problems behind them and move on. 'This last case was different, Peter. I know now that I was too emotionally involved. But I promise you it won't happen again.'

'Okay, Cassie, I'm going to take you at your word. Don't let me down.'

'I won't, sir.' Cassie smiled then. 'I wonder if I could get your advice on a personal issue.'

Peter was taken aback, he was unused to any of his team consulting him about their personal lives. 'I'm not sure I'm qualified to give advice, what's it about?'

Cassie took a deep breath. 'You know I've been seeing Mark Andrews.' Peter nodded. 'Well I think I may have ruined things on that front. I thought with him being a friend of yours you might have an idea of how I might set things straight.'

Cassie filled Peter in on the argument that resulted from her not showing up for their date. 'I'm afraid I got angry and didn't leave it well.'

'What I know of Mark is that he doesn't bear a grudge. I only know him through rugby, and you can't afford to be sensitive in a rugby team. We all get pissed off with one another at times, thinking a team member hasn't pulled his weight, for example, but we blow our tops and then it's all forgotten. In my opinion, I think he'd welcome some straight talking. Tell him how you feel, then it's up to him. If he's the man I think he is, he's not going to throw away a good thing after one silly argument.'

'Thanks, Peter. That sounds like good advice. Whilst we're talking about Mark, you said you'd tell me what the anchor tattoo was all about. It seems there's a mystery there.'

'I've been thinking about that, Cassie, and I've decided that what happens on a rugby tour stays on a rugby tour. If you want to know more, Mark will have to tell you himself.'

Cassie smiled. 'Well, I have ways and means,' she said seductively.

Before she could put her mind to speaking to Mark, Cassie wanted to contact Suzi. She had to ask her friend to return to the station for charges to be made, and used this as an excuse to find out how she was.

'What's happening, Cassie?' Suzi demanded as soon as she picked up. 'Have you got that bastard Penworth?'

'Suzi, you know I can't discuss the case with you. All I'm willing to say is that we're not looking at you or Simon for the murder now.'

'That's fantastic, does he know?'

'He will soon enough. We want you both back at the station. Someone's phoning him now.'

Suzi was tearful. 'Thanks for everything, Cassie. I'm sure you've had a hand in this, even though you might not admit it.'

'You were very foolish, though, Suzi, trying to take matters into your own hands. We would have got to this point sooner if you'd just called the police at the beginning.'

'I know, I know, but don't tell me off, Cassie. I did what I thought was best for Simon. You'd have done the same.'

'Okay. What's done is done. How are you feeling after all the excitement?'

'Excitement? It's been a roller coaster, Cassie. Mad but with its lovely moments too. I'll be okay when I know Simon is. It was really great seeing him. Don't you think he looks like Johnnie?'

'Peas in a pod, love. I just hope he hasn't inherited the seedier side of his dad.' Cassie was relieved to hear that the old Suzi was still there. 'Anyway, be at the station at two and remember, you still have serious charges to face.'

The charges were laid out to Susan and Sylvia Moorcroft. It was, as Susan had predicted, a charge of perverting the course of justice which, Peter reminded them, could carry a long prison sentence.

Susan had discussed possible outcomes with her solicitor, and was insistent that she was the one to blame. 'Simon was totally in shock and he just came along with me. I was the one leading. I was the one who could have called the police but didn't. I'm sure that, if Simon had been left to his own devices, he would have made a different decision.'

Sylvia didn't want her client to take all the blame, in order to reduce her sentence. 'Perhaps you were both caught up in events and made a mutual decision to leave the scene. A jury would understand, even if they couldn't condone your actions.'

But Susan was adamant. 'No. Simon really had no say. I drove him away, I found a place to hide out, I kept him there. He even asked me why I didn't call the police.'

Peter and Saroj listened as Susan repeated this confession to them. 'It looks like you had a great influence on Simon.' Peter said.

'I told you, he didn't know what he was doing. I'm used to crisis situations and could keep a cool head. I am the only one to blame, you have to believe that.'

Peter accepted Susan's assertion, despite believing that she was making it to protect her son. He read out the charge and told Susan that she would be released on bail. Her charge sheet set out the conditions, one of which was to report to the police station every week until her court hearing at the magistrate's court. She was given the charge sheet and again warned not to have contact with Simon Makinson. 'Do you understand the conditions, Susan?' She nodded. 'Okay, then you are free to go.'

Just as everyone was leaving, Peter asked Susan a final question. 'Just out of interest, Susan, where was the kitchen knife kept that was used on Carol?'

Susan gave a hollow laugh. 'Carol kept it by the sofa. She was terrified that Penworth would find her and she would need to protect herself. She wasn't wrong, was she, detective?'

Despite not knowing what Susan Delaney's statement would be, Simon's solicitor had persuaded him to go down a similar route to her. Speaking to him with his parents, the combined pressure convinced Simon that his hopes for the future would be dashed if he allowed himself to be imprisoned.

'You want to be a politician, Simon, that would not be possible with something like this in your past. You said yourself that Susan took over and that she led you away to the caravan,' urged Mr Makinson, desperate to keep his son out of prison.

Mr Bradbury weighed in. 'From what you have told me, Simon, I believe that Ms Delaney coerced you away from the scene and was in full control of the situation throughout. You said she took your phone away, and you stayed at the caravan until she decided you should leave. This looks like abduction to me.'

'No,' said Simon, 'it wasn't like that. She rescued me.'

'From what did she rescue you, exactly? You had committed no crime. If it had been up to you, you would have called the police, you said as much to me yesterday.'

Simon's head was in his hands. 'Oh, I don't know what to do,' he said. 'She was kind to me. She was just trying to help.'

In the end, a statement was prepared that minimised Simon's part in events and highlighted how Susan's experience and knowledge was a decisive factor in what happened after Simon had found Carol Lightfoot's body. Acknowledging that Susan had no intention of harming Simon, the statement claimed that it was Susan's overwhelming desire to protect her son that influenced the decisions she made. There was some measure of calculation in Susan's actions in that she removed the murder weapon, thus thwarting the police investigation, and made a deliberate attempt to hide herself and Simon.

Mr Bradbury was confident that Simon would be considered to have played no active part in the perversion of justice and allowed to go free with just a caution. This, in fact, was what happened, and Simon left the police station with his parents and Claire, all three shaking Allister Bradbury's hand warmly. Mr Bradbury had failed to convince Simon to bring an allegation of abduction against Susan, but he was satisfied that his client was free and that would have to do.

Simon was the only one of the party that looked miserable. He was desperate to speak to Susan but had been expressly warned not to by the police. He had no choice now but to go back home with his parents and then resume his studies in London.

Back at the hotel, Simon found a note under his door.

Dearest Simon,

I have found out that you have been let go with a caution. Cassie told me, even though she shouldn't have. I am delighted that the police got that right. There could be no blame attached to you. All the decisions were mine.

I want you to know that, despite the tragic situation we found ourselves in, spending that time with you was truly wonderful. It is my hope that you and I will be able to meet again in better circumstances. I will leave it up to you to decide whether to contact me when all this has blown over.

Take good care of yourself,

love Susan. X

Simon sat on the bed and re-read the note. He knew that they would meet up again, that was never in doubt. He also knew that, whatever happened, Susan would be okay. She was strong and resourceful. Now all he had to do was make her proud of him, and to do that, he'd have to stop moping around and get to work. He decided that he wouldn't go back with his parents, but return immediately to uni. They wouldn't like that, he was sure, but if he had learned one thing from his birth mother, it was to be true to yourself and be strong enough to go your own way.

Chapter Thirty-one

The day's interviews had been straightforward. The biggest surprise being Penworth's confession, and Peter realised he had Cassie to thank for that. She had managed to get under the man's skin, and he just couldn't help trying to justify his actions, much to his solicitor's disapproval. Peter knew that the claim of self-defence wouldn't carry any weight with the CPS. Their evidence was too strong for that.

Peter gazed at his drink. All of the team were in the pub celebrating and he told himself that he would have his customary one drink with them before giving his excuses. This evening, however, he was in no hurry to go home. He needed to relax and offload the events of the last couple of weeks. He would normally have been keen to use Rachel as his sounding board, but these days home was all about Charlotte, and Rachel was constantly tired. He felt guilty even thinking these things. It was what he wanted, after all. A wife he loved and a family. Why should that be so hard?

Cassie plonked herself down next to him. 'Penny for them, sir,' she said cheerfully.

'Oh, just going through the case. You know how it is.'

'I do, and I've got something to tell you relating to that.'

Peter perked up. 'Go on,' he said, interested in what Cassie could come up with next.

Cassie opened her bag and took out a padded envelope. 'I received this today. It's from Suzi.' She tipped out the contents. There was a letter and a flash drive. 'You may not know but Suzi's writing a book. It's about domestic abuse, but told through the stories of the victims. That's where this comes in,' she said, indicating the flash drive. 'Suzi interviewed the women who came into the refuge.' She paused for effect. 'One of those women was Carol Lightfoot.'

Peter was interested. 'So how does Carol's interview help us with the case against Penworth?'

'It doesn't. Not this case, anyway. But Carol told Suzi the truth about what happened when she was assaulted previously. The case I showed you that had been badly handled?'

'I know where you're going, Cassie. You want to re-open that case.'

'Exactly sir. I know the taped interview may not be admissible in court, but it should be enough to start an investigation. Especially now, as Penworth's been charged with her murder.'

'You could be right. Talk to me about it in a couple of days.' Peter held up his glass. 'Right now another of these would be nice.'

'Coming up,' said Cassie, wondering why the boss was lingering at the pub when he usually couldn't wait to dash home.

After downing his second drink, Peter decided he really should go home. He had spoken to all of his team and thanked them for their hard work. He now had no excuse.

An unfamiliar sound greeted him as he opened the front door of his house and walked into the hall. That's Jane's voice, he said to himself. What's she doing here? 'Hello,' he shouted as he walked into the living room.

Jane was talking to the delighted baby that she was holding on her lap. Carrying on a conversation as if the infant knew exactly what she was saying. Looking up, she said, 'Peter. I was just saying to Charlotte that it was time to send out the search party, and she agreed by the way.'

'It's great to see you, sis,' Peter bent to kiss his sister and Charlotte. 'An unexpected visit.'

'You don't mind, Peter? Only I am this little lady's auntie and she doesn't know me well enough. I intend to put that right. If you've got a spare bed, I'd like to stay for a couple of days.'

'No trouble at all,' said Peter, relieving Jane of his daughter and cooing at her. 'Where's Rachel?'

216

Jane smirked. 'Ah. I hope you don't mind me taking a liberty, but I've booked you a table at The Avalon and Rachel is currently making herself lovely. Not that she needs to make much effort.' Peter looked confused. 'A night out, Peter, remember those? Just the two of you in a romantic setting.'

Just then Rachel came into the room looking stunning in a blue silk dress that hugged her slim figure. 'Jane's going to babysit. Isn't that great?' Rachel looked so happy that Peter was stunned for a moment, being so used to his wife looking harassed lately.

'It's fantastic, love. Give me a minute and I'll freshen up.' He handed Charlotte back to Jane who was smiling broadly at her brother and sister-in-law, wishing that just once someone would look at her like that.

The restaurant was inviting, with white tablecloths and crystal glasses twinkling in the candlelight. Sitting opposite him Rachel looked equally beautiful, her black hair picking up the light, contrasting her ivory face, a touch of red lipstick being her only make up.

'You look gorgeous, love. This is the best surprise I could have had today.' Peter raised a glass of Champagne to his wife.

'Pity it took Jane to shake us out of our routine. But I'm glad she did.'

'Have you any idea why she turned up out of the blue?' said Peter.

Rachel fiddled with her glass. 'No, but I'm glad she did. There's something I want to discuss with you, and this seems like the perfect opportunity.'

'I never realised you were feeling like this,' Peter said. after Rachel had been talking for few minutes. She told him that she was missing being at work, the excitement and the challenge. 'It's not that I don't love being with Charlotte, especially as I am feeling more in control now, but I have nothing to exercise my brain. I feel quite envious of you, if I'm honest.'

Peter listened without interrupting, Rachel pausing only when the waiter came to take their order. 'So, what do you want to do?' he asked eventually.

'I want to go back to work,' Rachel said bluntly. 'Not immediately, but in a couple of months. That'll give us time to sort out some childcare.'

'I understand, love, and I want what's best for you and Charlotte. Just as long as we can find a good nanny.'

'A nanny! I hadn't thought of that. I was thinking daycare.'

'Can't you see, though, Rach, that a live-in nanny would give us far more freedom. Policing is hardly nine to five, so we need the flexibility. We can afford it I think, especially if you're working again.'

Rachel looked thoughtful. 'D'you really think so, Peter? A nanny. Yes, but it would have to be the right one.'

Peter smiled. 'That's a detail. The decision's made. Let's drink to it.'

Rachel beamed at her husband. 'I'll start looking into it tomorrow.'

Epilogue

After putting off the moment when she would tell Peter and the team about her future plans, Saroj knocked tentatively on her boss's door. Peter was stood by his filing cabinet but turned and smiled when he saw Saroj. He waved at her. 'Come on in. I intended to see you today to congratulate you on your input into the murder cases. It was good work.'

'Thanks, sir, I appreciate that. But I'm not here about the cases, I have something to tell you.'

Saroj told Peter that she wanted to leave immediately to pursue a different career. 'I want time to arrange someone to care for my mum. Sanjeed will expect his wife to step up if I'm not around, and I don't want that to happen to the poor girl. Then I'll need to find myself a place in London and sort out my study programme. It's going to take a few years of hard work, but I'm determined to get there.'

'Get where, Saroj? You haven't told me that yet.'

'I'm going to be a Forensic Pathologist.'

'That's great,' said Peter, genuinely excited for Saroj despite the disappointment of losing a valued team member. 'It'll suit you perfectly. With your detection skills and medical training, you'll be a real asset.'

Saroj was relieved that Peter was encouraging, and not putting up any barriers to her leaving quickly. 'Thanks, sir. Who knows, I might end up back here someday.'

A few days later at Saroj's leaving do, she and Cassie sat in a corner seat surveying the early evening pub crowd. 'I know we got

219

off to a bad start, Saroj,' said the DI, 'but I've grown to admire you as a detective and a person. I'll miss you.'

'Likewise, Cassie. I've learned a lot from you,' said Saroj. 'Sticking with something and not being put off, even if you bend the rules now and then.'

Cassie laughed, 'Well, before we get too maudlin with this mutual admiration, Peter's got a speech to make. I'll go and remind him.'

As Peter got into his stride, making sure he embarrassed Saroj as much as he could with tales of her first cases with the team, Cassie slipped out to make a call. She had been plucking up the courage to ring Mark for a few days, but she couldn't put it off any longer. He answered on the first ring.

'I hoped it would be you,' he said. 'I've been feeling terrible, the way we left things.'

'Me too, Mark.' Cassie took the plunge, bearing in mind Peter's advice about straight talking. 'Mark, I really like you and I want to make this work. It's not always going to be easy, but I want us to work it out.'

Although Cassie couldn't see it, Mark smiled broadly. 'I really like you too, Cassie, and I'm sure we can make it work. Want to meet me halfway? I mean literally. There's a nice small hotel I know that's almost exactly halfway between Callington and Truro. How about I book us in for a night or two?'

Cassie's heart leaped. 'I'd love to, Mark. I'll have to sort a date out with my kids but that shouldn't be a problem. Shall I call you tonight?'

They left it there, but Cassie knew that there would be lots of time to talk and make plans later. She wondered back into the bar feeling more settled and excited about the future. Looking around at the people she now called friends as well as work colleagues she reflected on the twist of fate that had brought her to the west country. If her life hadn't been threatened in Liverpool, she would probably still be there, stressed and lonely. Now, as well as challenging cases, she had a great team to work with. All this in a beautiful part of the country. And recently the added pleasure of an ongoing relationship with Mark to look forward to. She raised a glass in a toast to Saroj and felt very pleased with herself.